ALSO BY MARIAN THURM

FLOATING

WALKING DISTANCE

WALKING

DISTANCE

MARIAN THURM

RANDOM HOUSE / NEW YORK

Best Books for Public Libraries

Library of Congress Cataloging-in-Publication Data

Thurm, Marian.
  Walking distance.

  I. Title.
PS3570.H83W3   1987   813'.54   86-27947
ISBN 0-394-55147-8

This is a work of fiction. Any resemblance
between characters in this book and persons
living or dead is purely coincidental.

Manufactured in the United States of America
98765432
First Edition

DESIGNED BY JO ANNE METSCH

For my mother and father

WALKING DISTANCE

1

Without checking the rhinestone-studded Felix the Cat clock that hangs on the kitchen wall, its tail wagging, or the wristwatch that is jammed unwisely into the back pocket of her pants, Laura knows she is late. She has never in her life been on time for anything—an illness of sorts which she believes was transmitted through her father's genes. Ten years ago, on the night of her wedding, she tried to persuade her husband that she was cured, that from then on he could set his watch by her. What he did was set her watch and all the clocks in their apartment fifteen minutes ahead. Not a bad idea: instead of arriving everywhere half an hour behind schedule, she is usually only fifteen minutes late. Which, Laura knows, is as close to being on time as she is ever going to get.

"Let's put your jacket on, sweet pea," she tells her daughter. Mia is exactly four, a tiny, dark-haired wise guy who does mostly as she pleases.

"Which one?" Mia says, opening the hall closet and stretching toward a rack of coats and jackets beyond her reach.

"Any one at all will do just fine."

Mia turns toward her. "You're not wearing a jacket."

"I'm the mother and you're the child," Laura says. "It's like apples and oranges. You can't compare the two."

"That's your answer?" says Mia.

Laura bends her daughter's delicate arms into the sleeves of a miniature bleached-out dungaree jacket. "Move it, sweetie," she says.

"If you say so." Out the door, running to the elevator, Mia calls over her shoulder, "What day is it today?"

"Monday." Laura is now darting back and forth across the carpeted hallway from the tenants' elevator to the service elevator, observing the progress of each.

"Monday Monday Monday," Mia chants, as they step into the service elevator and arrange themselves around two large plastic bags of garbage and a metal pail full of ammonia and water. "Mundale and Ferraro."

"Who are they?" Laura says, amazed.

"What are you, crazy? Ferraro's running for President and Mundale's running after her."

"Actually, it's Mondale."

"Wrong." Mia's hands are resting on her hips, her Star Wars lunch box banging against her knee. "I'm the mother and you're the child and you're wrong."

The elevator stops on the third floor. "Let's go, let's go," Laura murmurs. A maintenance man, middle-aged and barely five feet tall, dressed in a dark blue uniform and red, flat-heeled shoes with pointed toes, joins them. His days are spent dumping garbage, waxing floors, Windexing the heavy glass doors at the entrance to the building. *"¿Qué pasa, chica?"* he says to Mia. His hair appears to be slicked back with Vaseline and his face shines with perspiration. There is a spray bottle of Fantastik in his hand; he aims the trigger at Mia and says, "Pow, *chica*, pow," making her laugh. He is a man eager to please, always smiling. Watching him, Laura wonders what it is that truly gives him pleasure. All that smiling, and still she suspects his life has never been anything but hard. She cannot look at the man without feeling an urge to comfort him.

At Mia's school, a newly renovated seven-story building across the street, the classroom doors are already shut tight. But on the fourth floor, the lobby opposite the elevator is filled with mothers standing in little groups, talking this fall morning in Manhattan about the sorrows of closing down their summer homes in Quogue and Sag Harbor. Housekeepers in white polyester uniforms, most of them from Central America or the Caribbean, stand in groups of three or four, talking of sorrows of their own. Some of the mothers, the ones in three-piece suits, are lawyers and doctors and psychologists; others, dressed in jogging suits and sneakers, are housewives. In colder weather, the housewives come in mink coats to pick up their children from school. Mink coats and carefully ironed bluejeans and high heels. Only Laura arrives in patched Levis that were once blue and now are nearly white. The other mothers think she is Mia's babysitter, perhaps a college student working as an *au pair*. Laura enjoys their confusion, enjoys knowing they have mistaken her life for someone else's. In her own mind, she has not yet settled firmly into adulthood. Out in the world, when she walks daydreaming through the neighborhood and someone yells, "Watch it, lady," she is startled and wants to say that she is not a lady, not a woman, not a mother, but just a girl unexpectedly grown older, someone living, by chance, in a cheap apartment in the most expensive of neighborhoods.

She kisses her daughter goodbye at the classroom door and then receives a warning: according to Mia, this is the last time she will ever be going to school. "After today, I'm going to stay home forever and keep you company."

"I'll be sure and mark it down on my calendar," Laura says.

"With a big red star."

"Absolutely."

Jaywalking outside as usual, Laura shoots across the street, pretending not to hear the taxi driver who is leaning through an open window to tell her exactly what he thinks. "Smart," he says. "Brilliant. Keep up the good work, genius." He flies up the street just as Laura reaches the safety of the sidewalk. Only a little embarrassed, she smiles at the stranger sitting under the awning of the apartment building a few doors down from hers. He sits there on an aluminum and plastic lawn chair every morning, usually reading hardbound books or a newspaper, and every morning Laura smiles at him, but never speaks. Always he responds with a nod, dipping his chin toward his chest; a nod so shy it's almost imperceptible. He is a youngish-looking man, and Laura finds his face very appealing—eyes nearly black, light, thinning hair, a narrow, elegant nose.

"I have to tell you something," the man says, and now she hears his voice for the first time. "I'm stopping you," he tells her, "because time is short and I want you to know the pleasure you've given me."

Laura's face goes red; she feels uncomfortably warm everywhere. She has no idea what the man is talking about. She focuses her attention on a schoolboy passing by, a boy in a tweed jacket, woolen Bermuda shorts, and knee socks, a nylon backpack on his shoulders. The boy is eleven or twelve, she guesses, with thick, white-blond hair that will never darken. On the lapel of his jacket is a Reagan-Bush campaign button.

"I'm dying," the man says, his voice low and calm, a lovely, pleasant voice. "I have cancer and I'm dying and watching you cross the street with your daughter every morning, last year and now this year, seeing you smile at me, has been an enormous pleasure."

Stricken, Laura breathes with difficulty; instantly, with no warning at all, she is in tears. She backs away from the man with a few tiny faltering steps. At this moment, she has forgotten everything about herself but this: she is someone whose heart has been broken at nine in the morning by the voice of an absolute stranger.

"Please forgive me for telling you all this," the man says. "I'm actually a fairly shy person, but I've recently found myself opening up to the whole world." He smiles at Laura. "Being a dying man does have its advantages." In his lap, his hands are quietly folded— very clean, soft-skinned hands. A wedding ring, possibly brand new, gleams from the bridge he's made of his fingers. His name is David Graham, he tells her. He is forty-two years old, ten years older than she. He is a marriage counselor, though since his illness, he has only been seeing a few couples a week in the tiny office he's set up in his apartment.

"I have to go to the supermarket," Laura says. "I can't remember what it is I have to buy, but I'm certain I have to go shopping. I think my daughter wanted some cereal, something truly awful, with green and blue marshmallows in it."

David hands her a handkerchief from the pocket of his jacket— a winter jacket with a fur-trimmed hood. It is mid-fall but warm as summer, and Laura doesn't like it; warm weather so late in the year makes her uneasy, as if life is not moving forward the way it should. At the end of his life, on a summery morning, David sits in winter clothes: thick socks, a flannel shirt, a furry hood. Why are you so cold? Laura wants to ask. When will you die? She opens the neat square of handkerchief he has given her, drapes it over her face.

"Tell me who you are," David says. "Tell me your name."

"I think I'll just continue crying for a while, if that's all right."

"You might consider crying and talking at the same time," David suggests. "Try it, and if it doesn't work out, you can always do your crying at a more convenient time."

Laura laughs; he smiles again. She wipes her face and winds David's handkerchief across her palm. She shrugs her shoulders. "Well, you know I'm Mia's mother. And I used to think I was an artist, but that turned out to be a mistaken notion. Over the summer, I painted barrettes with flowers and rainbows, silly stuff, and sold them to children's stores—that's the extent of my art these days. And I read stories for a magazine. Manuscripts. I drink Dr Peppers and read manuscripts, about two hundred a week."

"That's a lot of Dr Peppers."

"I sip them very slowly," Laura says. "That way I never get drunk." She settles herself on the concrete at David's feet, drawing her knees up under her chin. A bag lady drifts by, her face so filthy she might be wearing greasepaint. Her feet are in huge black basketball sneakers, ankle high, large as clown shoes. Under her arm she is carrying a stereo speaker in a wooden cabinet. The speaker appears to be in perfect condition.

"Don't fuck with me," she warns, and turns the corner.

David strokes his eyebrows with two fingers of one hand, the fingers making a V as they travel across his forehead. "I have a crush on you," he says. "If you'd passed me today, or any other day, without smiling, I probably would have started feeling sorry for myself."

It seems to Laura that the city has fallen silent. She listens for the sound of trucks shifting harshly into gear, of bumpers colliding, of the delivery boys in front of the deli around the corner dancing to the music of their enormous radios. Silence. She is in the middle of a small and peaceful town, where everyone knows everyone else's secrets.

"What the hell," she hears David say. "I'm thrilled to be sitting here talking to you like this."

"I won't stop smiling at you," Laura says. "Believe me, five days a week you'll get your smile."

"Rainy days are a problem," says David. "Rainy days I'm upstairs, in case you haven't noticed. Maybe later, when you're feeling comfortable with the idea, you can come up for a visit. You can show me your little barrettes with the rainbows. If the afternoons are better for you, you can bring some lunch over. I don't eat much anymore, hardly anything at all, really, but it doesn't bother me to watch other people. Of course, that's mostly what I do these days, sit here and watch other people walk past me. That, and stare at this maple over here." Near the curb, in a tiny fenced-in area, an unimpressive yellow-leafed maple stands. "It reminds me of the house we have in the Berkshires," David says. "All knotty pine, in the middle of a thick forest of silver birch, evergreens, and maples. I don't expect to be back there again. So I keep watch over this maple here in my front yard and it's as if I'm up in the Berkshires, in a quiet place of my own."

Laura rises, and her hand touches the fur of his hood. "I have to go."

"Don't forget the blue and green cereal at the supermarket."

She is in a daze, and walks back to her apartment house with her head lowered. She rides the elevator upstairs. She takes a can of Dr Pepper from the refrigerator and starts on a pile of manuscripts in the living room. Above her head, suspended from the ceiling by nylon wires, a six-foot-long pencil floats. A perfect replica of the one in her hand.

Dear Sir,

Please read my story about a girl whose friend decides he does not want to live anymore. He blows his brains out and finds his eternal peace.

Thank you.

What is she crying about? A dying man may mistakenly have fallen for her. He doesn't know it, but she is immune, shielded by the comforts of an old, familiar love. The man she has loved these past ten years, and the years before that, leading all the way back to high school, is a man who bought her a one-hundred-dollar, six-foot-long pencil for their wedding anniversary. It was either that or a gold bracelet, Zachary had explained. She'd nodded her head at this, understanding his choice perfectly. Above her head the pencil floats, a reminder that she has married wisely and well. Nothing could disrupt the perfect balance of their marriage. Not even a doomed man who says he thrives on her smile.

She remembers his apology: *Please forgive me for telling you all this.* An apology graciously offered. Could he know her that well: a soft touch, the softest touch in the world. Sometimes, children in the park where she takes her daughter, children she's never seen before, approach and ask her to dump the sand from their shoes, ask her for tissues, apple juice, pretzels. Their house-keepers sit on benches nearby, amused. Isn't that your babysitter over there? Laura asks. Still, she takes the sneakers offered her, turns them upside down and watches as the sand falls noiselessly at her feet.

2

In Brooklyn, in an apartment of tiny rooms in a miserably kept four-story red-brick building, Laura's grandmother, Sophie, sits in front of a small color TV set—a birthday gift from Laura and her husband. This morning, Phil Donahue has lots of questions for Geraldine Ferraro, who is wearing a red dress and looks very elegant, Sophie thinks. If she were a religious woman, she would pray for Geraldine Ferraro. But since she is only tired and pessimistic, she watches Geraldine Ferraro mournfully, knowing her defeat is just a few days away.

A sharp knock at the door, and Sophie gets up from her deep, soft chair to let her neighbors in.

"What's cookin'?" Aïda says. With her is her daughter Carmen, who was born on the same day as Sophie's great-granddaughter, Mia. Carmen wheels her Cabbage Patch doll in a stroller straight into Sophie's living room, straight into a mahogany end table that has seen better days.

Aïda thumps Carmen hard between the shoulder blades. "Moron," she says. "Watch where you're going."

"Not so hard like that on the back!" Sophie cries, wincing. "If you have to hit the child, for God's sake, don't do it like that on her back. You could cripple her for life." She finds it necessary to frighten Aïda just a little—Aïda, who is only a teenager and seems to know all the wrong ways, or at least very few of the right ways, to raise a child.

"A child is a flower," says Sophie. "A lovely flower that needs light. And very gentle care."

"Yeah, right." Carmen's hair is in corn rows: Aïda runs a fingertip along the space between two rows, kisses the top of her daughter's head. "Can you babysit for me for a couple of hours?"

"Where are you going?" Carmen is already at the TV set, switching the channels so that Geraldine Ferraro vanishes and is replaced by someone named Mr. Snuffle-upagus.

"I gotta have a *life*," Aïda says. "I gotta see my friends." She smiles at Sophie with her mouth closed. "What about *your* friend? Silverstein down there on the first floor. He wants you, baby. He wants you so bad it hurts to look at that poor old sad face. How come you don't want him?"

"Him?" Sophie says. "I've known Silverstein more than fifty years. And all that time he let his wife make him miserable, let her talk talk talk and blow cigarette smoke in his face until finally she died and he could breathe again. What do I want a man like that for?"

"You ought to marry him. I hear he's rich," Aïda says, smiling so that Sophie gets a good look at that dark empty space where her front tooth used to be, before Aïda's boyfriend knocked it out with his fist. Sophie was home that morning, scared to death at what she was hearing from the apartment next door. She called 911, but by the time the police arrived, Jimmie, of course, was gone, and all Sophie could do was call a cab and take Aïda to see a dentist, who stopped the bleeding and wanted to charge her hundreds of dollars for a new tooth. According to Aïda, no tooth in the world was worth that kind of money.

"If I ever get a hold of Silverstein's money," Sophie says, "one of the first things I'm going to do is buy you a new tooth. Then I can change my name to Sophie Rockefeller and we'll ride in a big black limousine to see the dentist."

"Just make sure it has a TV set in the backseat."

Silverstein's money is a hot topic of conversation among the tenants in Sophie's building. In good weather, a whole gang of them—housewives, mostly, but also a few old men—gather in the courtyard in lawn chairs and speculate about when the building is going to collapse. They also talk about Ronald Reagan (such lovely rosy cheeks, but such a pathetic clown), the roaches that march endlessly through their cabinets, and Silverstein's money. Sophie knows for a fact, actually having seen his bankbook (though in dim, grayish light and only for an instant), that the man is half a millionaire. The mystery is why a man like that would choose to stay in a building like theirs forever. Laziness? Fear of change? Insanity? Whatever the reason, Silverstein and his wife, Frances, absolutely refused to budge. Like Sophie herself, who has been living here on the second floor for thirty years, first with her mother, and now alone. Whenever her granddaughter, Laura, comes for a visit she says, "How can you live like this?" as if Sophie were sharing her apartment with rats and derelicts and steep piles of garbage in every corner. The truth is that Sophie is entirely comfortable here. She has two rooms and a kitchen and a bathroom all to herself, and plenty of neighbors to watch out for her. "Living like what?" she asks Laura. "You just stop trying to interfere with things that aren't your concern, Miss Nosybody," Sophie says, not without affection. "Why don't you go back to your fancy neighborhood and stir up a little trouble over there."

Silverstein, too, has nosy relatives—a son and a daughter-in-law who feel free to drop by unannounced, pack Silverstein up in their Lincoln Continental and take him out for a meal at the Palace of Naples, where he always orders the same thing, "a nice piece of fish, dry, very plain, as plain as they can make it." Sophie approves of his choice—she would order the same. Poor Silverstein, she thinks. Hard to lose a wife after fifty-five years, even a wife like that, who couldn't stop talking nonsense. On her death bed, her last words were, "Remember me like I was when I was a perfect size eight." She died fat, her skin gray, her hair unwashed and matted. This was almost a year ago, and still Silverstein shuffles around in his apartment unsteadily, missing the smell of his wife's cigarette smoke. Losing his wife, he'd also lost his balance. Even the simplest things seemed dizzying—going to the bank, the supermarket, the drugstore—all of these left him feeling lightheaded and weakened, he told Sophie. She helps him with his shopping, taking him along with her when she goes out to the strip of small overpriced stores a few blocks away. Sometimes he tries to hold on to her arm, and she shakes him off, saying, "Walk, mister. Just keep walking." "It's only for balance," he insists, and she has to hear him say this once or twice before she will let his arm rise up again to meet her own. For her, it is different. Her husband has been gone since 1938, when he was stricken by a massive cerebral hemorrhage behind the counter of the tea and coffee store they'd owned. Philip, her husband, was sweet-tempered and not very talkative, a man difficult to remember. His hair was red, thin as a baby's. What else can she remember? The sound of his voice, the shape of his fingernails, the feel of his bearded face against her hands—as hard as she tries, all of this eludes her. She thinks she loved him, and that he loved her, but it is difficult to be sure of these things. It has been years since she's talked with a man about love. Silverstein, of course, is another matter altogether. He thinks he is in love with her, comes right out and says so, but what he really means is that he cannot live without a woman to sew a button on a shirtsleeve for him. "What you need," Sophie has told him, "is a tailor. There's a very good one down the block. Charges reasonable prices, too. Let me introduce the two of you."

At this point in her life, what good would it do to be in love? Forty-five years ago, it would have made a difference in her life. Men were after her then, but not the right men. Widowers and bachelors who only wanted to ease their loneliness. She was too busy working then, raising her sons, battling her mother, all four of them living on top of each other, breathing down each other's necks. Loneliness wasn't the problem. She'd needed to slow down, to make a life for herself apart from her children and her mother, but it never happened. Once, there was someone she worked with, Morgan something, an Irishman, who flirted with her as if he meant business. And he did. He was too much to resist. Of course he was married. He and Sophie slept together perhaps ten times, in an apartment that belonged to a friend of his in Manhattan. As careful as they were, Sophie found herself pregnant. Her family doctor shook his head, saying he was disappointed in her. A head of a household. Two children. What could she have been thinking of? Of Morgan's perfect shoulders, the smooth skin below his ears, the light hairs that stuck out under the band of his wristwatch. (Why is it Morgan she remembers so well, and not her husband? she wonders.) The family doctor sent her to a nurse, who had no questions to ask, not even her name. And then it was over; the affair, its excitement, and the feeling that love was always a possibility.

Monroe Silverstein doesn't know who he's dealing with. He ought to, but he doesn't. If he thinks he's after the right woman, he's got another think coming.

"Go," Sophie tells Aïda. "Go out and enjoy yourself."

3

David is about to find out her name. With less effort than it usually takes him for even the shortest of walks, he travels the sixty yards to the entrance of Laura's building and chats with the doorman, Eduardo, about the motorcycle Eduardo has just bought. Knowing nothing about motorcycles, all David can do is admire the shining black finish, the wire wheels, the soft-looking leather of the seat. In the time it takes Eduardo to chain-smoke three cigarettes, he tells David more than he'd hoped to hear. The skinny couple with the little girl up there on the twelfth floor—very polite, thanking him each time he holds the door open for them—of course he knows them. They are just about the only tenants who want him to call them by their first names, Laura and Zachary. Laura's husband is very tall, he reports, and his clothes are almost always a mess—wrinkled shirts, badly scuffed leather sneakers, a dungaree jacket with big splotches of white in the back. And this is the way he went to work every morning, could you believe it? But even with those terrible clothes, you could tell this guy was very serious, a very intelligent person, Eduardo says. If everything about a man is in his face, his eyes, then this was the face of a man who was always thinking hard about things. The husband is some kind of professor, he says, and then Eduardo's hand begins to move across the seat of his motorcycle, massaging it, and David knows the doorman is bored. See you later, he tells Eduardo, and walks slowly toward home, one hand pressed against his side, against the pain.

He is exhausted by the time he reaches his apartment, but also exhilarated. He snaps a cassette of Bach's Concerto in C Major for Three Harpsichords into the tape deck, kicks off his shoes, and stretches out on the living room couch. Eyes closed, he savors the music, which starts out brightly, then turns dark and disquieting before its good-humored end.

The apartment, in mid-morning, is warm and peaceful—all his until late in the day. His wife is at work until six, his son at school until four. Usually David sits out on the street for a couple of hours in the morning, then comes upstairs to read and nap. Two afternoons a week he sees clients in his office, a small perfect square that had once been part of the dining room. (A risk, jeopardizing his status as a disabled person in the eyes of his insurance company. But a risk worth taking for a man who loves his work.) Often, he weeps in afternoon stillness, into his hands, listening to the breaking of his voice, the noisy endless breaking of his heart. Somehow he manages to pull himself together by the time Ethan returns home from school. Ethan is sixteen and very secretive about whatever it is that moves him deeply. David doesn't know the names of the girls he has loved, or whether he has slept with any of them. More important, he doesn't know what Ethan thinks about his illness and approaching death. Probably he is angry, hurt, despairing—logical assumptions that have not yet been proven. You can't get a word out of him on the subject. He will talk with enthusiasm about the stereo system that occupies most of his bedroom, the Porsche 928 he has his heart set on buying someday, the Bruce Springsteen concert he went to hear at the Garden last week. But he will not admit that his life has been altered in any dramatic way. From where he sits, life goes on and on and on, with no end in sight. Boring classes he endures in school seem endless; he is impatient with time that passes so slowly. He wants to be a grown-up and can no longer bear the waiting. What is happening to his father is so far beyond what he can imagine that he is simply unable to accept it. This is how David consoles himself and this is what makes him weep.

He weeps, too, for his wife, who is already lost to him. It is as if she is already in mourning, and he is not much more than a ghost. When Barbara talks to him, her eyes are focused on a point beyond him. She cannot meet his eyes or touch his hands or face, any part of him at all. "I can't live with a dying man," she told him a few months after he first fell ill. "I can't talk to a dying man. How can you tell a dying man that the sliding doors of the cabinet above the bathroom sink need fixing, that there's a corn on your littlest toe that hurts like hell, that the girl at the checkout counter at the supermarket was rude and almost made you cry today?" "You have to tell me all these things," he begged her. "Just don't stop talking to me." But most of the time she can't face him. She goes to the movies four or five nights a week, alone or with friends. Some movies she's seen three times, maybe more. She can't keep track, not that it matters. All that matters is that she keep moving—away from him and their life together. At first David was sympathetic, even flattered that she absolutely could not bear the thought of losing him. Then his sympathy waned. He was furious those nights he felt strong enough to make love and she could only go limp with weeping. The lightest touch of his hand on her breast and she turned wild with grief. Now he doesn't even try. He is a marriage counselor with a wife who will not sleep with him, who will not allow herself to be touched. *I love you*, she says half a dozen times a day, addressing a flower on the kitchen wallpaper behind his head. *I love you and it's killing me.*

A year ago, his doctors told him he could not expect to live more than nine months. Talking to him, his internist and oncologist looked in different directions: one down at the floor, the other toward an empty corner of the room. He has survived three months longer than expected, and now has been officially informed that he may survive considerably longer, possibly another year. And still no one will look him in the eye. No one except Laura. This alone is nearly enough to make him fall in love with her. She is young, though only a few years younger than his wife, and her face is sweet and round and peaceful, a face he could watch forever. What he likes best about her is the way she walks, with spirit, and her shoulders held back beautifully. Eyes closed, David can see her walking with her daughter across the street, the two of them holding on to each other's hands, or Laura's arm lying across the little girl's shoulders—clearly a mother to be counted on. His own mother always seemed to be in a daze, her feet not quite touching the ground. A space cadet, Ethan would say. David remembers his mother taking him to the Museum of Natural History long ago, when the subway fare from Brooklyn was a nickel and he was young enough to ride for free. At the end of what was a long and exciting day, they went back down into the subway station, David hoping for nothing more than to sleep with his head on his mother's shoulder all the way home. The train approached just as he and his mother entered the station. Reaching into her purse for the fare, all his mother managed to come up with was three pennies. The train came and went and she was still explaining herself to the clerk in the change booth. Not surprisingly, the man wasn't the slightest bit interested in her story. David was five or six, and close to tears. He thought he would spend the rest of his life in the subway station or that he and his mother would become beggars on the street, pleading for help from strangers. But his mother had other ideas: grabbing his hand as a new train appeared, she raced to the turnstiles and ducked under one of them, dragging David along with her, forgetting his ride was free. In his mind, she remained forever someone who could not be trusted, a mother who could not protect her child, when all it took was something as small as a nickel.

He means to tell this to Laura, and every other story he can think of. He will tell her everything, and then she will have no choice but to fall in love with him.

He checks the newspaper for tomorrow's weather; rain is predicted. It will rain tomorrow and the day after that and every day for the rest of his life and he will never see Laura again. So he will get himself a neon yellow slicker and stand out in the rain like a big dopey kid; a ridiculous lovesick dying man waiting to be noticed.

4

Waking up to light, noiseless rain that falls from a dust-colored sky, Laura is disappointed. Then relieved. Then disappointed. In her bathroom, in the shower, she decides not to think of David. She shuts her eyes, ducks her head under the water, and succeeds, for a moment or two, in keeping her mind a perfect smooth blank.

The bathroom door swings open and Mia sits down to pee. "I'm not going to the dentist today," she announces.

"Can't you say good morning first?" Laura calls from the shower.

"Maybe tomorrow. Today I can only say I'm not going to the

dentist." Mia flushes the toilet, stealing Laura's cold water and scalding her. Then she walks out, absently flipping off the light switch as she leaves.

Laura finishes her shower in darkness, pretending there is nothing in all the world that she is afraid of.

Dear Editor,

Does this story have anything valid to say? I wrote it during a time of joy, pain, and frustration. I have worked for seven years as a receptionist for a manufacturing company that makes plumbing supplies, but I am currently unemployed and in search of myself.

P.S. Can you believe it? It has taken me this long to learn that life is what you make it.

Dear Sir,

I hope that you will feel free to criticize my writing. When I first entered the working world, I turned to the usual go-go dancing and cocktail waitressing. Then I began to study creative writing at a local college. As luck would have it, my husband soon sickened and died of meningitis. I immediately left school and went to Alaska to work on the Pipeline and work out my grief. Enclosed is part of my latest novel.

Dear Friends:

Might you be interested in an up-to-date boy-loses-girl love story? Both characters have M.B.A.'s and silver BMW's. In addition, there is also a lonely and pathetic widowed Mother involved. Am waiting breathlessly to hear from you.

Laura is on her second Dr Pepper when the phone rings. It is Sophie, calling to say she accidentally locked herself in the bathroom this morning.

"But I'm fine now," she reports. "You ever spend an hour counting rows of bathroom tile? Rows and rows of dirty little octagons. I'm such a pathetic housekeeper, let me tell you."

"How did you get out?"

"Oh, Silverstein came by looking for a little company. I heard him knocking on the door and hollered as hard as I could. He went and got the super, and the rest is history."

"What's new with you and Silverstein?" Laura says. She takes the phone to the living room window and watches a pair of teenage girls walking in the rain eating pizza, the hoods of their forest green sweatshirts drawn up over their heads.

"After the super left, I made him a cup of tea. He tried to thank me by putting his hand in a very private place, right near my pacemaker."

Laura smiles. "I hope you weren't too hard on him."

"You bet I was hard on him. I said, 'Walk, mister. Put one foot in front of the other and march yourself right out of this apartment. And don't set foot in here again until you can behave like a human being.' "

Laura imagines Sophie crossing her arms over her wide bosom, staring Silverstein down until the man hangs his head and shuffles along a path of buckling, yellowish linoleum that leads to the door. "When are you going to give the poor guy a break?" Laura says.

"I don't know what you're talking about," Sophie says, and hangs up.

After school, Laura carries her daughter eight blocks through light rain to the dentist, Mia kicking at Laura's thighs and howling all the way. They arrive late, both of them breathing hard, barely able to speak. The waiting room is filled with expensive toys—

jeeps that roll across the floor on their own, tiny video games that play electronic music, computerized spelling games that speak in unearthly voices.

"I think this may actually be a toy store," Mia says respectfully. "Do you have any money in your wallet?"

One of the dentist's assistants, a woman in white wearing mouse ears on her head, comes forward with a Polaroid camera after Laura checks in with the receptionist. "I'm going to take your picture for our album," the assistant in mouse ears tells Mia. "Can you smile for me?"

"Maybe Friday or Saturday. I'm busy right now."

"No problem." The woman squats opposite Mia on the floor and snaps her picture.

"Is this Disneyland?" Mia asks. "What's the hat for?"

"Dr. Steve likes the way I look in this hat. Do you?"

Mia doesn't respond. She's pushing buttons on two games at once, laughing at all the electronic noise.

Another assistant, this one dressed in a jumpsuit patterned with Winnie the Pooh characters, approaches. "Dr. Steve is so excited to see you." Miraculously, Mia takes her hand, Laura following behind them as they enter a bright room with walls painted shining white. From the ceiling, soft-sculpture mobiles hang— crescents of moons, stars, rainbows, unicorns, spinning slowly overhead.

The dentist turns to face them. He shakes Mia's hand, saying "I'm Dr. Steve." To Laura he says, "I'm Dr. Bennett." He is wearing a red plastic fireman's hat, a short-sleeved Ralph Lauren shirt, and Gucci loafers. He shows Mia his chair, pressing a button so that it rises and then falls, like something breathing very slowly. "Want a ride in my magic chair?" Mia climbs up onto it and the dentist says, "Mommy is going to stay in the room with us, but she's going to stand in the silent corner and stay quiet as a mouse." He gestures to Laura so that she knows exactly which corner is the silent one. Obediently, she sinks down into her corner, wondering whether a dunce cap will be lowered from the ceiling and dropped ceremoniously onto her head.

"Now," says the dentist, "this is a very bright light that I'm going to be shining in your face, and these are the sunglasses you're going to wear so your eyes will be protected." Laura has to laugh; lying back in the chair with heart-shaped sunglasses covering half her face, Mia looks like a starlet in a chaise longue getting a tan.

"Mommy," says the dentist, "may I remind you that you're in the silent corner. That means we're not going to hear a peep out of you. Otherwise, you'll have to leave." He removes his fireman's hat and hands it to his assistant, who puts it on and salutes him.

"Do me a favor and please don't call me 'Mommy,' " Laura says.

"Here we go again." The dentist sighs. "Would you say I've lost the facility for talking to grown-ups?" He seems to be speaking to his assistant or perhaps to himself. Surely not to Laura. "My wife thinks I have. She can't stand listening to me anymore—according to her, everything I say comes out sounding moronic and condescending." He examines Mia's teeth in silence for a few minutes, then says, "People don't realize what a tough business this is. They think it's all fun and games, but really I'm part man of science, part entertainer, part artist, or sculptor, if you will. A Renaissance man of sorts."

"Not a bad thing to be."

Straightening up, drawing back from Mia, the dentist says, "Listen, if you're going to talk to me, you'll have to move away from the silent corner."

Laura drifts toward the window, casually running a finger along remarkably clean Levolors. She hears the dentist offering Mia a choice of fluoride flavors: chocolate mousse, cantaloupe, coconut. She thinks of her conversation with her grandmother, imagines Monroe Silverstein's hand slipping under her grandmother's dress, then David's soft clean hands reaching out toward *her* to touch her throat. She is startled: she cannot remember the last time she fantasized for more than a moment or two about any man at all. Since she was fourteen years old, there has been only Zachary. She fell in love with him when she was fourteen, but would not sleep with him until the day after their graduation from high school. She drove Zachary crazy with her excuses, her fears. Trying to calm themselves, they smoked pot together nearly every weekend their last few months in school, up in Zachary's attic while his parents were out at the movies or visiting friends. At last she had given in. Dreamily they undressed to the sound of Janis Joplin's exhausted wail floating from the little transistor radio they'd brought upstairs with them. They were fascinated, as always, by each other's bodies—Zachary's long white limbs, long delicate feet, the framework of his ribs so evident Laura could count every one of them with ease. He admired the freckles on her chest, her fingernails that were small as a child's, her thick hair that hung in his face when she bent over to kiss him. All he wanted in life was to sleep with her, and when finally she gave in, he lifted his hands in front of her so that she would see the way they shook. Afterward, Zachary walked her home along dark and quiet suburban streets, holding her hand tightly, but saying nothing. Years later, she can hardly believe that there was ever a time when the sight of her had caused him to tremble.

Zachary's smooth spare body is all she knows. Probably she will pass through life knowing only him, and this seems a blessing to her, something to shoot for—a perfect record of absolute loyalty. In her memory, Zachary is groaning, half teasing: *Jesus Christ. I know you've had a few fantasies now and then. Come on—let's hear them.* Unlike Laura, who is too embarrassed to tell him what he's waiting to hear, Zachary willingly admits to fantasies of his own, dozens, hundreds of them. *Come on*, he says, pretending to be exasperated at her impoverished imagination. *What are you thinking about all day?*

What does David think about? she wonders. She wonders what it is like to awaken every morning and be faced with *that*. All that fear. And the certainty that he is mortal. Secretly, Laura is not convinced she will not live forever. If she told this to David, he would probably smile and say that was a luxury reserved for the healthy—a luxury he cannot afford. As promised, she will always return his smile. Perhaps she can be the simple cure for his loneliness. For a few minutes every morning she will sit at his feet on cold concrete, tilting her face up toward his, trying to read his mind.

"Look!" Mia shrieks. "Look at me!" The dentist has placed a large green star-shaped sticker over her heart. The sticker says "Dr. Steve Adores My Wonderful Teeth."

"May I speak now," Laura asks, "or do you want me back in the silent corner?"

"What a silly goose," says Dr. Steve. "You won't have to stand in the silent corner for another six months."

"That's a relief."

Mia lowers her heart-shaped sunglasses to the tip of her nose and looks out at Laura imperiously. "I want to come back tomorrow," she says.

At dinner, while Zachary arranges a John Lennon album on the turntable, Laura tells him about meeting David. She tells him because it has always been her habit to tell him everything, even things that have been revealed to her in the strictest of confidence. And in the telling, one thing becomes obvious: all that David has is her sympathy; surely, she thinks, not a rare thing, but something he must encounter everywhere. There is sympathy for him now in her husband's dark, worried eyes—sympathy and horror and curiosity.

"Who?" says Mia. "Who are you guys talking about?" Ignored, she leaves the table and does a handstand against the living room wall, the toes of her bare feet pointed gracefully.

"Wait, I know the guy," says Zachary. "I thought he was sitting out there guarding a new Jaguar that's always parked in front of his building. I guessed he was someone with nothing better to do than sit and watch his car."

"Guess again."

"I'm trying," says Zachary, "to imagine what it's like listening to someone tell you he's dying."

Laura leans out of her seat and raises Zachary's work shirt above his chest, pressing her head against him. She listens to his heartbeat, a steady succession of reassuring thumps.

On the stereo, John Lennon sings, so confidently, "Grow old along with me/The best is yet to be."

"You can't imagine," Laura whispers.

5

David fantasized that there was a note waiting for him downstairs in the lobby. He wanted to buzz the doorman to ask about it, and several times during the day he got up and went over to the intercom in the kitchen and actually lifted his finger to the buzzer. Asshole, he thought each time, and walked back out to the living room to watch the rain falling in an annoying half-hearted drizzle.

He knew exactly what the note said: "Just wanted to tell you I'm obsessed with you." Fat chance. The woman had a husband and a child and a life of perfect contentment. Just his luck to fall for someone who loved her husband. He had no proof, of course, but his instincts told him she was a woman sure of her happiness. He could see it in the way she walked, the narrow shoulders thrown back, head raised, arms swinging. Most of the women who had come to his office over the years, alone or with their husbands, moved differently; sluggishly, weighted down by disappointment. He grieved over the stories they told him, though he knew he wasn't supposed to. Sometimes he watched with excitement as they vaulted over one obstacle after another— selfishness, boredom, an unreasoning, explosive temper—to finally arrive at some measure of happiness with their husbands. It was the women who most easily won his sympathy. Their husbands usually seemed inarticulate, stubborn, embarrassed at the thought of opening their marriages to him. One man he was still counseling always sat slumped in David's swivel chair with his back to his wife. Months went by; finally, inexplicably, he swiveled around to face her, and silently David celebrated. He loved his work, as he always had. He was blessed with patience and a willingness to forgive the awful things people told him. In all the years he had been in practice, there was only one client he had chased from his office. The man was a chronic womanizer, so selfish and blind and dumb that finally David could not bear listening to him any longer. "You're making me crazy," he told the man. "All that garbage coming out of your mouth is making me sick and crazy." The man looked bewildered at first, then recovered and told David to go fuck himself.

Not an episode he was proud of; in his mind, an unforgivable loss of patience.

In fact, he was not as patient as he had once been. He wanted Laura *now*. He wanted her by his side all day, every day, for as long as he had left. He felt greedy, and excited by his greed. He would have liked to have gone to Zachary and said, *Let me borrow your wife.* And he would have promised her return in a year's time, possibly less. *Dying men don't lie,* he would have said.

*They are men of honor, men to be trusted. Please. Please don't
say no to me.*

You are wacko, he told himself. He went to the small oval
mirror framed in stained glass on the wall above the fireplace.
In the mirror his skin looked yellowish and dry. What was left
of his hair was lifeless straw. "Smile," he said out loud. It is the
end of your life and you have fallen in love one last time.

Someone was standing in the hallway outside the apartment
shifting packages around on the floor.

"Good to see you," his father said when David opened the
door. He kissed David first on one cheek and then the other.
"Always good to see you."

"How you doing, Pop," said David. He helped his father with
the packages, two large plastic shopping bags and a white paper
bag with a flat cardboard box sticking out of it. "Doing your
shopping in the neighborhood and just thought you'd stop by?"

"I went to the health food store for you. Got you a tofu frozen
pizza, a carob-coated Bio-Bar, yogurt-wheat germ chips, and lots
of other terrific stuff." George was six feet tall with an enormous
stomach and surprisingly small feet. His hair was thick and wavy,
and completely silver. An impressive head of hair. He'd recently
celebrated his seventieth birthday and recently lost his second
wife. He'd been so depressed about being a widower again that
he hadn't had much time to be depressed about David.

"You're looking good, cookie," George said. "Let me give you
another kiss." They put the packages on the counter in the kitchen
and sat down at the table. "Feeling okay?" George asked, and
didn't wait for an answer. He opened the flat narrow box in his
lap and showed David two Liberty print flowered ties, one yellow
and green against a red background, the other orange and pink
against black. "What do you think?"

"They're striking," said David. "Really."

"I thought they'd go nicely with all the white I wear down in
Florida."

"Perfect for Florida."

"I'm going down a little early this year. Next week, in fact."
George looked worried or ashamed, head lowered so that David
could study his beautiful hair. "Is it safe to leave you? If it isn't,
I'll stay around a while longer."

"I promise not to die without giving you some advance warning," David said agreeably. "You know I wouldn't do that to
you."

"Please," said George. "I hate it when you talk that way. I
hate those words. I'm sick when I hear them."

"What words?"

"What words? *Die dying death.* I look at you and I swear that
I'm seeing an ordinary person, not much different from anyone
else. How can it be possible that I'm wrong?"

David clamped his palm over his father's mouth. "No more,"
he whispered. "Enough." His father nodded; David took his hand
away.

Wiping his eyes with his fingertips, his hand moving slowly
across his face, George said, "Do you think there's a woman for
me down in Fort Lauderdale? It's been four months, and I feel
like I've been alone forever. I need the kind of company a man
can't give you, do you understand what I'm saying?"

"Ah," said David, and smiled. "Sex rears its ugly head."

"That too, but what I miss most is the smell of hand lotion
on the pillow next to mine, the bottles of nail polish all lined
up along the bathroom counter. And a voice yelling at me to get
a move on, to stop taking so long to get dressed in the morning.
You should see me in the morning: I'm there on the edge of the
bed staring at who-knows-what, nothing in particular, just staring
and staring, waiting to be rescued."

"Yes."

"What do you mean 'yes'? It's terrible to feel so weakened, so
completely at a loss. I'm a grown man and the goddamn dish-
washer breaks down and floods my kitchen floor and I'm in tears."

Funny, David thought, that old age was something he'd been

terrified of. Terrified at the thought of his hair going gray, his legs slowing down, his hands turning mottled and shaky. Ludicrous to be afraid of such things. Pure vanity. He had done the impossible: caught up with his father, both of them now in their old age, facing the end of their lives. Forty-two and he was as old as he was ever going to get. On his fortieth birthday, his wife had presented him with a framed needlepoint wall hanging she'd made for him. "Life Begins at 40" it said across the front in perfect tight blue stitches, the words surrounded by clusters of wildflowers. He'd believed it, too. Fool. Blind to the possibility that things could be otherwise, that he would not necessarily live out the years he'd naturally assumed to be his. He could still see parts of that future so clearly—see his son edging toward adulthood, reaching it finally, the two of them with much to say to each other, always amiable in each other's company. Who would cheat him of this, making him vanish while his son was still only a bewildered boy? And Barbara. He and Barbara would be as they had been before his illness—the solid center of each other's lives, affectionate in a thousand ways, never distant, passion and love always within their reach. Growing older, little would change between them; nothing that was good would sour.

Goddamn son of a bitch obscenely outrageously rotten luck. He refused to take responsibility for his illness, to pretend that he had brought it upon himself, that too much work and too much worrying about his clients and not enough sleep had left him vulnerable, unable to protect himself from that one cancerous cell that was eventually going to ruin him, destroy him, until he was nothing nothing nothing gone from the earth vanished as if he had never been there at all.

He kicked over the table they were sitting at, a small round white Formica table good for nothing but a hurried breakfast.

"Cookie," said his father, ignoring the fallen table. "Look what I have here for you." He held up a paperback book. *Miracle Medicine Foods.*

David glared at it, then at his father.

"Look," George insisted. "It's got chapters on arthritis, heart and lung problems, high blood pressure, nerves. Nothing on cancer, but who knows what you can learn from it."

"You want to save my life?" David said. "Forget it. My goose is cooked."

George shook his head wildly: No. Don't.

"There's nothing to feel guilty about," David said. "No one's done anything wrong."

"If I could take ten years from my own life and give them to you right now, would you take them? Would you do me a favor and take them?"

David was smiling. "I'm so greedy, I'd probably take twenty."

"Let's see," his father murmured. He reached for his wallet and removed a check. "Got a pen?"

"It's all right."

"Get it."

David stood, and searched through a cabinet drawer that was a jumble of rubber bands, plastic bottle caps, and supermarket coupons, until he found a pencil. He watched as George balanced the check on his thigh and wrote "Twenty years" in the space where it said "dollars." Slowly, meticulously, taking his time, his father signed his name at the bottom.

"You take this," he ordered in a whisper, "and you cash it in. And promise me you won't waste a day of it."

David held the check in his palm, staring at his father's careful signature.

"It's what I want to do," his father said. "It's all I want."

6

Barbara is in a small dirty theater in the Village, watching *The Graduate* for the sixth or seventh time in her life. She is with her friend Anita, who is legally separated from her husband and delighted not to be alone tonight. Anita feels sorry for Barbara, but even sorrier for herself. Her husband is in perfect health, living in Connecticut with a twenty-three-year-old named Beige. If she could, Anita would perform miracles: she would will the cancer from David's body and have it settle somewhere in Beige's. In a just world, that is the way things would be, she thinks.

On the screen, Dustin Hoffman's Alfa Romeo is running out

of gas. He is in trouble, but he is young and healthy and deter-
mined to get what he wants.

Barbara clenches her fists, leans forward in her seat as Dustin
Hoffman wisely abandons his Alfa. Run, she urges him, run.
Her favorite scene is coming up, the scene in the church where
Dustin Hoffman screams "E-lainnne!", putting his soul into that
scream, a scream full of passion and courage.

She has no courage. She cannot look her husband in the eye,
not even for a moment. What would she see there that is so
frightening? Just the wounded look of a man who knows he is
beyond hope.

He seems, sometimes, so at peace with his dying, which in-
furiates her. He's said that he has never felt much anger, that
anger is really fear and that he has no fear of dying. No fear at
all? How can she be expected to believe this? How can she be
expected to believe any of this?

Like Dustin Hoffman, she would like to shriek the name of
the person she cannot live without.

David, she says in a whisper. David, she murmurs.

"What?" says Anita.

"Nothing."

"Do you want to go?"

Dustin Hoffman is grinning, understanding perfectly what a
lucky son of a bitch he is. He has stolen someone's bride right
from the altar! Barbara weeps for him, overcome by his good
fortune.

Soon the lights in the theater go on, revealing walls with
blistering paint, aisles full of squashed paper cups, shallow pools
of spilled soda studded with bits of popcorn. There are perhaps
two dozen people in the theater, all of them still in their twenties
and thirties. Barbara can see that Anita is looking them over,
looking for possibilities.

"Every goddamn time," a man says excitedly, "that movie just
blows me away."

"Mind-blowing," the man behind him agrees. "Intense." They are drifting down the aisle just ahead of Barbara and Anita, two curly-haired men in dungarees and sweatshirts.

"Excuse me," Anita says when all four of them reach the lobby. "Are you members of the Woodstock nation?"

The men smile immediately, knowingly. "Was 1969 the greatest year of your life or what?" one of them says.

"This guy," the other one says, pointing to his friend, "dropped acid over two hundred times during his college career. That there's anything left of his brain is a major miracle."

"I'm Warren," the former acid freak says. "I'm a tax lawyer, honest to God."

"Believe it," says his friend, whose name turns out to be Reynolds. "I'm in the litigation department at the same firm. The two of us dress up in perfectly pressed suits and ties every day and work our tails off for corporate America. A sick joke. But try not to hold it against us."

Barbara yawns delicately, her hand flying to her mouth. "I have to get home," she says.

"Don't go," says Warren. "Couldn't we all go out for coffee or something?"

Barbara signals Anita, letting her know that this is out of the question. "I really can't," she says. "I'm sorry."

"Her husband isn't feeling well," Anita says.

"What about *your* husband?" Reynolds asks.

"My husband," says Anita, "is in Connecticut with his girlfriend."

Reynolds looks surprised for an instant, then seems pleased. "So I guess he wouldn't mind if you went out for coffee."

"Barbara?" Anita is staring at her, demanding generosity, sympathy, loyalty. Her eyes are extravagantly decorated tonight— upper and lower lashes brittle with royal blue mascara, lids dusted with too much pink shadow. All the effort that went into those eyes: clearly Anita will be unforgiving.

"You know I can't," Barbara mumbles.

"What I know," says Anita, "is that you can."

This is what it will be like, Barbara thinks. When she is a widow. Men will come her way and she will not know what to make of them, what to do with them. She is furious at David for what her life will become once he is gone. How can he leave her so vulnerable? They have talked about these things together, in the days when they were still talking to each other. She told him she will never marry again, that she will move from the city back to the small town in Oklahoma where she grew up. Like her mother and father, she will live out the rest of her life in a trailer camp; admiring the view from her front door, gossiping with her neighbors, examining the sky at night for stars, utterly content. *Old Widow What's-Her-Name. Once she was married and lived far away in a city that sometimes seemed as large as the world, but her husband took sick and then she came home again.*

Took sick? She remembers that David was laughing, reminding her not to forget the part about her new job at K mart.

As a cashier or a manager, Barbara wanted to know.

Definitely a cashier, David told her, still laughing. A friendly down-home cashier, the kind who asks you how your tendinitis is doing, and whether your brother Red ever got back from his big trip to Oklahoma City.

They were both laughing so hard, wheezing with laughter. And then the tears started.

Lie to me, she said. Tell me all the lies I want to hear most. In his lap, the two of them squeezed into a single lounge chair in the living room, she listened for lies; the one about how the doctors had promised to save his life, and the one about how things always, inevitably, worked out for the best. She waited and waited, fell asleep waiting, though it was three in the afternoon and she never slept during the day like that. When she awakened, she was still in his lap and it was almost sundown.

For almost two hours, David had watched her sleep, watched the comforting rise and fall of her chest. That was the truth, he said, and it was all he would tell her.

Now she is studying Warren, admiring his reddish, curly hair and wire-rimmed glasses. He looks pleasant and eager and perfectly healthy. She does not know what she is looking for or what he can give her, only that at this moment she will go anywhere but home.

Taking his arm, surprising them both, she says, "Tell me what it's like thinking about taxes all day."

7

A bright morning, the sky a sharp blue, just as the weatherman promised on the eleven o'clock news last night. Laura dresses with cold hands, though it is warm in her bedroom, even with the window half open. Another summery day. She holds her hands under hot water in the bathroom, watches them turn red. Steam rises above the sink; she barely pays any attention. Soon she will be lecturing to herself out on the street, mumbling furiously, oblivious of everything but the sound of her own voice.

"Why is there smoke in here?" Mia says, arriving on bare feet, slamming the door open so forcefully that the knob makes a crescent-shaped bruise in the metal clothes hamper recessed into the wall.

"Steam," says Laura, and shuts off the faucet. "Not smoke. And please don't push against the door so hard. Check out what you did to the wall."

Mia refuses to look. "I want to wear a bathing suit to school today," she announces. "A bathing suit and my Wonder Woman flip-flops."

"Dream on," says Laura.

"Does that mean yes or no?"

"What do you think?"

"I think I *will* wear my bathing suit to school."

"Guess again."

"Shit," says Mia, with just the right note of mild frustration.

Laura pretends to stiffen, forces herself to look severe. She doesn't much care about this kind of thing, but she knows she is supposed to and so she says, "Do you want me to wash your mouth out with soap?"

"Great!" says Mia exuberantly. "Let's do it right now. This is great!" Hopping on the toilet seat cover, she perches at the edge of the sink and opens her mouth wide, waiting for something wonderful to happen.

"Close that mouth," says Laura.

"You said we could," Mia cries. "You said and now you're not going to do it."

"It was an empty threat. Can't you tell an empty threat when you hear one?"

"I'm so sad," says Mia. "It's summertime and you won't let me wear a bathing suit."

"It's November. It's almost winter."

"It feels like summer. So I think it *is* summer."

"Trust me. It's almost winter."

"Summer," says Mia.

"Winter," says Laura.

"I'm the mother and I say it's summer."

"You're too short to be the mother," Laura argues.

Mia stands on the scale wedged between the sink and the toilet. "I'm thirty-two pounds and thirty-two years old and I'm the mother."

Whisking her off the scale, Laura carries Mia into her bedroom, where she dresses her in a two-piece bathing suit patterned like leopard skin, and overalls and a T-shirt. "This," she says, "is what is known as the layered look."

"Actually," says Mia after a moment, "I *like* the layered look." She holds the top of her shirt away from her chest and squints down at her bathing suit underneath. "Yup, I really think I do."

"A small victory," says Laura, "but a victory nevertheless."

"I'm a child," says Mia. "Don't talk to me like that."

She can see David from a wall of windows opposite the elevator on the fourth floor of Mia's school, Laura discovers. Not all of David—only David from the knees down. The rest of him is hidden under the canopy of his building. Watching him from four stories above, she gazes at his knees in tan corduroy pants, his shining, polished loafers tapping against the pavement. It is all she has of him; she will make the most of it. She imagines the sound his shoes are making, the clear, magnified sound in a movie, of a single pair of shoes on an empty city street. It occurs to her that a stranger watching would think that all he was seeing was an ordinary pair of feet belonging to an ordinary man. But she knows better; there is nothing ordinary about David.

At this distance, the sight of his restless feet in gleaming loafers moves her nearly to tears.

Ignoring the small crowd of mothers and housekeepers gathering to wait for the elevator, she sits on the window ledge and watches as David's hands move down to his knees and rest there, one hand cupping each knee.

"What you looking at down there?" a janitor asks, coming by with two child-sized chairs under each arm.

Hands and feet.
Haven't you ever seen hands and feet before?
"Nothing," she says out loud.
"Nothing or something; either way it's perfectly all right with me."

The crowd is gone now; Laura enters the elevator along with a worried-looking baby in a stroller and a housekeeper dressed in designer jeans. The baby's brow is furrowed and her hands are clenched in her lap.

"Hey, you, McMillan," the housekeeper says. "You stop that. People don't want to look at a baby with a face like that. So whatever it is you thinking about, you just stop it right now."

McMillan begins to cry.

"Did I hurt your feelings?" the housekeeper says, sticking a green plastic pacifier into the baby's mouth. "Jesus, McMillan, you going to be sensitive like that, how you ever going to go out into the world along with the rest of us?" To Laura she says, "This baby worries about *everything*. She probably even worrying about you now."

The elevator lands gracefully, with only a slight shudder. "Relax," Laura whispers in the baby's ear. "You've just got to relax."

Crossing the street against the light a minute later, she sees David gesturing to her, hand raised stiffly above his head.

"There's no escaping me," he warns as she approaches. "Here I sit day after day, a permanent fixture under the canopy. If you want to avoid me, the only solution is to move across town." His winter jacket with its furry hood is thrown over his shoulders; pale arms, thin as Zachary's, rest now at his waist.

"It rained yesterday," Laura says, and wonders why she sounds so apologetic.

"You're forgiven."

"I'm innocent," she says. "So there's nothing to forgive."

"Of course not."

She seats herself on a smooth square of concrete and faces

him. "I took my daughter to the dentist yesterday. What did you do?"

"Yesterday?" His ankles are crossed, his loafers knocking quietly against one another. "Yesterday I missed you, and I almost convinced myself that you'd written me a letter and left it off with the doorman." He smiles. "Jerk. There's no excuse for that kind of dopiness."

"The dentist made me stand in the silent corner."

"I have no idea why I expected you to write to me. Pretty romantic notion, isn't it, the idea of someone writing you a letter and then delivering it personally."

Somewhere in close range a telephone rings, and Laura watches, surprised, as David pulls a one-piece phone and receiver from his coat pocket. "Excuse me," he says, and speaks into the phone. Laura can hear the voice at the other end perfectly. "Just wanted to see how you are," a woman's voice says. "You were sleeping when I got in last night and pretending to be asleep when I left this morning. Are you all right?"

"Can I call you back?" David says. "I'm out on the street now and I'm not feeling very talkative."

"Sure," says the voice, clearly disappointed. "Fine." She hangs up noisily.

David slips the phone back into his pocket. "I don't know why I bother to carry this thing around with me."

"I assume that was your grandmother," says Laura.

"She's ninety-seven years old and very cranky. She's going to live forever, of course."

Closing her eyes for only an instant, Laura says, "Do you have a happy marriage?"

"I'm a marriage counselor," says David. "What kind of marriage do you think I have?"

"An exemplary one?"

His face is impassive. "And you?" he asks.

"I've been lucky, all these years. Luckier than most of the world, from what I can see."

"And it's hard for you to imagine things ever changing."

Laura nods.

"You get fooled into believing that life simply goes on, in the way it always has, one day after another, without end."

"When I was a kid," Laura says, "I thought that everyone lived to be a hundred. I remember turning eight and thinking, nervously, that now I only had ninety-two years left."

"Sounds like a good deal to me," says David. "And I guarantee you I'd spend the next fifty-eight years pretty constructively."

Half smiling, shaking her head slowly from side to side, she wonders if he is ever free of this; if there are ever easy moments of real happiness, or if he has already lost everything.

"What," he says. "Tell me."

Everything she wants to ask seems so dangerous; even the simplest of questions could wound him deeply. "I don't know anything about dying," she says. "I don't know what you're feeling."

"Right now?"

"Or anytime."

"Right now," says David, "I'm feeling lucky. As if anything at all might be possible."

"Miracles?"

Just last week, he tells her, his father had arrived with a postcard from a neighbor of his in Fort Lauderdale. On the back of the card, in beautiful italicized letters, the woman wrote that she'd gone to church to light a candle for David, and prayed that he'd be healthy again. Reading the postcard in the lobby of his building and again upstairs in his living room and again in bed before he went to sleep, David had cried, picturing the woman on her knees, praying for a miracle. He felt humbled by her generosity and faith, and ashamed of his own faithlessness.

Miracles? "Put it this way," he says now, "if one came my way, I wouldn't run from it."

The phone rings in his pocket again.

"I'm a very popular guy," David says. "As you can see."

It is a man's voice this time, loud and exuberant. "My father," David mouths.

"Cookie," says George. "Are you listening to me? I met someone at the library last night, a very tall reference librarian, almost as tall as I am. Married, but not really. She and the guy have separate bedrooms and apparently they go their separate ways. I sat around in the periodical room reading old magazines for two hours, waiting for her to finish work. We had dinner together in a coffee shop and our legs kept bumping into each other under the table. Accidentally, of course, because we both have such long legs. She wears a size ten shoe, what do you think of that?"

"Very impressive," says David, rolling his eyes at Laura.

"She says her marriage has been dead for years. Her husband goes to bed right after the seven o'clock news every night. He's up at five A.M., doing the laundry and going out to the twenty-four-hour supermarkets looking for fresh produce. He used to be a drunk, but no more. Now he's a professional shopper and sleeper."

"Just be careful," David warns. "One day at five A.M., while his laundry is spinning in the dryer, he just may decide to pay you a visit with a sawed-off shotgun."

"To tell you the truth," says George, "I could use a little excitement in my life."

"Oh, well, I'm only a marriage counselor," says David. "What do I know?" Back into his pocket goes the phone. "I can't remember what we were talking about," he tells Laura.

"Miracles," Laura says. "And it would be a miracle if my father ever called me with good news like that. Or my mother. They get me in the middle of the night, a few times a year, one of them usually calling to complain about something outrageous the other has done. They've been divorced for almost fifteen years and they still have it in for each other."

Those middle-of-the-night phone calls terrified her—the phone an intruder shrieking in the dark, catching her off guard, leaving her heart knocking crazily. There was never anything new to say. If it was her mother, she began or ended by telling Laura not to forget that she was in love with someone else when she married Laura's father. If it was her father, he had to remind her that her mother had deliberately gotten herself pregnant to force him to marry her, merely to make her ex-lover jealous. She can hear her father whispering drunkenly, *And of course I had to do the decent thing and marry her. A man has obligations. A sense of responsibility. Idiotic misguided notions ruined my goddamn life.* He had never even wanted children, he'd told Laura a hundred times. They'd had four—each of them an accident—and would have continued having accidents if her mother had had her way. Instead, she had her tubes tied when Ben told her it would be the end of their marriage if she didn't. Their marriage had already turned cold and hard by the time Laura, the second of their children, was born. She believes, as she always has, that her mother loves her but is too crazy to admit it, and that her father loves her not at all. Once, on a childhood vacation on the coast of Maine, she and her father were standing out in the ocean, hands at their sides, not saying a word to each other. A wave washed over them, knocking Laura underwater. On her hands and knees, she struggled, in a panic, to rise to the surface. She had thought then that she would drown, that her father had no interest in saving her. She was six years old and already knew that her father had not wanted to be anyone's father; perhaps, she thought, he had even brought her there to the ocean hoping she would go under. When at last she managed to get to her feet, choking on swallowed water, her hair streaming past her eyes so that she could barely see, her father did not embrace her or reach for her arm to steady her. "Got to watch out for those breakers," he said, as if he had been talking pleasantly to a stranger, acknowledging the weather, the color of the sea or the sky, merely to be polite. Needing to grab hold of his hand, but not wanting to, Laura watched as her hand found his and slipped inside it.

Her father swung their arms high and then low, over and over again, joyously. She was afraid of him and he seemed not to notice or not to care. Eleven years later, he moved out of their home in northern New Jersey and into an apartment in Stamford with his lover, and Laura was no longer afraid.

In her nightmares, she is a child drowning as her father looks on, silent, both arms swinging high above the water.

She tells David all of this, and is grateful when he does not say she has lost sight of one simple fact: that all parents love their children, no matter how inept they are at showing it.

What he says is, "These days, I try not to think so much of what's been lost, of missed opportunities . . ."

"The past, you mean."

"I fantasize about the future, mostly about my son. But that's wrong, too. The future is just one more missed opportunity, as far as I'm concerned. I'm like an old man; there's nothing there for me."

From her seat on the sidewalk, Laura imagines that his face is in her hands, his skin under her fingertips. She can do so little for him, but surely she can touch him, warm him. She wants to rescue him, but there's no lifeline in reach, no matter how far she stretches.

8

The end of the world is near; or at least the end of all life in America. Aïda and Sophie are holding hands on a flowered love seat, their eyes on Sophie's television screen. Carmen is in her mother's lap, drawing triangles with her index finger into the velour of Aïda's blouse.

"Oh my," says Sophie. "I'm telling you." Aïda loops an arm across her daughter, squeezes Sophie's hand. In the movie they are watching, a woman is standing over the corpse of her small son, which is wrapped in a colorful Marimekko sheet. (It's a sheet Sophie recognizes from her great-granddaughter's bedroom—a sheet and matching comforter, patterned with cars and trucks and buses.) The woman's husband has been missing for weeks, and now only two of her three children are left. All of them are dying of radiation sickness; it is only a matter of time.

"Those fucking politicians," Aïda moans. "This is what they're going to do to us."

"Oh, come on now, Mr. Reagan has grandchildren," says Sophie. "Do you think he would let that happen to them?"

"They're adopted, those grandchildren. They're not his flesh and blood. What does he care about them?"

It's the son who is adopted, Sophie starts to say, but she is not going to argue the point. A waste of energy. She thinks of Mr. Reagan's rosy cheeks; could be rouge, or maybe the glow of power. She would like to write him a letter about that glow: *You ought to be ashamed of yourself, Mr. Reagan. You are an old man and growing foolish in your old age. You and your millionaire friends are going to destroy this earth with your pride and your greed. Your heart is in the wrong place; what is the matter with you? My hands shake and my mouth goes dry when I think of all the stupid things you have said and done during your years in the White House. Your face looks so nice and sweet but I feel sure that you are a dangerous man. I see in the New York Times that you and your adopted son haven't been together in years. And that you have never even met your new granddaughter. Shame on you. A man who can't deal properly with his own family has no business dealing with the Russians and the Arabs and those people in El Salvador. I have no faith in you; what you inspire in me is despair. Mr. Roosevelt, whose policies I understand you despise, was the last President I could love. A wealthy man, who, unlike yourself, had sympathy for the needy. Never mind that he was unfaithful to his wife; he saved this country from going under and all the rest can be excused. He had brains and a heart, while you are empty-headed and prideful. The newspeople ask you a question about the Middle East and what do you tell them: you say you are too busy to answer the question, that you have to watch a football game on the television, the Super Bowl, I think they call it. This is the kind of President the American people deserve? A man who avoids the issues by running off to watch a football game? God knows, if I could shake some sense into you, I would.*

"Maybe I'll go back to Puerto Rico," Aïda is saying. "Do you want to come with me?"

"What?"

"It might be safer there, who knows."

"I want a Pepsi," says Carmen.

"No Pepsi in this house," Sophie says. "In this house children drink milk."

The woman on TV is sitting in her car along with her last surviving child and a neighbor's retarded son, now orphaned. The car is in the garage; the garage door is shut tight. The woman turns the motor on. She speaks her son's name. "I know," says the boy. What is there to say? The woman turns the car off. "I can't do it," she says. There is no hope, but at least there is life.

"This is the saddest I have been in a long, long while," says Sophie. "It tears your heart out."

Aïda sighs, and says the roaches are going to inherit the earth. "They can survive anything," she says. "Even a nuclear war."

"Try a little Ajax," Sophie suggests. "Sprinkle it under the kitchen sink and at the back of the counter and you'll see what I mean."

"Yeah, right. The thing is, I'm so depressed, the roaches hardly bother me anymore." Aïda gets up to turn the television set off. "You still want that Pepsi?" she asks Carmen.

"I want to go to sleep."

"Good news," says Aïda. "Great."

"I want to sleep *here*." Carmen arches her back along the love seat, rests her head in Sophie's lap.

"She's got to have a blanket," says Sophie.

"It's warm," says Aïda. Carmen's eyes are already closed. Quietly, Aïda goes down the hallway to Sophie's bedroom and returns with a black cardigan sweater she drapes over Carmen. "I'm going to have a baby," she whispers, backing away from Sophie, bumping into a chair against the wall, then falling into it. "Maybe that's why I'm so depressed. Hormones."

"Jimmie?" Sophie says. "He knocks out your front tooth and then you get into bed with him and make another baby?"

Aïda shrugs. "He's got a bad temper. I've sometimes got a bad temper. It's the way some people are. Not so terrible, really." She takes a cigarette from the pocket of her blouse and lights it. "Anyway, Carmen's been wanting a baby for a long time now."

"You're going to be on relief for the rest of your life," Sophie says sorrowfully.

"The welfare? I don't know, I might borrow your typewriter and teach myself how to type. And be somebody's secretary, answer their phone, work the Mr. Coffee machine, easy stuff like that."

Smoke from Aïda's cigarette spirals toward the ceiling. Watching it, Sophie remembers the night her father had caught her with a lighted cigarette in her mouth. It must have been seventy years ago that he'd seized the first thing within reach—an old wooden kitchen chair, its joints already weakened—and broken it over her back. They had called it a bad temper then, too. "Savages," she remembers her mother saying after her father had slammed out of the room, "that's what the savages do to each other." It was one of the few times Sophie and her mother had agreed on anything. Her mother, Lillian, had lived into her nineties, and only at the very end had she softened the slightest bit. She raised four children and one by one they broke free of her, moving out and as far away as Florida and Pennsylvania and Massachusetts. Only Sophie, the oldest, stayed behind in the city, first with her husband and later, alone with her children. She could not manage long without her mother once she'd lost her husband. Both of them widowed within a year of each other, and then Lillian moving in with Sophie and her sons, taking charge while Sophie went off to work. Taking charge of the cooking and cleaning and the conversations at the dinner table and everywhere else. Always her eyes were bad and the cataracts returned two and three times and finally her sight was gone for good. But still she was in charge of the household. Of Sophie's home. What Sophie felt was an explosive mixture of gratitude and resentment. They fought over everything—over the arrangement of silverware on the table, over the tea in their teacups, and later, Sophie remembers, much later, the McCarthy hearings and the Rosenberg trial and every now and then Sacco and Vanzetti, dead twenty-five years but still worth fighting over. Often Sophie's boys sided with their grandmother, the three of them informing Sophie that she was dead wrong about everything. Whose house is this? Sophie would holler. Who's the mother here? She and Lillian slept in the same bed at night, a double bed with a cherry wood headboard against which Sophie would sometimes knock her head lightly, over and over again, while her mother slept beside her. At last Lillian was gone. Like Silverstein, who missed the smell of his wife's cigarette smoke, Sophie missed the sound of her mother's disapproval. She was lonely without it. Sometimes, in bed, in the pitch dark, she listens for it. Her mother has been dead for eighteen years, though that seems impossible. And in her bed where she has slept alone these eighteen years, Sophie still listens hard.

Aïda has put out her cigarette in a cut-glass candy dish. The dish was filled with sour balls wrapped in cellophane, which she dropped in handfuls into a planter holding a dusty-looking, pink-veined coleus.

"You going to grow candy in there?" Sophie asks.

"What I really want," says Aïda, "is to work at Bloomingdale's. Behind the counter in the makeup department, wearing a white coat like I was a doctor or something. I bet they let you try on all the makeup you want if you work there. Estée Lauder, Revlon, Charles of the Ritz, all that fancy shit," says Aïda dreamily. "If I could have a job right there on the main floor of Bloomingdale's, I'd be happy forever. Customers would come to my counter for advice: you know, like what kind of foundation is good for oily skin or dry skin or combination skin. I'd have all the answers for them."

"This is your dream?" Sophie narrows her eyes.

"Oh, yeah, definitely. I think about it all the time. Like when I found out I was pregnant a few weeks ago, I thought, oh, wow, if I was working at Bloomingdale's, they'd have to get me a special maternity smock so I could go on waiting on customers until the very end."

"Better you should dream of being Vice President of the United States. Or an astronaut. Something that matters."

"Makeup matters," says Aïda, looking insulted. "It's very important to look nice."

"It's even more important to use birth control."

"Get off my case," Aïda says quietly.

"You're eighteen years old and there's no one telling you what to do," Sophie says. "You still have such a long way to go before you're grown up. Sometimes it pays to listen to people, to hear what they have to say."

"Someday," says Aïda, "you'll come and visit me at my counter at Bloomingdale's. I'll make you up nice and afterward you'll be very impressed with me. I'll be a professional lady in a clean white coat. A very serious lady who knows what she's doing." She lifts Carmen from the love seat, wipes away the silvery trail of saliva at the corner of her daughter's mouth. "You can babysit for me tomorrow?" she says.

"Aïda, darling," says Sophie, "you make me feel real bad sometimes. 'Get off my case'—how do you think I feel when I hear that?"

"*Lo siento mucho*. Really." Aïda does look apologetic, her

lower lip drawn downward, her eyes glimmering with something, which, to Sophie, looks like remorse.

At the door, Sophie says, "Promise me you'll take vitamins this time. And that you'll eat real food, not garbage."

"You mean like one bag of barbecue potato chips every day instead of three?"

"That's right," says Sophie. "A pregnant woman can't afford to get heartburn."

Out in the darkened hallway, inches from her rubber doormat, Sophie sees something she can't believe. "You think I don't know who did this?" she says. "Those two big dogs next door, that's who. Pigs those people are. Immigrants from Russia, and they let their dogs do their business at my front door. You do that in the Soviet Union and they take you away and you're never heard from again. Internal exile, they call it."

"I keep telling you," Aïda says, "but you never listen. Marry Silverstein and move to someplace nice, to a house with a door-man, and lights and carpeting in the hallways, where dogs wouldn't dare to—"

"Let me let you in on a little secret," Sophie interrupts. "A man isn't always the answer."

"I'm not talking about any man, I'm talking about your friend, a man with money. Even if he won't spend it, at least *you* could spend it."

"My whole life I've never had it," says Sophie. "What do I need it for now?"

"You've got to be joking," says Aïda. "You could live like a queen. Three flavors of Häagen-Dazs in your freezer, a lady to come and wash your kitchen floor for you, to wash your dishes. And then another lady to do your hair for you, zip up your dress for you every morning, help you on with your coat . . ."

"A lady-in-waiting," Sophie laughs.

"Is that what rich people call it? Those people don't do anything for themselves. All they do is sit back and snap their fingers and the world comes running to them. Now, wouldn't you like to live like that?"

"I've always thought," says Sophie, "that resourcefulness was a virtue. And I'm going to continue to think that."

Aïda looks puzzled for a moment, then says, "You keep talking like that, turning down all my great ideas, and I'll just have to marry Silverstein myself."

Now Sophie laughs so loudly that Carmen begins to stir. "You think you could pass yourself off as Jewish? Because I don't think he'd marry a gentile girl like yourself."

"Oh sure," says Aïda. "I know all about that kosher shit, no eating meat on Fridays just like the Catholics used to have to do. Or is it just no pork on Fridays?"

"Right," says Sophie. "Either way, you're right on the nose."

"And Saturday's their big day, right?" Aïda is excited, moving closer and closer to Sophie, reaching for her arm and grabbing hold of it in the dim light. "A lot of fasting and no talking. Just a lot of praying and thinking about their evil deeds. Shit, I could spend every Saturday thinking about my evil deeds and not even cover half of them."

"Don't you say that," Sophie says quietly. "I know you're a good girl. So go inside and put your baby to bed. And then come back here and help me clean up this mess in front of my door. It's so dark out here, I'll never be able to see what I'm doing."

"What we gotta do," says Aïda, "is get ourselves a lady-in-waiting."

9

" 'In the middle of the night,' " Laura reads, " 'Miss Clavel turned on the light/And said, "Something is not right!" ' "

"Carvel," says Mia. "Miss Carvel. And you're sitting on my blanket. Get off it."

"*Please* get off my blanket, darling Mother," says Laura, pushing the blanket out from under her elbow. She is lying on her stomach on Mia's bed, her legs raised in the air. "The sacred blanket," she says. "How would you like it if I took your sacred blanket and cut it up into a thousand pieces and sold them on the black market?"

"What are you, crazy?" Mia says. "You're the craziest mother in the whole world."

"You think so?"

"Just read the book," Mia says, her voice edged with weariness and also mild contempt. She flips her dark straight bangs out of her eyes and then sits on her hands. "Come *on*."

Laura sweeps Mia's bangs entirely off her face and kisses her perfectly smooth forehead. "That face," she says. "Zachary," she calls out to the living room, "come in here and look at this face."

"Do I have to?" Zachary yells back. "I'm busy grading papers."

"It's the wonderful face of your one and only child. Soon she'll be in college and your opportunities to look at her will be severely limited."

"I don't want to go to college. I only want to stay here with you," Mia says. "Forever." She puts her arms around Laura's neck. "Please don't make me go to college."

Zachary darts into the room with a ballpoint pen clamped sideways between his teeth. "Just another pretty face," he teases. "No big deal." He lifts Mia from her bed and puts his face next to hers. "Cute is not enough," he says. "Always remember that." Dropping her back on the bed, he kisses her all over.

Laura looks on with pleasure, gratefully. Then she pushes Zachary out of the way and swoops down over her daughter.

"Cut it out, you guys," says Mia. "You guys are crazy."

Dear Editor,

I have written a story better than LOVE STORY, which really isn't anything. This story of mine is terse and concise fiction sprinkled with outright humor.

I know that you, the editor, are a lovely woman, true of heart and mind and that you will make the right choice after reading my work.

Dear Editor,

Enclosed is my story "Misdirected Love." If you decide not to publish it, I'll slit my throat.

The knife is poised.

P.S. I live in Cleveland, Ohio, but I belong someplace else.

Sir:

A quick plot summary: Ellen Sylvia Berkowitz is a fifty year old with the mental ability of a four year old. She is lost in Yellowstone National Park. Ellen Sylvia will make you laugh, but her story will make you cry. The child in all of us will ask WHY?

P.S. We have a totally disabled teenaged son who I care for at home. I rarely get out into town and have many hours that need to be filled. Could you use someone like me to read manuscripts for you?

Laura and Zachary are side by side on the living room floor, surrounded by manuscripts and student papers. Zachary is wearing headphones and he is tapping his pen against his knee to music Laura cannot hear. Across the room, the television set is tuned to a football game with the sound off.

"Listen to this," Zachary whoops, and reads from the paper in his lap: " 'The Muslims have only one supreme being and his name is Allan!' " Because of the headphones, he has no idea he is shouting. "All hail mighty Allan!"

Laura lifts the headphones from his ears and tosses them to the floor, feeling as if she has done something intimate, as if she has already begun to undress him. She gets up and closes the Venetian blinds, letting the plastic-tipped ends of the cord linger in her palms for a moment.

"What's happening?" says Zachary softly.

She moves from lamp to lamp, snapping switches. The only light left is the one coming from the silent TV set.

"Pretty presumptuous of you," Zachary says, but his pants are off now and his shirt open to the waist as he lies back on the floor. Gently she falls over him. She slips her hands into the sleeves of his shirt. She closes her eyes: such warmth from his lean, light body.

"Allan be praised." Zachary sighs.

It is the broken, irregular sound of Mia's coughing that awakens Laura from a dreamless sleep, and she springs from her bed just as Mia begins to call for her. Racing in the dark to her daughter's room, flicking on the overhead light, she sees Mia standing on the floor at the side of her bed, looking down at her feet.

Mia is crying. "Look at the terrible thing I did," she says. Her lovely perfect feet are covered in vomit. She heaves suddenly; Laura has no time to run for anything, but stays where she is, instantly, automatically, making a bowl of her hands. Afterward, she walks with great delicacy to the bathroom, as if holding something of value. Returning for Mia, carrying her to the bathroom, she hears herself whisper sympathetically. *Poor poor baby doll.* In her arms, Mia smells sour everywhere. Together, knees pressed against cool tile, they lean over the toilet. "More," Mia says, crying now as Laura strokes the back of her neck, the softest place her hands have ever been. Her child rumbles strangely, breathing sounds that are violent and colored with pain.

Remembering her own mother's voice on nights like this long ago, Laura suggests crushed ice, a lollipop, the smallest sip of ginger ale—all refused with a shake of Mia's head.

"You stay with me," her daughter says.

A few minutes later, while Mia watches from her bed with one eye open, Laura kneels on the carpet, surrounded by spray cans of deodorizer and rug shampoo, cans making extravagant, hard-to-believe-in promises. It is three in the morning and her hands are in pale blue rubber gloves, scrubbing halfheartedly at a patch of ruined carpet. Her mind travels quickly from Mia to David, making connections she cannot forgive. What kind of a mother is she? Mia will have to stay home from school tomorrow, and all she can think of at this moment is that David will know nothing of this, will know only that she has let him down again. Head bowed over the evidence of her daughter's misery, she grieves over a stranger's disappointment.

"It's you I'm worried about," she says out loud to Mia. "You know that's true."

"It stinks in here," Mia observes.

"How are you feeling, sweet girl?"

"Not good," says Mia. "Not good at all."

"I'll get my blanket and pillow and I'll be right back." In her bedroom, her hands reach for the sharp blades of Zachary's shoulders. "Wake up," she whispers, and then, improbably, the phone begins to ring, once, and twice more until finally she answers it. She sits at the edge of their bed with the receiver in her lap, trying to decide whether to speak into it.

"Darling," her mother yells into her lap.

"Not so loud," says Laura.

"I couldn't sleep," says Ruth Elaine. "I was lying in bed thinking about how much I missed you and I realized I just had to hear the sound of my favorite daughter's voice."

"What?" says Zachary. He grabs the phone from Laura and says into the receiver, "What's going on?" He listens for a moment, then hands the phone back. "I'm going to kill her," he says. "I'm going to fly out to California and get her right between the eyes."

"Mommy," calls Mia. "Daddy. Somebody. Anybody."

"Go," Laura says, pushing Zachary from the bed. "She's going to be sick again." To her mother she says, "You're not going to like this, but I'm telling you right now I'm going to be hanging up in sixty seconds or less. I have a sick child to take care of."

"What kind of sick?" her mother says, sounding skeptical.

"You missed her birthday again last month." Laura stands in darkness next to the window: there is a draft on her face and hands and she is trembling slightly. Just beyond the window, a dozen stories below, an excavation site sits in spooky stillness. A huge graceless crane, a dump truck, and a cement mixer are at rest, looking, in the light of streetlamps, like ghostly prehistoric creatures. During the day, the machines wheeze and grumble ceaselessly, as they have for months. Laura hardly notices anymore; the noise has become mere background music, a radio in a distant apartment that someone has forgotten to shut off. She stares now at mountains of overturned earth, at piles of lumber and steel beams stacked haphazardly, at the Port-O-San erected off in a far corner at street level. In the soundless dark, all of this seems frightening, unfamiliar, and she has to turn away.

"How come you never call any of your other favorite children?" she asks her mother.

"You're the best of my children," Ruth Elaine says. "Or at least the kindest. All the others speak rudely to me. Impatiently."

Laura sighs. She can see her mother, a stocky, wide-shouldered woman with thin arms and legs, delicate ankles and wrists, see her mother opening her fingers wide and waving them, insisting, *These are the hands of a thin person, can you understand that? It's a mistake that I'm fat; anyone looking at me can tell I wasn't supposed to be this way.* Her mother's face is soft and unlined, her eyes teary with disappointment. "If you made your telephone calls at a decent hour, things might be different," Laura says.

"I know it's late, but that's when I'm loneliest. Does that make any sense to you?"

Zachary is back, flinging himself noisily across the bed. "The kid wants you to sleep with her," he reports.

"Please don't go," says Ruth Elaine. "It's been months since we talked. There are so many things I have to tell you."

"How about tomorrow? Can't I call you tomorrow afternoon?"

Laura reaches to stroke Zachary's temples. Her hand drifts down his face to his mouth; he kisses her palm, warming it.

"She's never going to stop," he says behind her palm. "With any encouragement at all, she'll go on like this forever."

"Let's be honest here," Ruth Elaine says. "You'll never call me. That's why I can't let you go right now. And while I've got you on the line, I want to tell you about my latest asthma attack."

Clamping the receiver under one arm, muffling her mother's voice, Laura runs with the phone to Mia's room. The plastic cord just reaches to the doorway; Laura collapses with her head on the wooden threshold and the rest of her stretched out along a wall of closets filled with Mia's things. There is a rustling sound as Mia drags her blanket across the carpet. She slips her head under Laura's arm and is, in the next moment, asleep.

"I'm no fool," Ruth Elaine is saying. "After they pumped me full of adrenaline, I told the resident in the emergency room that I was fully aware of the connections: I told him that almost every time I finish talking to my ex-husband, I'm hardly able to breathe. I begin to wheeze and then I go into a panic, but even in my panic I'm thinking, Why did I ever agree to marry a man I felt no love for? It's a mistake, you know, to think you can learn to love someone, gradually, over weeks and months and years; that if you pay close attention to the smallest details, you'll eventually find all kinds of reasons to love anyone at all." Ruth Elaine's voice is growing shrill. "Absolutely untrue!" she yells. "There's nothing to learn—it's all instinct and you know in a moment, no longer than that, exactly what's what."

"Excuse me," Mia says in her sleep. "Excuse me," she begins again, clearly alarmed, as if what she has to say next cannot wait another moment. But she offers nothing more, only the sound of her breathing, light and untroubled.

"It always comes back to this," Ruth Elaine says softly. "No matter how far I think I've traveled, it seems I've gone nowhere at all."

10

Seated on a metal bench against the wall in David's office is a life-sized, large-nosed papier-mâché woman. She is in a floor-length calico skirt, cradling a baby dressed in white linen. The figures, along with the bench, were given to David by the artist, a former client of his. He is always soothed by their presence and sometimes finds himself gazing at the woman's placid face, looking to her for answers as his office fills with the sound of his clients' confessions, accusations, and denials.

He is in his office now, listening in silence as a young gay man with sleepy eyes complains about the faithlessness of his lover, who is middle-aged and clearly bored, both with what is being said and with the affair itself. David has been counseling the couple for over two years now, and he notices, for the first time, that both of them have bitten fingernails painted with clear polish.

"When did you guys start biting your nails?" he asks.

"What are you talking about? I don't bite my nails," says Reid, the older man. "I just like to keep them very short and very clean." He is in a three-piece suit and there is an opal stickpin in his tie. He is a salesman in a men's clothing store on Fifth Avenue and is here on his lunch hour, which he thinks of as a major sacrifice. He would probably dump Adam, his lover, in a minute, if only he could believe Adam would take it in stride.

"The man's lying," says Adam. "He quit smoking a few weeks ago and now he's taken to biting his nails. As for myself, I've been smoking *and* biting my nails since I was six months old." He is only twenty-nine, but always sounds, to David, like a defeated old man. His hair is frosted gray-and-blond and he is very thin, gaunt as a sick man, though he used to be slightly overweight. He drinks endless cans of Tab and eats a whole head of lettuce for dinner each night, along with a tiny can of tuna fish. This, he confided to David, is because Reid likes him lean, likes to be able to feel the bones beneath the skin. What about you? David has asked him. Is this the way you like yourself to be? Adam had laughed bleakly. "Me? What I want has nothing to do with it." What he wants is to stick with Reid forever, for the two of them to think of themselves as a family, a partnership that cannot be undone by selfishness or lust or boredom. Talk like this makes Reid crazy; makes him want to move to the other end of the earth, and fast. Listening to talk like this is a nightmare, doesn't Adam understand that? Adam doesn't; he is a romantic. He wears a picture of Reid around his neck in the empty silver casing of a pocket watch. He snaps it open a dozen times a day for a quick look, keeping the picture upside down in the case for easier viewing.

In separate sessions with Adam alone, David has told him to

look within himself for answers; to try to discover why he has chosen to love a man who gives him so little. "I'm a masochist," Adam said. "An idiot. A man with lousy judgment. So what? It's all beside the point." David said this was precisely the point: discover the reasons for self-destructive behavior and then determine how to alter the behavior itself. "I don't *want* to alter my behavior," Adam hollered at him. "I'm the one who's doing everything right, who's bending over backward to please. It's Reid who's doing everything wrong. Why can't we alter *his* behavior?"

"I'm on my goddamn lunch hour," Reid is saying now. "Can't we get this show on the road?"

"You're a beast," says Adam. "A selfish beast. We know all about those lunch hours you've been sacrificing but we're still not very impressed, are we, David?"

David laces his fingers together and rests his chin on them. "I think Adam is angry about something," he says.

"What else is new?" says Reid, looking at his watch and frowning.

"Drop dead," Adam says. "Do us all a favor." Instantly he blushes. "I'm so sorry," he says.

Reid seems surprised. "I don't know that I accept your apology."

"Not you, asshole. I was talking to David."

"No need to apologize," says David. "But I do think we need to know what it is you're angry about."

Except for the click of Adam's cigarette lighter and the sigh as he exhales smoke, there is silence.

"I'm waiting," says Reid, "for *my* apology."

"Then you're out of luck," Adam says.

"*You're* out of luck," Reid says, rising from his seat and heading for the open door, his footfalls so heavy that David half expects the old woman living in the apartment directly below to bang on her ceiling, as she sometimes does, with a broom handle.

Adam waits for Reid to disappear from the apartment before he speaks. "Men," he says finally, and rolls his eyes.

David gives him a small smile, then breaks into laughter, thinking that long after he is dead and buried, Adam and Reid will still be together, torturing one another in familiar ways.

As a marriage counselor, he has come to believe that there isn't a marriage in the world without aches and pains, that there is no marriage so well made it cannot be shaken by the most unlikely things. It is not only his clients who have convinced him of this, but also his friends: over the years, every close friend he has ever had has approached him at least once to confess that his marriage was foundering.

This is what keeps him feeling hopeful about Laura, despite what she has told him about her marriage. Somewhere within the safe harbor of her marriage there have to be weak spots, points of vulnerability that he can go after quietly, so quietly that she won't even notice when the damage has been done. Of course this is unethical, immoral, especially for someone in his profession, but who the fuck cares?

He is dying, and just doesn't have the time to play by the rules anymore.

He sits slumped on the metal bench next to the papier-mâché mother and baby, one arm around the mother's brittle shoulder. "Do you believe me?" he asks her. He looks into her dead eyes, incapable of reflecting anything at all. "Can you actually believe this maniac?"

He is angry at Laura for not showing up today, though he knows this is unreasonable. Awakening early this morning, just after six, he had been excited by the ordinary sight of the sun in the sky, and had been downstairs and under the awning by eight-thirty, earlier than usual. He skimmed all four sections of the *Times*, then piled the paper under his chair, and turned his head toward Laura's building, waiting for her to emerge, as she always did, in a hurry—jaywalking across the street with her little girl marching obediently beside her. He watched the men and women heading for the subway, swinging attaché cases, a small boy on a tricycle wearing a ski hat patterned with Playboy bunnies, and an even younger child in a stroller eating a frankfurter wrapped in a white paper napkin. He watched a dog walker, a tall woman in a jogging suit, struggle up the street with seven dogs on leashes— long-legged Great Danes and weimaraners and a beautiful white borzoi. He listened, with amusement, to a man saying to a woman, whose hand he held, "You've known me all these months and you never knew I was a balletomane?" and also to a well-dressed woman walking alone, saying, "I didn't hate it, but I thought it was the worst piece of mediocrity I've ever seen and they should be ashamed of themselves for making it." No one smiled at him, except the woman who talked to herself, and he did not smile back. At ten o'clock he gathered up his newspaper and folded up his chair and took the elevator to his apartment. He looked for Laura's number in the phone book, wrote it on a corner of the newspaper, and dialed from the wall phone in the kitchen. When she answered, he hung up, feeling as if he were a teenager again, too cowardly to ask the girl of his dreams for a date. Love and madness, he decided, were closely linked—who else but a dying madman would even think of pursuing a woman so lovingly tied to her husband and child?

He had called his father, hoping to hear of further success with the reference librarian with the size ten feet. Perhaps he and his father would move together along a parallel course toward love. But his father, who hadn't been around to answer his phone, was already way ahead of him—he had already had dinner with the librarian and their legs had touched under the table. Knowing his father, he'd probably made extraordinary progress since yesterday. Unlike David himself, whose hand had yet to graze any part of Laura at all. The only physical connection between them— so tenuous he doubted Laura even remembered it—had been when her hands rose to touch the fur of his hood the first day they'd talked. She had not touched him, only the fur that touched his head, but at least she'd been unafraid.

In the afternoon, before his clients arrived, he'd gone to Laura's building with a note. The note said, "Please call me (I'm the one with the rose in my teeth.)" No signature, just a telephone number.

She's had the note for three hours when at last she calls.

He leans away from the bench to reach the phone at his desk, knocking over the papier-mâché mother so that she slides on her back until she is lying alongside him, her head in his lap.

"Is this the man with the rose in his teeth?" Laura says.

"You've got him."

"I found your note when I went downstairs to pick up the mail. I had to wait until my daughter fell asleep before I could go down."

"You sound tired," he says.

"Wiped out," she says. "I was up with Mia and her stomach virus all night."

"I know how miserable that kind of thing can be," David says. "When I go in for chemo every month, it's like that for me, too. All that vomiting . . ." Surely she doesn't want to hear the rest. "Poor Mia," he finishes.

"I think your sympathy is extraordinary," says Laura. "Under the circumstances."

"Hardly." He smiles into the phone.

"No, really. If it were me, I'd have no sympathy left for anyone at all. I'd be impossible to live with."

"Maybe I am."

"Not you," says Laura. "You're . . ."

"What?" he says. "What am I?"

"You're really something," she murmurs.

"Tell me again." He knows she thinks she has gone too far. That she is going to back away now. "Don't hang up," he says. "Please."

"I'm too nervous to talk to you right now."

"Listen, I have to tell you there's a woman lying with her head in my lap even as we speak," says David.

"What?"

"She's made out of papier-mâché and she can't talk, but her breasts are tremendous."

Laura is laughing. "You're disgusting," she says.

"Disgusting yet wonderful. That's what makes me so special."

"I can hardly see straight," says Laura. "I was up with a sick kid all night. You've got to take pity on me and let me hang up."

David bares his teeth, as if she could see them. "I take pity on no man," he growls.

"See you tomorrow nevertheless," says Laura, sounding buoyant as she disconnects him.

Slowly, David pushes the papier-mâché woman from his lap and arranges her upright against the bench. He calls his father, who says, "I have here in my hand a copy of *Salt Watchers Quarterly*—America's first low-sodium lifestyle publication. Should I bring it over the next time I drop by?"

"How's the reference librarian?"

"She's terrific." George lowers his voice. "The deed was done," he says, articulating each word carefully.

"Why are you whispering?" David says, smiling.

"I balled her brains out!" George hollers, then whispers, "Excuse me. Forgive me for talking like that, but it really was unbelievable. Spectacular."

"Good," says David. "When's the wedding?"

"Ha ha," says George. "But seriously, she's a lovely human being. Sweet, bright, impassioned. Too bad she's married to that joker."

"At least she's not happily married."

"Yes," says George. "Thank God for that." He pauses, and says, "What's up with Barbara? You people getting along all right?"

"About the same."

"She still going to the movies every night?"

"It seems that way."

"Do you talk to each other at all?"

"Not much, I guess."

"Funny," says George, "it seems like there should be so much to say. So much holding on to each other. If I were Barbara, I'd quit my job in a second and stay home and just *be* with you."

"That's because you're such a romantic," says David.

"No," George says. "It's because I love you. But I'm your father, not your wife. I don't have the right to be hanging over you, breathing down your neck every minute. Not even at this stage of the game."

David puts his head down on his desk. He listens to the sound of his own breathing for a while. "I'm in love," he says.

"I'm confused," says George.

"The thought of happiness excites me," says David, straightening up in his seat. "My life is coming to an end, but there's still time left for something unimaginable to happen. And it's happening already. I'm in love!"

"So you said."

"I don't owe you any explanations," says David.

"And I'm not asking any questions."

"But you are. I can hear it in your voice. You want to know who the hell I think I am."

"You've suffered so," says George, his voice shaky. "The surgery and the chemo and more chemo and more misery and to tell you the truth I don't even know that I would have brought you into the world if I had known that this was what was waiting for you. Funny that when you reached twenty-one I thought you were home free. That I was home free. I'd seen you through diaper rash and fevers of one hundred and four and the measles and chicken pox and you survived. We both survived. And then you were a teenager driving my car and I kept thinking every time I gave you the keys, How do I know he'll be back in one piece, how do I know there isn't a drunk on the road heading right now in David's direction? How do I know it isn't preordained that tonight is the night the brakes are going to fail? After a while, after you'd had your license a year or two, it got easier for me, I calmed down a little. But at three or four in the morning I'd be in your room, watching you sleep, as if you were a baby, as if there were something miraculous about your presence. And then when you were twenty-one and out on your own, I was so relieved. I'd gotten you to adulthood—the rest was going to be easy. I thought you were safe. Safe! You were a married man with a child, working hard, successful, happy. Safe. You tell me, cookie, what could have been done differently. What?"

"Nothing," says David.

"Is it fate, then?"

"If it's somebody's will, you can believe it sure ain't mine. I want to live," David says, laughing a moment later, realizing he has just recited the title of some movie about a convicted murderer sentenced to die. "Susan Hayward?" he says.

"What?" says his father.

"I want to live," he says again. "But not without some measure of happiness."

David's son arrives at the dinner table shirtless, his smooth chest still faintly darkened from occasional afternoons spent at the beach last summer with his friends.

"Attention," says Barbara. "Patrons without shirts will not be admitted under any circumstances."

"Boy, is she strict," says Ethan.

"Next thing you know she'll want us here in ties and jackets," says David, winking at his son. He is dressed in a hooded velour bathrobe that reaches almost to his ankles—a gift from his father when he went into the hospital for exploratory surgery a year ago. A time of innocence; before he even knew about the tumors at all, let alone that they were inoperable and would surely kill him.

"Great," says Barbara. "You look like a monk and he looks like a surfer, and neither one of you makes the slightest effort to look presentable at the dinner table."

"Lighten up," David says. "If it means that much to you, I can always dress for dinner in white tie and tails."

Ethan snickers. "And patent leather shoes."

"Thanks a lot for undermining my authority, creep," says Barbara. "Things are going to be swell around here once you're gone, let me tell you."

David tells Ethan to go and put a shirt on. He turns sideways and leans over his seat to brush his lips against the side of Barbara's face, something he has had neither the courage nor the desire to do in weeks, possibly months. Her cheek grows warmer under his touch. She is blushing, he realizes, as if this were her first kiss, the one she had been daydreaming about all her life. Her skin is flawless, and very fair. He strokes her face with two fingers, tilts her head back for another, deeper, kiss.

"No," she says. "Please." There are tears in her eyes.

Tightening his hands around her face, he sinks his fingers into her flesh. Probably he is hurting her, and there is satisfaction in that. "Please what?" he says. "Please take your goddamn hands off me? Please divorce me? Please drop dead immediately?"

"I love you," she says, then corrects herself. "I hate you."

He loosens his grip on her, studies the crimson marks he's left against her skin. He knows she would be relieved if he died tomorrow, or, even better, today. He understands the relief she will feel when it is finally over for her. How can he blame her? She wants to get on with her life, to live among healthy people again, people who are obsessed with their lives, not their deaths. It is not difficult to understand that all her hopes lie with his death.

"Do you want a divorce?" he asks her. He selects a child-sized portion of salad from the Lucite bowl at the center of the table and lowers it onto his plate with serrated wooden spoons.

"Are you crazy?" Barbara says. Wiping her eyes with the backs of her hands, she shakes her head "no."

"Salad?" he says, hands poised at the edges of the bowl. Patiently he waits for an answer.

"No olives," she says.

No olives, no divorce. A handful of French fries, three small slices of London broil. He arranges the food on her plate and watches her eat, watches the delicate working of her jaws. She is the slowest eater in the world tonight, but he is infinitely patient. The salad on his own plate remains untouched; the rest of the plate shines, empty. In a while, his son returns to the table, dressed in a dark gray pin-striped suit, a pink button-down shirt, and a maroon tie. Under the table, his bare feet are in thick rubber thongs.

"Go ahead and start without me," his son says. "See if I care."

11

Sophie is in the supermarket, navigating a shopping cart down narrow aisles with Silverstein. It is eight in the morning and already the store is crowded with elderly people and young mothers pushing babies in strollers as their older children trail behind them. The young women are either Puerto Rican or ultra-Orthodox Jews, and many of them are pregnant with their third or fourth child. Sophie pities them; so early in the day and already they look exhausted, defeated by the persistent demands of their children.

"Men," she says, "have it easy. If I were a man, my life would have been entirely different."

"Maybe different," says Silverstein, "but no easier." He reaches into a refrigerated case for a container of milk.

"Don't you worry about your cholesterol level?" Sophie says. "You put that back and get yourself a quart of the ninety-nine percent fat free. Do yourself a favor." She thinks all the way back to her childhood and her brothers, the three princes, Prince John, Prince Harry, Prince Howard. Allowances were made for them because they were boys; they were permitted to behave like children all through their childhood. Sophie was the oldest and the only girl; at the age of nine she was on her hands and knees washing down the wood floors of their apartment every Friday, covering them with sheets of newspaper to protect them while they dried. After school, in the afternoon, she worked in her parents' store, making buttonholes, covered buttons, pleats and hems on skirts. Outside in front of the store her brothers played baseball, shot marbles in the gutter, chased the fire engines that rolled up the streets of Harlem. Seventy-five years have passed and still she envies them for what they had then—endless hours to do as they pleased, time stolen from her and never paid back. The three princes. An accident of birth was all it was. Now a moment of vaguely remembered happiness comes to her: a dress that had been bought as a gift for her by her father in Bauman Brothers department store, on Third Avenue, a beautiful flowered dress on sale for twenty-nine cents. Twenty-nine cents!

"Imagine that," she says out loud.

"Saltines or the Ritz?" says Silverstein. "Which should I take?" They are standing in front of shelves packed tight with boxes of crackers and cookies. Silverstein shakes his head wearily, mournfully, as if it is too much to make such a decision. He is a tiny man, hardly taller than Sophie, and much thinner, with hazel eyes that seem to have lost most of their color over the years. His face is sweet and kindly, his head almost entirely bald. He reminds her of General Eisenhower at the end of his life.

"You are pathetic," Sophie tells him. "Another prince who can't lift a finger to help himself."

Silverstein's head droops. "In the morning, sometimes, I like to dip a cracker in my coffee. Which would be better for dipping, do you think?"

"Can't you do anything for yourself?" Sophie hisses. She grabs a box of Saltines from the shelf and also the Ritz crackers and boxes of Wheat Thins and Oysterettes and Triscuits and Wheatsworth. "Take them all," she says, throwing them into the cart one by one. "Enough to last you the rest of your life."

Silverstein looks frightened—the sight of all those crackers in the wagon unnerves him. "Don't get so angry like that," he says. "Have a little patience."

"Monroe," says Sophie, and begins putting the crackers back on the shelf. "What am I going to do with you, Monroe?"

"Keep the Ritz," Silverstein orders. "Those are my favorite, I guess."

"For a man of means," says Sophie, "you are sorely lacking in self-confidence."

"It's losing Frances that did me in. A hundred little decisions to make every day and she made them all. She kept a lot of secrets from me—I don't even know what kind of toilet tissue she used to buy."

Sophie puts a hand on Silverstein's elbow. "Don't tell me things like that, Monroe. It's too personal; I don't want to hear things like that from a man. Between women, it's different. Women can tell each other anything, it's only natural. But a man and a woman have to be careful what they say to each other."

"Why?"

"Men are men and women are women. You can't ignore that."

Silverstein moves forward, matching his soft cheek with her own. "Sophie," he says in her ear.

"Back off," says Sophie. "Back off or you'll find yourself doing your grocery shopping alone. Forever."

Holding his hands over his head, surrendering to her, Silverstein says, "You amaze me."

"I'm tough," says Sophie. "I do fine on my own." She steers the shopping cart down the aisle, heading for the meat counter across from the no-frills section—black-and-white bags of popcorn starkly labeled "popcorn," black-and-white cans of carrots labeled "carrots," jars of mayonnaise labeled "mayonnaise."

"Have you ever tried any of that bargain-basement stuff?" she asks Silverstein.

"That's food for poor people," he says. "Dog food disguised as people food."

"Says who?"

"Frances," says Silverstein.

"Frances said a lot of ridiculous things in her time."

"She was your best friend," Silverstein says sharply. He goes off by himself to the meat counter, where he gets in the way of a couple of serious shoppers examining Styrofoam packages of hamburger covered in cellophane.

"Do you mind?" says one of the women, who is young and wearing a pink sweatshirt decorated with a drawing of Mickey Mouse behind the wheel of a convertible. "You're blocking my light."

"I beg your pardon," says Silverstein, moving to the right of the woman. "How's that?"

"Who took my sirloin tip?" says the woman. The drawing on her sweatshirt is outlined in rhinestones that glitter spectacularly as she turns toward Silverstein. "Have you got my sirloin tip?" she says. "I had my eye on it and now it's gone."

Sophie approaches, hands at her hips. "Now what makes you think he's got your sirloin? He's a vegetarian, for God's sake."

"Is that so," says Silverstein.

"Then why didn't he say so instead of standing there looking guilty?" says the woman in the glittery sweatshirt.

"He's very shy," says Sophie, hooking her arm through Silverstein's. "He lost his wife some months back and he's still not quite himself." She remembers him at Frances's funeral last year, held up on either side by his son and daughter-in-law as the three of them made their way down the center aisle of the little chapel to their seats in the front row. Sophie sat two rows behind, watching as Silverstein slipped lower and lower in his seat until the top of his head could barely be seen. Later, at the cemetery on the North Shore of Long Island, propped again between his son and daughter-in-law, he seemed to have been made smaller by his grief, to have shrunk to the size of a child. Returning with his family to the hearse that waited at the side of the road for them, Silverstein had passed Sophie without a word for her except her name, whispered so softly she would have missed it had she not been searching his face so carefully. His face was vacant as a mannequin's, an unearthly white tinged with blue—a face whose emptiness she'd had to turn away from. She thought then that he would be buried before too long; that there was nothing to anchor him to life. But after three weeks at his son's house he returned, his clothing stuffed into a pair of tiny paisley-patterned suitcases trimmed with plastic piping. Not long afterward he invited Sophie down for tea, and mumbled, across the table, that he loved her, making her laugh so hard her eyes ran and her head ached.

"He's not quite himself," Sophie repeats now. "And that's the truth."

"I'm no vegetarian," Silverstein announces. "I like a nice piece of flank steak as well as the next man."

"Quiet," says Sophie.

"Crazy old people," says the woman in the sweatshirt. "Steal my sirloin tip right out from under me." She walks off, hands clenched at her sides.

"People are peculiar," Sophie says. "As far back as I can remember, people have always been peculiar."

"And how," says Silverstein, with enthusiasm.

Sophie gives him one of her darkest looks, wrinkling her eyebrows and making her mouth into a small tight knot. "Be a mensch, Monroe," she says. "Learn to do for yourself. You like steak? Let's see you buy a piece and cook it in the broiler for lunch today."

Silverstein grips her wrist with cool dry fingers. "I couldn't," he says. "I wouldn't even know what temperature to put the oven on."

Letting out a little whoop of disbelief, Sophie says, "No oven. No temperature. Broil is broil. You've lived on this earth for eighty-five years and you don't know that broil is broil?" She reaches into the brightly lighted case full of meat and sorts through the packages until she finds something for Silverstein. "We'll take this home and put it under the broiler for you and you'll see how easy it is. In your old age you'll see how easy a lot of things are."

Silverstein is skeptical. "There are so many things that are mysteries to me. They've always been mysteries—it may be that I'm meant not to know about them."

"What are you, afraid to cook a piece of meat?"

"Why are you afraid to marry me?" says Silverstein.

From Sophie's chest an uncomfortable warmth begins to spread outward into her shoulders. "Heartburn," she says. "You talk to me like that and I want to strangle you. Because you keep confusing need with love. You *need* a housekeeper—a cook, a maid, a laundress, whatever. You need someone like that, you get the Yellow Pages. You hire a woman in a white uniform for two hundred dollars a week and you're all set. I wouldn't do those things for a man for two thousand dollars a week. Not because I'm too old and too tired but because I just don't want to. I'm not some dummy who's going to fall into a trap and get stuck there for the rest of my life."

"You're hollering," says Silverstein. "In a supermarket. People are listening." All around them women are studying chicken parts and turkeys and bloody-looking packages of beef, weighing them in their hands, sliding their fingers over plastic, looking for signs of spoilage, of something gone wrong. No one is staring at Sophie, paying her the slightest bit of attention.

"They're not listening," says Sophie, "but they should. They might learn a little." But she falls silent, and allows Silverstein to wheel their shopping cart up to the checkout counter, where she stares at the headlines of a skinny little newspaper that never tells the truth about anything. The front page promises the story of a blind boy whose sight was restored after a dentist pulled one of his teeth. This reminds her of her mother, who lost every tooth in her mouth in a single visit to the dentist. The teeth were pulled to cure her mother's arthritis; fingers, wrists, knees so swollen at times her mother simply sat in a chair and cried. The day she returned from the dentist's office with an empty mouth, cheeks puffed in pain, she was comforted by the hope that at last the other pain would be gone. What connection could there possibly have been between the two? A joke: you pull a mouthful of teeth and the patient's arthritis is cured. That was what the doctor had promised fifty years ago and the dentist, too, and her mother, who had such respect for professional men, doubted their word not even for a moment. Anger at that doctor and dentist, names long forgotten, fills Sophie now, as if it were yesterday or last week or last year that she had listened to their promises.

"Idiots," she says out loud.

"We'll settle up later," Silverstein is saying as he hands the cashier a twenty-dollar bill. Their groceries are in two white plastic bags; trying to impress Sophie, Silverstein lifts them both from the counter with a muted groan.

"Don't be foolish," says Sophie. "Give me the heavier one." Instead, he offers her the lighter one, filled with rolls of paper towels and boxes of tissues and cylinders of Ajax. "I bet I've got fifty pounds on you, Monroe," she says. "Fifty pounds of muscle. So don't be so stubborn."

"I'm strong," says Silverstein, gesturing to her to pass in front of him through the door that opens for them automatically. "I used to wrestle in high school."

"Like fun," Sophie says. "You were in night school, just the same as me. So don't tell me fibs about the wrestling team. I know where you were during the day—pushing a mop across the filthy floor of that walk-up your family owned."

"It wasn't filthy. Those floors were immaculate, thanks to me."

They are out on the avenue, walking past a drugstore that pretends to discount its prices, a laundromat that swallows whole handfuls of change and is steamy all year round, a superette that stays open until midnight and charges ninety-eight cents for a quart of milk. Soon they have come to the beginning of their street, which is crowded with two-family red-brick houses, lawns well trimmed, metal garbage cans lined up neatly at their curbs. These are the homes of very religious Jews, families with seven or eight or nine children, all of them carefully dressed in clean clothes, and, as Sophie likes to say, polite as they can be. Sometimes they see Sophie climbing the few broad stone steps to her building (the only eyesore on the block), her arms loaded with packages, and in an instant, they fly to her side, a flock of boys and girls clamoring sweetly to help her up to her apartment, to carry her packages for her. She offers each one a quarter or two, and always they refuse, saying it is a *mitzvah* to help her. Sophie smiles at this, but what she really wants to say is that she isn't needy or suffering, as they imagine her to be, and that she is someone who pays her own way. Even the candy she presses into their hands is refused because she cannot offer proof that it is kosher. Watching them from her window on Friday nights as they troop off to the synagogue around the corner with their parents, all she feels is guilt. She is a woman without faith and will not apologize for it, yet still she feels guilty. No faith in God, no faith in a lasting happiness, no faith that things turn out as they are meant to.

Home now, standing in the lobby in front of the ornamental fireplace that, like the walls surrounding it, is covered with graffiti, Sophie searches through her purse for her wallet. "How much, Monroe?" she says.

"What about my steak?"

"What about it?"

"You said you'd cook it for me."

"It's nine in the morning, Monroe."

"I'm hungry; I've been up since five."

"Since when do you eat meat for breakfast like the gentiles?"

Silverstein shrugs. "Why not? Will you come to my apartment?"

"I don't go visiting in a gentleman's apartment so early in the day," says Sophie. "If you want a meal, you'll have to come upstairs."

"With pleasure."

On the landing between the first and second floors, Sophie pauses to catch her breath. A grimy half-open window looks out on an alleyway full of undernourished cats, and laundry hung on a clothesline stretched taut from one windowsill to another across the way. Nearly a dozen cats, their tails held stiffly in the air, pace the concrete. They are awful-looking animals, Sophie thinks, gaunt and sharp-faced, and the sounds they are making are awful, too, something like the insistent wail of a newborn baby. Years ago she used to feed them, bringing them leftover tuna fish on an aluminum pie plate, but after a while it began to seem like a futile gesture, as if they would always be hungry and she would never have enough to silence them.

"I can't bear to look out there," says Silverstein. "It hurts my eyes, if you know what I mean."

"You," says Sophie, "you could have a view of Park Avenue, if you wanted. So don't tell me what hurts your eyes."

"I'm too old to move," Silverstein says. "You settle in someplace and you get accustomed to things and before you know it thirty years have passed and you know you're not going any-where."

Slowly they travel up the stairs together. The hallway sur-rounding Sophie's door is so dark it is hard to believe that outside the sky is actually light; fitting a different key into each of her three locks seems nothing less than a magic trick.

"Need any help?" says Jimmie as he closes Aïda's door behind him. He is six foot four and slender; in Sophie's eyes all that is needed to make a young man handsome. He speaks beautifully, too. Even though he was born in the islands, Sophie has no trouble following him. Jimmie is in some kind of technical school now, as she understands it—a school where they are teaching him about air conditioning and heating and refrigeration, useful things to know.

"I hear you're going to be a papa again," says Sophie. Three locks click one after another and then the painted metal door to her apartment swings open.

"I'm not worried," Jimmie says. "I think it'll be okay."

"The important thing is that you'll be good to Aïda. No fight-ing, no punching. A pregnant woman has to be treated nicely."

"Are you kidding?" says Jimmie. "I just made her some toast. I sat right over her and watched her eat it. Plain toast and a warm Pepsi—a real fine breakfast for someone with morning sickness, right?"

"Tea would have been better, but you did pretty well, Jimmie."

"It's not going to be bad," Jimmie says, smiling in the wedge of weak light that comes from behind Sophie's door. "It's going to work out. I'm nineteen years old this time around and I know it's going to be all right."

"Nineteen years old," says Sophie. Seeing his smile, she thinks of Aïda's ruined one, of Jimmie's fist aiming straight for his lover's smile. "Nineteen years old," she repeats. "Of course."

Silverstein follows her into the apartment, into the kitchen that is just wide enough for a table pushed against the wall. On the table is a plastic flowerpot; rising from its center are tall, thick tube-shaped stems that end in spectacular orange-and-white blossoms. "Wow," says Silverstein, reaching to touch one.

"Hands off my amaryllis," Sophie says. "Watching them bloom this week has been the joy of my life." She takes off her coat and arranges it over the back of a chair, then heads for the oven and lines the broiling pan with aluminum foil. "Don't get excited, but I'm going to add a little garlic powder," she warns. Noticing that Silverstein is still standing, she says, "Sit down, please."

Silverstein remains standing. "There's no danger of falling into a trap," he says. "There's only the danger of a little happiness." Approaching her at the stove, he stares at her for a moment and then his arms lightly circle her waist.

Sophie's arms are at her sides. Her eyes are closed. "After a while," she says, "after so many years alone, you lose interest. You don't mean for it to happen, but it does." It hurts to say this, as if it were an admission of calamitous failure.

"I'm talking about love," says Silverstein. "It's like music. Why would you ever stop listening for it?"

"Love?" Sophie says, nodding her head so he will know she understands. Telling herself, over and over again, that for her it will be like listening to unfamiliar music, nothing more than that.

12

Zachary wants to keep Mia home from school one more day.

"Why?" Laura says. "She's fine. You can see that for yourself." Mia is sitting in a chair in the living room watching *Happy Days*. In her lap is a small glass bowl of pretzel sticks. There's a slice of American cheese in her hand; laying out ten pretzel sticks in a row, she rolls the cheese in a cylinder around them. "Her appetite's back," says Laura. "Her color's good. Why can't she go to school?"

"Yeah," says Mia. "What's the big ideal?"

"The big idea," says Zachary, "is that there should be no sign of the virus for at least twenty-four hours." He sticks a banana in the side pocket of his briefcase and gets into his dungaree jacket.

"There's shaving cream on your moustache," says Laura. "And I think your big idea stinks."

Zachary examines himself in the mirrored wall opposite the kitchen. "I don't understand what's happening here," he says. "Why can't she stay home and rest one more day? What's your objection?"

"My objection is it's not necessary," says Laura, appalled at her willingness to start an argument with her husband knowing that he is right, and worse, that she is absolutely wrong. "You stay home and take care of her," she says. "I have things to do."

"I don't believe what I'm hearing," says Zachary over his shoulder. "I'm talking about the kid's health and you're worried about 'things' you have to do? What things? What the hell is wrong with you?" He slams out of the room so violently that the doorbell rings behind him.

"I'm ready to go to school now," says Mia.

"Not today, sweetie."

"What?" Mia says, pronouncing the *t* as if it were a separate syllable.

"Daddy thinks you should rest today."

Swiveling around in her seat, Mia faces the door. "He's gone," she says. "Let's go."

"Can't," says Laura. "My conscience won't allow it."

"You *want* me to go. I know you do."

Laura can see David in his woven plastic chair, tapping his feet, waiting impatiently for the best part of his day. He has never said so, but she suspects that this is the truth; that his pleasures are meager and even fewer without her. The best part of his day? Surely an exaggeration of her importance. "I'm an egomaniac," she says out loud. "Without a doubt."

"Like Superman and Clark Kent?" says Mia.

"What?" says Laura. Then, "That's alter ego, sweetie."

"Right, right. Like Batman and Bruce Wayne and his young ward Dick Grayson, who's really Robin and Hal Jordan who's really Green Lantern and—"

"You watch too much TV," Laura says.

"Do not," says Mia. "I could turn off *Happy Days* right now and not even cry a minute." She darts to the television set and snaps it off with her palm. Running to Laura's side she says, "Look at my eyes. See how they're smiling?"

Laura drops to the floor on one knee. She folds her arms around Mia and squeezes. "Love you," she says.

"Love you one hundred and fifty-nine million miles an hour." Mia seizes her mother's hand and examines her diamond engagement ring. "Can I have this?" she says. "Wouldn't it look pretty on my thumb?"

"You can have it when I die," says Laura. "Until then it stays put on this finger."

"Will you die tonight?"

"If I die," says Laura, "you'll never see me again." She looks at her daughter's impassive face. "Do you understand what I mean?"

Mia nods. "Do you think you could die tomorrow?"

"Go to your room immediately," says Laura, but she is already laughing. Mia starts to walk away, head lowered. "Never mind," says Laura. "You want to go out for a while?"

"Outside?" says Mia. "Terrific."

"First tell me you love me." There is no one in the world who has heard these words from Laura, no one she could so fearlessly bribe. And she feels no guilt, only a little thrill at how easy it is to evoke her daughter's loyalty.

"I do," Mia says eagerly. "I really do."

Out on the street, David takes Mia's hand. "Will you shake hands with me?" he says.

"Are you a stranger?"

"This is my friend David," Laura offers. "It's all right to shake his hand, but not too hard." A mistake: Mia shuts her eyes, pleats her brow, and squeezes David's hand as hard as she can.

David looks at her disappointedly. "Well," he says. "That wasn't very friendly, was it?"

"Did I crack your bones?" Mia says. "My daddy always tells me to try and crack his bones."

"Your father may be strong, but I'm not," says David. "I'm very weak and very sick and that's why it makes me sad that you tried to hurt me like that."

Mia searches his face. "Are you a wimp?" she asks.

Laura has to laugh; David's laughter arrives a moment later. "That's one thing I don't remember ever being accused of," he says.

"So you're not a wimp? I was just curious," Mia says.

"That's enough," says Laura. She is embarrassed and wants to say that she has raised her daughter to be sweet and lovely, that she has tried her hardest to teach her kindness, generosity, and courtesy, but that sometimes, inexplicably, Mia feels compelled to show only the worst she has to offer.

"So," says David. "Tell me your news."

"That's my school over there," says Mia, pointing across the street. "I'm not there today because I'm supposed to be home resting."

"But instead you're out here talking to me."

"Yeah," Mia says. "How come? Do you have any toys I can check out? Because if you don't, I'm going home."

"I have an idea," David begins, but then Mia is sailing down the street toward home, shrieking for Eduardo the doorman. Laura and David watch as she confers with Eduardo, gesturing at his motorcycle parked opposite the doorway. In a moment they can see him lifting Mia onto the seat and Mia's arms outstretched on the handlebars.

"You shouldn't let her run away like that," David says.

"I shouldn't," Laura says, but does not leave his side. She keeps her eyes on Mia as David talks.

"I think about you too much," he says softly. "A lot of day-dreams leading nowhere." Laura continues to look away. "Does it scare you to hear me say things like that?" David says.

Laura shivers slightly. There is a khaki wool army blanket resting on David's lap; she would like to drape it around her but does not want to ask even the smallest of favors of him. She kneels at his side. "Are you afraid of dying?" she says.

"Yes, ma'am," says David. "But only sometimes. Some days, when I'm not seeing clients, when I'm alone and feeling crazy, I can just weep the afternoon away. I sit in the most comfortable chair in my living room and mourn my losses. I think of myself turned to bone, shut away forever in a steel-lined box. Forever! It's sickening to contemplate, and sometimes my legs begin to tremble uncontrollably and I think to myself, 'There's nothing worse than this, you are as low as you are ever going to go.' And I force myself out of the chair and walk to the window and see a person going by in the street, a stranger whose life I envy. I know nothing about him but for an instant I envy everything I imagine is his—health, love, hope. I beat my fists against the window but the stranger is gone and then it's just me slamming around the apartment, knocking books off shelves, kicking over chairs, until I'm exhausted and ready to sleep."

"You think I'm someone who can make you happy," Laura hears herself say. She is still on her knees and can't seem to manage to pick herself up and go after her daughter. Facing David, she is confused by his cool, placid face, his unblinking eyes that refuse to turn away from her. As if his confession of misery, moments ago, had cost him nothing. She has a glimpse of him in another life, a life untouched by illness, and she is certain that he was demanding, unyielding, perhaps even a little arrogant. Not someone she would ever have been in danger of falling in love with.

"If only you would let me sweep you off your feet," David says. "And I don't mean with stories of myself as a tragic figure. I mean with my charm. If I had the strength, I'd romance you in a thousand ways. I'd take you to a rooftop restaurant where you can see the whole city, where a string quartet from Juilliard plays for hours. I'd go around and find you tiny perfect gifts that you never knew you wanted. I'd make you know exactly what it feels like to be in love."

"If you had the energy for all that, if you weren't sick—"

"If I weren't dying," says David.

She can't repeat his words but can only say, "You wouldn't have gotten even this far with me."

She has hurt him and wants to make amends. But even taking his hands in her own seems beyond the distance she wants to go, seems to suggest that anything is possible. She wants to protect her life, to safeguard what is her own. This is only natural: why can't he see that?

"In your mind," says David, "I'm merely a tragic figure. Have I got that straight?" His voice doesn't sound dark at all, only curious.

It's true that for her, he is defined by his illness. He is a man in early middle age, a married man, a marriage counselor, but none of these facts has much meaning for her. He is a doomed man and that is what draws her so powerfully to him. Is this something to be ashamed of? On a television documentary she saw months ago, a man said of his friendship with a dying man: "I feel guilty for feeling curious about how he feels about dying." She knows just what he meant.

There is something else that cannot be ignored. The face that is staring at her now is a face that compels her irresistibly; a face more intelligent than handsome, but finely drawn, lovely in its elegance. Laura sighs, and rises on bruised knees from the concrete. "I want to keep looking at you," she mumbles.

"Say it again." David's hand is on her arm; immediately she shakes him off.

"Don't smile at me, please," she says. She leaves him without saying goodbye, running to her daughter, who is leaning over the doorman's motorcycle and sounding its horn with great pleasure. "Get your finger off that button," Laura says.

"Why?"

"Because it's painful to listen to."

Depressing the button with quick stabs of her thumb so that the horn bleats in staccato, Mia says, "Are you going to get a headache?"

"You bet."

"Well-ell," Mia drawls, "it's simple. You can go upstairs to the medicine cabinet and take some extra-strength pain relievers." She smiles sweetly. "You can just do that, right, and everything will be fine."

13

Barbara is walking along First Avenue with Warren, the tax lawyer. It is a Saturday night and they have just seen a John Sayles
movie about a pair of lesbian lovers. Sitting next to Warren in
the darkened theater, watching two women falling in love with
each other, Barbara struggled with the feeling that everything was
wrong. The movie made her uneasy, along with the warm hand
that Warren insisted on resting along her thigh throughout the
movie. (She is a small-town woman who has spent half of her
life in the city; she will always think of herself as small-town.)
She and Warren have been to the movies together half a dozen

times over the past two months, and half a dozen times they have gone to his apartment in a brownstone on East 79th Street and made love in his narrow, high-ceilinged bedroom. This is the first time Barbara has experienced passion without romance, without love, and she has found it surprisingly satisfying. (She does feel some remorse for betraying David, but not enough to keep her from Warren.) Warren is generous and good-natured, and also slightly loony. Sometimes, when he has smoked a little dope, he talks endlessly about the Kennedy assassination and Lee Harvey Oswald, and also about Lincoln and John Wilkes Booth. He sees parallels between the two assassinations, which he has explained to Barbara numerous times, but she never listens, preferring instead to roam through his apartment in her underwear, examining his books and record albums, most of which are in cartons on the floor, as if he had just moved in. Once, they were in the living room eating chocolate cake straight from the box with their fingers, when Barbara noticed sauce-covered strands of spaghetti hanging from the wall above the butcher block table. Warren peeled them off without embarrassment and explained that he'd had a fight with his girlfriend the night before and that she'd thrown a plateful of food against the wall. "She's an attorney, too," he said. "And a very aggressive one." Barbara smiled, glad to hear he had a girlfriend. Spending most of their time together in movie theaters, she and Warren know not much at all about each other, which suits Barbara fine. She thinks of the two of them as sexual companions who take enormous pleasure in each other's bodies. She is grateful for this, and also for Warren's lack of interest in the rest of her life. He knows the names of her husband and son, and the seriousness of David's illness. ("Heavy," he'd said knowingly. "A real downer.") His father had died of leukemia two years ago, so Warren knew something of Barbara's pain. He never encouraged her to talk about it, though, because, as he said, "Some things are just *too* heavy." And she had to agree that this was so.

"Do you want some ice cream?" he says now as they pass one

dessert shop after another. "Gelato? Tofutti? Watermelon-flavored popcorn?"

Eyeing the mostly young, mostly cheerful crowds all around them, Barbara feels momentarily lost. It is Saturday night and she is out on a date of sorts, while her husband lies across their bed exhausted, reading a book called *Getting Well Again*. She will go back to Warren's apartment, where she will allow him (encourage him) to remove every bit of her clothing and then make love to her. "Perform sex" would be more accurate. A line she has never forgotten from a Woody Allen movie. "Do you want to perform sex with me?" she says out loud.

"What?" says Warren. "You do want Tofutti?"

"My husband is dying," says Barbara. They are stopped at a corner, waiting for the "Walk" sign to flash in their direction. "He's forty-two years old and he's dying." Warren takes her hand and kisses it out on the street, something he has never done before. Recklessly, Barbara leans her head against his shoulder.

"You poor man," says an elderly woman in a red wool turban standing alongside them. The woman's face is chalky-white, ghostly looking. "Have you tried prayers and fasting?"

Warren gives her a dirty look, which of course the woman does not understand. She shrugs. "The Lord," she says when the light changes, "works in ways utterly mysterious to man. May that be a comfort to you and your loved one over here."

"I'm not his loved one," Barbara says, but the woman is gone. "And I have to make a phone call."

"We'll go to the apartment," Warren says.

Barbara's head is still across his shoulder as they turn off First Avenue and walk up 79th Street to the townhouse where Warren lives. Certainly she is not his loved one. What is she doing slumped over him romantically like that? She snaps her head up and moves apart from him.

"Come back," says Warren, patting his shoulder. "It was kind of nice, wasn't it?"

"A moment of weakness," says Barbara. They trudge up a steep staircase that always leaves her winded. "In fact, all of this is weakness," she says.

In the apartment, Warren slips off her down jacket and stuffs it into a corner of the couch. Watching, Barbara smiles. She thinks of David, whose coat is hung up in the closet the instant he returns home. Who gets down on his hands and knees (or used to, before his illness) to realign the tassels on their Persian rug. Whose closet and dresser drawers are extraordinarily well ordered, arranged according to some mysterious system she has never bothered to contemplate. Compulsive, David calls it, rolling his eyes, but secretly he is proud, Barbara thinks. Like Warren, her instincts lead her to sloppiness. Chaos, even. At college, her roommates despaired over Barbara's half of the room, where bras were somehow tangled around notebooks and cake crumbs littered the doily spread across her dresser. According to David, she clearly had no desire to order her environment, to exercise control over it. David, for whom control is everything. Devastating for him to sit, hands tied behind his back, while deep in his body, cells multiply endlessly, shamelessly betraying him.

Warren stands facing Barbara in his living room, his fingers unbuttoning her blouse. He is broad and muscular; a gymnast in college before he became so interested in drugs. His body feels sturdy under her hands as she runs them along his back.

"I have to use your phone," Barbara says. Locked together, they move clumsily toward the bedroom, Barbara walking backward, trusting Warren to maneuver them safely through the narrow doorway.

"Later," says Warren, and they fall into his unmade bed.

"Now." She grabs the phone from the night table and sits up straight against the brick wall to dial. Warren untangles himself from her and leaves her on the bed alone. "Hi," she says into the receiver. "How are you feeling?"

"A stupid question," David says.

"Just trying to make small talk," says Barbara.

"Small talk is for strangers."

Across the room now, Warren is stepping out of his underwear. He flicks his jockey shorts through the air like a Frisbee; they land on the bed, at Barbara's feet. She frowns at them and then at Warren. "The movie's over," she says. "Anita and I are going to get something to eat and then I'll be home. Is that okay?"

"Don't rush back on my account." His voice is flat, emptied of everything, even weariness.

"I hate this," Barbara says, thumping Warren's pillow with her fist. "Goddamnit."

"It's the best we can do, apparently," David says, and hangs up on her.

Warren approaches her cautiously. He sits on the edge of the bed and watches her for a while. "I'm sorry," he says. "I've never said it before because it seems so insubstantial, so little to offer. And I figured you've heard it a hundred times from a hundred other people. That you're sick of hearing it." He slips down under the covers. "My father was always the healthiest guy in the world. He'd never even been in the hospital. When he got sick, when he found out how sick he really was, he was stunned. He wasn't good at being sick; he was cranky and demanding and impossible to please. He kept saying how wrong it was, how unnatural it felt to be so helpless. After a while, he began to talk about how much he wanted to die. I believed him; I knew he was telling the truth." Warren tugs lightly at Barbara's hand and the next moment she slides next to him and under a soft rumpled plain white sheet. "Is that what David wants?" he says.

"He wants me to feel," Barbara says slowly, "I don't know, almost comfortable, I guess, with what's happened, with what's going to happen. He thinks I should be able to look at him and talk to him as if very little had changed, as if for us, like everyone else, the future was uncertain, undecided. But that's impossible. I look at him and think, Our marriage is coming to an end. We've been married seventeen years and that's all there's going to be. I wake up at four in the morning and my face is wet, my pillow is wet. I've been crying in my sleep. I'm a coward; I don't want to be left alone." She does not tell him that while David sleeps, she kisses his eyes, his ears, his throat. She strokes his hair. She whispers to him to forgive her. She hears herself whispering, but it's like a dream, something happening so quietly in the dark. In bright daylight she has to look away. She's overcome then, overwhelmed by the sight of him. She's close to tears every minute; holding them back seems to take up all her energy. A look from him, the right word from him, and she is lost.

"These are secrets you've told me," says Warren. "And I have no secrets for you."

"I don't want to know them anyway."

Warren lowers himself over her, breathing warmly at the side of her face. He's too close, his body too heavy for her.

"I need to breathe," Barbara says, almost apologetically. "Please."

Instantly easing off of her, propping himself up on his elbow, Warren says, "Do you want to hear about the day I spent in jail?" He means to entertain her: how can she refuse to listen? "I got caught selling a few tabs of acid to some minors," Warren explains. "It was all a mistake. I was in college, in upstate New York, and they took me to some little jail where they kept bringing me Cokes and peanut butter sandwiches every hour. I sat there in a cell with an old man, a vagrant, a sweet guy, really. He gave me a lot of advice. I remember him saying, 'A man has to have a trade or a profession, the one thing that can't be taken away from him.' "

"And that's why you went to law school," Barbara says, smiling.

"No," says Warren. "In fact, I can't remember *why* I went to law school."

Barbara takes a guess. "Your father was a lawyer?"

"Do you think that could have been it?" Warren says. He sounds plaintive, bewildered. Absently, Barbara plays with his hair, which is curly and full and nearly red.

"You have beautiful hair," she murmurs, though they have never felt the need to compliment one another. Warren doesn't answer. His eyes are closed; perhaps he is asleep.

"My cellmate," he says suddenly, "the guy who lectured me? He was a one-man band. Out on the street his whole working life. It was hard work and it wore him out. One day he just didn't have the strength for it anymore. He abandoned his instruments right there on the street. That still seems so sad to me, all these years later."

Sad? Barbara is no longer moved by the lives of strangers and their suffering. Her own sorrows are as keenly felt as an unrelenting toothache. She is always in pain, even in her dreams. "Sad?" she says to Warren. "I don't even know what you're talking about."

14

Though Laura is beginning the third month of her pregnancy, she has not yet felt a compulsion to share the news with anyone. The pregnancy was unplanned and perhaps, she thinks, this is the reason why it feels the slightest bit illusory. She and Zachary had always assumed they would have another child, and for weeks now Zachary had been trying to convince her that the timing was of little consequence, that they had no reason in the world to regret what had happened on the living room rug in the light of a silent TV set. Laura has come to see the wisdom in his casual acceptance of things; she is able to say out loud that she is happy about the new baby. Listening to her voice, she is satisfied that she is speaking the truth. And still she is content to keep the news to herself.

At night, in bed, she does not know what to do with her breasts, which have suddenly grown too full for her narrow body, spilling out beyond her rib cage, pressing painfully against her arm or Zachary's spine. If not for this awareness of pain, she would hardly know she is pregnant at all. And so most of the time she finds herself concentrating on other things. Except when she is with David. Over the past few months (and it amazes her when she thinks of this), she has spent more time with him, and spoken more intimately with him, than with anyone except her husband. He has earned the right to know everything of importance about her: clearly she is deceiving him by withholding the fact of her pregnancy. She has seen him early every weekday for two months, David wrapped in an army blanket over his jacket and she in her sheepskin coat, sometimes hopping from one foot to the other to keep warm, and always, unhesitatingly, refusing his offer to go upstairs where of course it would be more comfortable. What does she think will happen if they go upstairs? he wants to know. She does not want to find out.

One morning he calls her just as she is about to leave with Mia for school. "Listen, you idiot," he says cheerfully. "The wind-chill factor is minus six. If you think I'm going to sit out there and freeze to death just for the pleasure of your company, you're nuts."

"Let me think about this," Laura says, taking a handful of her hair and sweeping it across her mouth, stroking her face with it, always a comforting gesture.

"There's nothing to think about. I'll see you upstairs in a couple of minutes."

In the kitchen, Zachary is standing with his back to the refrigerator door, eating yogurt from a plastic container. "Who was that?" he asks.

"David. He says it's too cold to sit outside this morning."

"Sounds reasonable."

Laura frowns at the spoonful of yogurt coming in her direction, but opens her mouth wide anyway. "He wants me to go up to his apartment."

"So?"

"I don't know." She brushes her hair across one eyelid and then the other.

Feeding her more yogurt, Zachary pins her against the sink with his hips. "If he has any etchings to show you, just look the other way." Both of them laugh at this, at the absurdity of it. "What do you think, I'm going to be jealous of a dying man?" Zachary says.

Afterward, when David's doorman buzzes him to signal Laura's arrival, he smiles at her and says into the intercom, "Your lady friend is here to see you."

"The wind-chill factor is minus six," Laura explains.

"Freezing cold out, yes." The doorman, Rodney, a courtly man in a black uniform with flat silver buttons, grabs her hands. "He's a very sick man and you are a very lovely woman. A good person. It's something to be proud of, to be the friend of a man like that."

Embarrassed, eyes slightly teary, Laura escapes into the elevator. She rides up to the fifth floor, and when she gets out, there is David standing at his open door, wearing a baggy gray jogging suit. She walks over thick pale green carpeting to meet him.

"Nice building," she says, meaning nicer than her own. There are only four apartments on the floor, and the walls in the hallway are decorated with Impressionist prints framed in metal and glass. An oval mahogany table, highly polished and holding a ceramic vase of silk flowers, rests against the wall opposite the elevator.

"Are you rich?" Laura says.

David closes the door behind them. "Very," he says. "In fact, just the other day I was considering giving the butler a raise. Actually, we bought the place for a song a thousand years ago."

He shows Laura around the apartment, which is overheated and smells of furniture polish. The living room looks strikingly ordinary, everything in expected places—a couch and matching armchairs upholstered in Haitian cotton and separated by an octagonal-shaped glass-topped coffee table; a black leather lounger with a folded newspaper on its seat; a few posters advertising museum exhibitions dry-mounted and hanging on the walls; to the side of the couch, an upright piano with yellowish keys; a small bookcase filled with a set of encyclopedias and the complete works of Sigmund Freud and Winston Churchill and Ernest Hemingway. In David's bedroom, there is a Persian rug on the floor and a king-sized bed carefully covered by a white comforter decorated with a faded rainbow that runs the length of the bed. A small dressing room is beyond the bedroom; on a bureau with clawed feet is a photograph of a serene-looking bride, a narrow pink ribbon threaded through eyelets at the hem of her gown and also through her hair. Laura studies the picture with her hands behind her back.

"A long time ago," David says in a murmur.

Laura nods; she knows all about Barbara, whom David loves but barely speaks to. She cannot imagine such a marriage, such suffering. Whenever David talks of Barbara, his voice becomes a mumbled monotone, so that Laura has to strain to understand him. He suspects Barbara of having an affair, he told Laura recently, shrugging it off as if it were of no interest. As a marriage counselor, he said, he had always been prepared for anything. He told her stories of men running off with their fathers-in-law, mothers-in-law, stepdaughters, stepsons. The possibilities, he said, were infinite. Sometimes he tried to get Laura to talk of her own marriage, but there was nothing she could say that David wanted to hear. And she didn't want to sound smug in her happiness. Her parents' marriage was a disaster; wouldn't he like to hear more about it? A look of despair came over his face at that, a look that said he had given up.

"Let me show you my office," he says now, leading her back

to the living room, across the small dining room, to the other end of the apartment.

Laura's eyes open wide at the sight of the papier-mâché mother and child. "Neat," she says and settles on the bench next to the figures, feeling them delicately with her hands. She strokes the baby in its white linen gown, strokes its bumpy skull. "I'm pregnant," she says.

"What?" David says, a little harshly, she thinks. "You're kidding." Making room for himself beside her, he gives the papier-mâché woman a little shove.

"You're the first person I've told."

"Great," says David. With his knuckles, he raps against the papier-mâché breasts. "I'm jealous, of course," he says. Rap go his knuckles, a little harder this time, across the woman's breasts. Laura flinches. Covering his hands with her palms, she quiets them. It is the first time they have deliberately touched.

"What is there to be jealous of?" she says.

"Think about it: for a man in love, there have to be a thousand things to be jealous of."

"A joke?" says Laura in a tiny voice, the strongest she can manage.

"No joke." Then, turning toward her, "I'm going to kiss you now."

"You are?" Laura says, and is silenced sweetly. They kiss chastely, with their hands at their sides. "No joke," Laura says when at last David draws back.

"You'd better believe this is serious business," he says, not smiling.

This is just what she does not want to believe. But there is the booming of her heart, her chilled hands, her mouth full of dust. All the signs of a coward in danger. She falls against him and feels his arms close in a circle around her back. She wants to know just how much he loves her. She thinks of her daughter saying, I love you one hundred and fifty-nine million miles an hour.

David's hands are under her sweater now, discovering her swollen breasts, and then her soft belly, already puffy and unfamiliar to her.

"This isn't me," she says. She misses Zachary, who knows her so well; who does not need to be told that this new rounding out of her body is so strange, such a surprise. But David knows her only as she is now, soft, bones nearly gone.

Her clothes are gone, too, and David's. On the floor, on thin industrial gray carpeting, they lie side by side. Now he is moving toward her, matching his chest against hers. This isn't me, she says silently, but of course it is a lie. She locks her ankles around him so he cannot get away. "Stay," she says.

She blinks her eyes and it is over.

Afterward, she opens her mouth to speak, discovers she has lost her voice. Lifting her head, she stares at the silvery pink scar that runs from David's groin to his sternum. It looks a bit raw, still; more pink than silver. She would like to touch it, but is afraid of hurting him.

"A souvenir," he says. "From the exploratory surgery."

Bending over him, she kisses the trail the surgeon left behind. Then she dresses, slipping her clothes back on, dreamily, noiselessly. The apartment is silent as she leaves it, as still as if it were just before dawn.

Later, at night, after making love with Zachary in the darkness of their bedroom, she runs her finger along the smooth unmarked path from his navel to his neck, and weeps without a sound.

Once a month, David disappears into the hospital for a couple of days for his chemotherapy treatments, which he refuses to discuss with Laura, saying only that they are ghastly. When next Laura sees him, he always looks wearier than she remembers, his pallor more pronounced, his face leaner, skin papery. But it is the chemo that is keeping him alive, and so she doesn't worry too much when he vanishes.

This last time, though, is different: she has not heard from him in a week. Panicking at the thought of this long silence between them, she calls the hospital and learns that he is in intensive care. No explanation is offered, of course, and there is no one she can call for one. She is only a friend, and the wrong kind of friend at that—not the kind who can ask the family for details.

"No problem," Zachary says that night when she tells him. "Why don't you call his wife, or something."

Or something, she thinks. Lamely, she says that David and his wife are having problems, that they are angry at each other a lot, that in any event she does not want to bother his wife.

"That's a lot of horseshit," says Zachary. "You can't make a simple phone call?"

"I can't," Laura says. A mistake to talk about this with Zachary, even to mention David's name, though occasionally, over the months, it has been Zachary who brings up the subject, who asks how David has been feeling. Zachary has no idea that she is no longer someone to be trusted, that she no longer trusts herself. "I love you," she tells him now, but it doesn't much ease the prickle of guilt that will always take her by surprise.

Zachary rests his hand on her stomach. "Just hearing David's name always depresses me," he says. "Doesn't it depress you to be with him?"

"He's lonely," Laura says. "We talk and then he's less lonely."

"Are you?"

"Am I what?"

"Lonely," Zachary says.

"What do you mean?"

"It's been *ten* years," Zachary says, sounding amazed. "And every now and then it hits me that for days we've hardly been paying attention . . . it's as if some part of me has been dozing and then suddenly I'm wide awake and thinking, Days have passed and we've forgotten each other, God knows the things we've missed."

"We?" Laura's hand falls on top of his; together they travel in wide circles across her stomach.

"You, too," Zachary says softly. "Where have you been?"

At four in the afternoon, as Mia sits mesmerized in front of the TV, thrilled by a hideous-looking cartoon character named Skeletor, Laura telephones David's apartment. She is counting on the probability of his son's being home alone and is relieved when an adolescent voice, not quite manly, answers on the third ring.

Explaining that she is a friend of David's, Laura says, "I've been so worried."

"Yeah," says Ethan. "I know what you mean." In the background, Laura hears Bruce Springsteen singing of sailors in satin shirts.

"What happened?" Laura says. Talk to me, she urges him silently. Tell me what I want to know.

"Okay, see, like they injected some junk into his stomach," Ethan says, "some experimental stuff, and he got a real high fever, an infection. But he's better now, just got out of I.C.U. this morning. He'll be all right, I guess." His interest is fading; Laura can hear him snapping his fingers in time to the music. "Look," he says, "do you want to leave a message?"

"Have you seen him?" Laura asks, reluctant to let go.

"He doesn't like people to visit him when he's in the hospital. He hates for anyone to see him when he looks so awful. Even my mother's not allowed."

Laura listens as the music grows louder, overpowering. "Thank you," she says. "Thank you for talking to me." She is grateful that he is sixteen and self-absorbed; that he will probably forget the details of their conversation, forget that she called at all. Quickly, before she has a chance to lose courage, she dials the hospital and asks to speak to David. She does not recognize his voice, which is lifeless, somewhere between a moan and a whisper.

"It's Laura," she says.

"Laura." There is no change in his voice, no sign that her name means anything to him. "I was more dead than alive," he says. "But I'm back from wherever it is I was." A long pause while he breathes heavily. "Just in time for my birthday."

"When is that?"

"Tomorrow," he says. "Bake me a cake with a hacksaw inside."

"A hacksaw?"

"Isn't that what prisoners usually ask for?"

"I don't know, but will you let me come and visit?"

"That would be lovely," David says in this ruined voice which she cannot get used to.

"Are you sure?"

"Just come," he says. "Whenever you can."

Marching up the street with a Mylar balloon tied firmly to her wrist, Laura returns the smile of anyone who grins in her direction. It is a bright, windy day and the balloon, which has "Happy Birthday" printed across it back and front, sways above her, knocking noisily in the wind. At the toy store where she bought it, Laura had asked for a plastic bag to carry it in, and the salesman, a blond who was dressed entirely in black, had challenged her, saying, "What's the matter, you don't want to be seen with a balloon on the streets of New York?" Behind the counter, two other salesmen were laughing—at her, Laura assumed. But when the salesman all in black came around to the front of the counter to fasten the balloon to her wrist, Laura saw that taped to his back was a sign in red letters saying, "Kiss me, I'm gay." The others salesmen were gay, too, she realized; a private joke among the three of them. "You want to be noticed in this world," Laura's salesman told her, holding on to her wrist. "Trust me, this balloon will do the trick."

On a side street bordering the hospital, a man is selling flowers out of a rusting station wagon, his German shepherd lying calmly on the roof of the car, one front paw crossed neatly over the other. "Bird of paradise?" the man says. "Freesia? Or maybe the birthday kid would like some roses."

Laura ignores him and enters the small pavilion where David stays every month. She reaches his room with no difficulty and peeks inside, her feet staying just behind the threshold. David is seated at the side of the bed, eating his lunch from a maroon plastic tray that has been placed on top of a metal cart on wheels. He is wearing a pajama top open to the waist, and gray sweatpants. His hair sticks out from his head in all directions, giving him the look of a gentle madman.

"Hi," Laura says, and walks toward him.

"Hello." He glances at her, then goes back to his lunch: a gray hamburger on an open bun, black, soupy spinach, melting vanilla ice cream in a Styrofoam cup.

"Happy birthday." Laura releases the balloon, which floats off into a corner. She stares at the floor, at David's white feet in green foam rubber slippers, curved along a bar at the bottom of the cart.

"Right," says David, nodding at the balloon. He gulps down a cup of tea, then eases himself onto his back, groaning quietly, terribly, his eyes shut tight. He continues to groan, on and on and on; eerie music Laura cannot bear to listen to.

"Stop," she murmurs. She thinks of the worst pain she has known, of the half hour before Mia's birth, of wanting to die. "Given the choice between life and death," she'd screamed at Zachary, "I choose death." He'd smiled in confusion, not believing her, the words making no sense to him. He tried to comfort her, but it wasn't possible. She had only contempt for his meager offerings—spoonfuls of crushed ice, a damp washcloth for her forehead, kisses for her fingertips. She'd only wanted to die, had never wanted anything more desperately.

"I think I should go," she says. "I don't think I should be here." No response from David. "Maybe I'll come back in a couple of days."

"Whatever," David says. The groaning has stopped and Laura

can look his way again. He has pulled the bed sheets up all the way to his nose, hiding everything from her but his eyes, which are pink-rimmed and only half open. Watching David, Laura imagines herself as his wife, someone with ties to him reaching back over the years to another life. The pain of remembered happiness. The inevitable, unbearable loss, easy enough to imagine, impossible to live with. If she were his wife, she could not survive any of this.

"Let me do something for you," she says. "You tell me what."

"There's nothing," he says.

A silver-haired man in white shoes, peach-colored pants, suspenders, and a gray polyester shirt pulled tightly over an extraordinary stomach, walks into the room. "Cookie," the man says, a little too loudly. "My birthday baby." In his hands are sprays of three different colors of freesia—red, yellow, and white. The man's face is very tan, and unnaturally shiny, as if he were wearing makeup.

"Hey, Pop," says David. He does not introduce his father to Laura. "Sorry to see your tan's fading."

After bending to kiss David's forehead, his father lays his cheek on David's pillow. "How can you be so sick on your birthday?" he says. "What miserable timing."

"Did I forget to mention this is Laura?" David says. "And the old guy is George."

"Ah," says George. Smiling at Laura, he says, "I thought so."

Laura says, "Truthfully, I was just on my way out. Really."

"I came at the wrong time," George says. "I'm sorry."

"You both came at the wrong time," David says as George lifts his head from the pillow. "Why don't the two of you get lost for a while."

"Cookie," George says. "What's with you?"

"I hate birthdays," David says. "And I'm used to my solitude, nurses and doctors popping in for a word or two, nothing more. I've lost the knack for pleasant conversation. If someone asks

'How are you?' I laugh, because it's a joke. Notice I didn't ask how you are. I didn't ask because that's a joke, too—I couldn't care less." All of this is delivered without inflection, making it sound all the more menacing.

"Well," says George after a moment. "You're entitled, I guess." Taking Laura's arm, he steers her out the door, both of them looking over their shoulders at David, neither of them saying goodbye. At the elevator George says, "I'm not taking this personally, and don't you either."

The elevator arrives, carrying a little boy about Mia's age and his father. The man steps back to make room for Laura and George, but the little boy stays up front. "Move," says the man, yanking his son back.

"Bug off, buffalo breath," the boy says fiercely.

Startled, Laura laughs out loud.

"That's right," the man says, "encourage him. Let him think he's a first-class entertainer."

She is still laughing as they leave the building. On the steps leading down to the street, George throws his arm around her shoulder. "Always better to laugh," he says. They begin walking crosstown, still joined by the arm he's looped across her. They are strangers, but she likes the comfortable weight of his arm around her neck.

"You have a child," George soon says, "so you know what they are."

"Irreplaceable."

"Even when they're grown, when they have children of their own, lives of their own, you want to protect them. My son's life is in danger, and I can't rescue him. Every day it's as if he's running out into the street, running closer and closer to some car that's eventually going to get him for sure. I'm watching from a window, paralyzed. I can't make a move to help him. I'm watching from close by, listening for the squeal of tires, for that thump just before the body goes flying into the air."

Two mimes in white-face pass by. They are dressed in tuxedos and black ballet slippers, their hands in white cotton gloves. They are talking about pastry crust. "Some people swear by Crisco," one says, "but for me it's butter all the way."

"I'm not going to argue with you," the other one says.

George stops, and stamps his foot on the pavement. He looks up toward the sky. "You miserable miserable shithead," he yells.

The mimes turn to stare at him.

"Why don't you get lost," Laura says to them, but softly.

One of the mimes steps forward, leaning all his weight on one bent knee. He cups a hand around his ear, raises his eyebrows. In the center of all that white, his eyes look intensely dark, something to be afraid of.

"You heard me," Laura says.

In an hour's time, she has led George back to her apartment and into her living room, a place that David has never seen and most likely never will.

George admires an entire wallful of books and the giant pencil hanging high across the window. "Forget my place here in the city, but you should see what I've got in Florida," he says. Laura is making tuna fish salad for their lunch, grating half a carrot into it now; George stands in the doorway of the kitchen, facing her back. "Everything's avocado," he says. "Carpeting, refrigerator, stove, cabinets, electric can opener, you name it. My wife—my second wife, not David's mother—picked everything out. Then she died, leaving me with all that avocado. Kind of a nauseating color, actually."

"Do you miss her?" Laura brings the tuna fish to the dining room table; George sets out the plates and silverware she hands him.

"Too much," he says. "Sometimes, when I'm down in Florida, shopping at the Pantry Pride, I stop at the frozen food and pick out some Sara Lee pound cake, just the plain kind, because that's what Helaine likes best. I'm paying for it at the checkout counter, three boxes of it, and then it hits me that she's gone, that I don't even *like* such plain cake, but the cashier's already rung it up and what am I going to tell her: 'Void those numbers. I accidentally bought cake for a dead woman'? So I go home and put the cake away, and every time I open the freezer I think, Fool. Poor dumb fool. After a while, in a few weeks, maybe, I carry the three boxes out to the hallway to the compactor and in a flash that stuff is down the tubes." George taps his huge belly. "And for a man like me to throw perfectly good food away . . ."

"Have some tuna," Laura says.

"Packed in water or oil?"

"I'm sorry," says Laura. "But at least I used low-calorie mayonnaise. Or maybe I didn't. Do you want me to check the jar?"

George laughs. "Why bother?" he says. "Let's face it, I love to eat. At this late date, what's the difference if I'm fifty pounds overweight or fifty-one?" He tastes the tuna fish and says, "The carrots are a nice touch, for which I'm grateful." He tells Laura about his new girlfriend in Fort Lauderdale. "A working girl, so she doesn't have too much time for me. Like my friend up here, but this one doesn't have a husband, thank God."

Laura looks down at her plate, then at George's dark gleaming face.

"So," says George. "I understand my son thinks he's in love with you. It's not hard to see why."

"It's not?"

"I think it's a beautiful thing," George says. "At first I didn't; I thought, What if she doesn't love him back? What if it's just pity and he's mistaken it for love? Then I realized it didn't matter. If you're good to him, I don't care what your reasons are. I don't care that you've got a husband you love. So what? David's got a wife he loves but there's so little happiness there. Let him be happy, let him think he's discovered love all over again. What else is there for him?"

"It's *not* pity," Laura says, as if she has been accused of something unforgivable. She would like to reach across the table and grab George by his suspenders, lift him out of his seat and then let him go, watch him fall back clumsily into his chair, or maybe have him miss the chair entirely and end up on the floor, his limbs in a tangle. She sees herself bending over David to kiss his scar, remembers her mouth against his skin. Surely not pity. Love? Passion? She did not ask for any of it, and is uneasy contemplating it. She never smiles to herself when thinking of David, she realizes. Never? She is smiling now, remembering the two of them on the floor of his office, the scratchy industrial carpeting under their backs, each of them staring at what the other had to offer. Kissing him, allowing herself to be kissed, to be touched, she had left her old scrupulous self behind. She thinks of Zachary, who is heartsick every time a student hands in a plagiarized paper. Oddly, some of the guilty ones claimed they had no idea that what they'd done was wrong. They seemed surprised that there was actually a word for it.

Unlike Laura, who knows all the words.

"I love him," she says out loud.

George nods. He looks relieved. He finishes all the food on his plate and then asks for more.

15

"I hear," says Aïda, smiling, "that you and your boyfriend been spending a lot of time together. You making it yet?" She pokes Sophie in the stomach with her elbow, but lightly. "Don't be shy. You can be straight with me." They are sitting on a bench in the neighborhood schoolyard, watching Carmen sweeping downward along a stainless steel slide that leads into a sandpit, watching her dribbling handfuls of sand now through her fingers. Aïda lights a cigarette, throws the match over her shoulder.

"You think your baby likes all that smoke going down into your lungs?" Sophie says. "Shame on you."

"At least you guys don't have to worry about you getting pregnant," Aïda says. The thought of Sophie pregnant makes her giggle; choking on inhaled smoke, she slaps her chest sharply a few times, bends her head toward her knees.

"Very funny," says Sophie. "Ha ha. See what you get for laughing at me?"

Carmen has been joined by a pale-faced little boy a few years older than she is, dressed in dark green bell-bottomed pants and a nylon windbreaker that barely reaches to his waist. They play in silence at opposite corners of the sandbox, ignoring each other.

"So you two going to live happily ever after?" Aïda asks when she's breathing normally again. "Let's hear the dirt."

"There's no dirt," Sophie says. "There's just the two of us, Silverstein and myself, looking out for each other, cheering each other up now and then."

"That's all?" says Aïda, disappointed. "Jimmie says he saw the old guy leaving your apartment real early one morning last week, creeping away with a big smile on his face. I heard that and I told Jimmie, 'They're making it, all right.' I got a big kick out of it, thinking of the two of you like that."

Not for anything would Sophie admit to her that Jimmie saw exactly what he thought he saw that morning. Spending the night with Silverstein—the two of them clinging shyly to the bedsheets all those hours on Sophie's big droopy mattress—had been sweeter than she'd expected. "Why sleep alone when the alternative is *this*?" Silverstein said, dropping kisses so loudly in her ear they hurt. "Get away, you," Sophie told him, but she had let him stay until morning, had even kept her glasses on so she could study his face from time to time in the near-darkness. Beyond her window, two blocks away, the elevated train periodically flew past with its muted rumble, a sound that always saddened her but that night did not. A man had shared her bed and here she was smiling at the memory of it. The last time, she had been the mother of young children and Mr. Roosevelt had been President. How had she managed for more than half a lifetime without it?

"I suppose it's true you can get used to anything," she says out loud.

"What?" says Aïda. Then, "Just a minute." She rushes over the pavement to Carmen's rescue; Carmen, whose scalp has been sprinkled with sand by the little boy in bell-bottoms. "You do that to my daughter again and I'll break your head," Aïda warns him. "You get the picture?"

"*She* told me to do it," the boy says. "She said, 'Put sand in my hair, Russell, and then I'll put sand in yours and we'll be twins.' "

"Great," Aïda says. "The idiot twins."

"I did not," says Carmen. She scratches her head with the fingers of one hand, her tiny nails painted with pumpkin-colored polish that is half chipped away.

"Remind me to give you a manicure," Aïda says as she walks off, back toward Sophie, who is holding an open compact up to her face and putting on lipstick in bright winter sunlight.

Aïda shakes her head. "That color is all wrong for you."

"Plain old red," says Sophie. "What could be wrong with it?"

"Too much for you. You need something softer."

"You're not working in Bloomingdale's yet," says Sophie. She flips the compact shut. "Once, you know, a very long time ago, so long ago I'd forgotten about it, I worked there myself, in the children's department. A temporary job, just for the Christmas season. And there I was, working at my station, when who do you think wants me to wait on her?" Aïda shrugs. "Take a guess," says Sophie. When Aïda doesn't answer, Sophie says, "Fanny Brice, that's who. What do you think of that?"

"Who?" says Aïda.

"Fanny Brice, a very famous actress. She picked out a fancy navy blue velvet coat, for her little girl, I suppose. I wrapped up the coat nicely for her in a box and she thanked me, and that

was that. It must have been very exciting for me, wrapping something up for such a famous lady." But it is the coat she remembers
most of all, made of the softest velvet, with velvet-covered buttons
and a matching hat that tied with ribbon.

"Oh yeah? You don't sound too excited," says Aïda. "If I was
working there and someone like Michael Jackson or Prince came
in and wanted to buy some makeup from me, I'd probably freak."

"Your prince I don't know about, but I read all about this
Michael Jackson in the *New York Times*," Sophie says. "I hate
to tell you, but his big hobby is watching cartoons all day like a
baby. He doesn't sound like much of a person to me."

"Those cheekbones." Aïda sighs, eyes closed, hands folded
along the globe of her belly.

Sophie laughs. "It sounds to me as if you're in love."

"Don't tell Jimmie." Soon, seizing Sophie's hands, Aïda says,
"There goes the little guy again. Want to check him out?"

Under her palms, Sophie can feel the baby, like a pulse thumping against Aïda's middle. "The sweetest thing in the world," she
murmurs, "to feel life right under your fingers." Overcome, for
only a moment, she kisses Aïda's cheek. "Your *mazel* should be
good, that's the main thing, what you have to hope for," she
says.

"Is that Jewish talk or English?"

"It's luck I'm talking about, sweetie pie, just plain luck. Everything in this world is so much harder without it."

"Money is what would do the trick for me," Aïda says. "If you
have enough money, you can *buy* your own good luck. Rich
people do it all the time." Suddenly she is out of her seat, racing
to her daughter, shrieking sounds but no words. Straining through
the tops of her bifocals, Sophie sees a child near Carmen holding
something between his fingers, arms stretched down toward his
knees, head lowered in concentration. She thinks that perhaps
what he holds in his hands is a tiny bird, something fragile and
in need of protection. What Aïda sees, even more clearly now

as she draws near, is an arc of amber liquid falling at her daughter's feet and the look of mindless rapture on the little boy's face, a look that changes to annoyance marked with the slightest trace of doubt when he notices Aïda's approach. "You little bastard," she says to the boy, grabbing Carmen and pulling her away from the foaming puddle in the sand. "You think the world is your toilet?"

"I had to go," Russell says. "At the beach, at Coney Island, I go in the ocean. Here, there's no ocean, only the sand." He zips up his fly languidly, taking his time, as if knowing he can do nothing to appease Aïda, he might just as well continue to infuriate her.

"You," Aïda says, and waves a fist close to his face. "Your *mazel* should be all bad, the pits, the worst."

The boy looks at her without interest. "I have a cousin who has a knife," is all he says. He climbs up the slide and out of the sandbox on his hands and knees, then runs across the playground and beyond the chain-link fence, down the street and out of sight.

"There's nothing to worry about," Aïda comforts Carmen. "I chased him away with an old Jewish curse. They're the best kind."

At the Palace of Naples, seated next to Silverstein on a stained velveteen throne, Sophie slaps her laminated menu shut. "I'll have the fish, very plain, very dry, no butter," she tells Mac. Mac is Silverstein's son, a big broad man whose real name is Milton. He brokers heavy industrial machinery and makes a good living at it, as he will be the first to tell you. His house on Long Island has a Jacuzzi in one of the upstairs bathrooms, a shining black tub as wide and deep as a small pool, according to Silverstein. Hearing this, Sophie was not impressed. She has always thought of Mac as indelicate and thick-witted, though she assumes his success as a businessman must, in some very small way, have something to do with brains. (Or maybe, she thinks, listening to Mac now, it's just what they call "business sense," a shrewdness that operates entirely on its own, separate from intelligence.)

"Sophie, honey," he is saying, "why do I bother to bring you to an elegant restaurant like this when the best you can do is a boring piece of fish? You and my father are some pair."

"It's the hypertension," says Silverstein, glaring at his son. "She has to watch what she eats. Not that it's any business of yours."

Sophie puts a hand at the back of Silverstein's neck. "And how is Audrey?" she asks Mac. Audrey, his wife, is at their condominium in the Virgin Islands perfecting her golf game, Mac says. If she were here with them in the restaurant, Sophie knows, she would be calling Silverstein "Grandpa" and drinking down one Scotch and water after another, finding life sadder and more overwhelming with each successive drink.

"Audrey," says Mac warily, "is Audrey."

"A terrific golfer," Sophie offers.

"When she's not half crocked," Silverstein whispers in her ear.

"No fair," says Mac. "If you're going to tell secrets you're going to have to speak up so everyone can hear."

"How's the Jacuzzi?" Silverstein says in a loud voice.

"Leaking through to the kitchen ceiling," Mac says. "Don't ask." He goes on to tell a complicated story about the plumber who tried to repair it and left muddy footprints on their new white carpeting. Sophie loses patience almost immediately, and turns her attention to a large oil painting in a heavy gold frame positioned on the wall opposite her. It is a portrait of a middle-aged man dressed in a suit, and a woman, who reminds Sophie of Ann Landers, in a low-cut gown with a crucifix around her neck. The man and woman are staring straight ahead, as if into a camera, looking grim, Sophie thinks. Hanging on the wall above the painting, dangerously close to their heads, is a pot of plastic flowers. Sophie laughs, imagines the flowers falling, the identical fixed expression on the couple's faces turning to horror.

"What's so hilarious?" says Mac. "You think a fifteen-hundred-dollar plumbing bill is funny?"

A waiter named Joseph arrives to take their order. "Ah," he greets Silverstein, "don't tell me: a nice piece of fish, dry, very plain, as plain as they can make it." He is a tall young man in a satin-edged jacket. Shining at the very tip of his ear, miles from his ear lobe, is a tiny diamond stud.

"This is my oldest and most beloved friend in this life or any other life," says Silverstein, gesturing toward Sophie now. "She'll have the fish, too."

"I was just admiring your beautiful diamond up there," Sophie says.

"Were you? My lover found it in the dirt in his backyard when he was growing up. He was digging for worms out behind his bedroom window and look what he comes up with. His mother cleaned it off, wrapped it up in cotton and promised him that someday it would be his pleasure to offer it to the girl of his dreams. Forty years goes by and there's not a single girl he's been dreaming about. Then along I come—"

"And the rest is history," finishes Mac. "The romance of the century. I'll have the lobster, the Fra Diavolo, please."

"A lovely story," says Sophie, reaching for Silverstein's hand. "And so romantic."

"Would you like to see his picture?" says Joseph. He hunts in his pocket for his wallet and withdraws a glossy snapshot of an older man with a gray beard and moustache. "And that's the sweater I knit for him. You can't tell from the picture, but those are some really spectacular cables there. Not that they were appreciated. In fact, this picture is the only proof I've got that he actually wore the goddamn sweater."

"Make that the Chicken Rollatini," says Mac. "It seems to me I had lobster tails for dinner just a few nights ago."

"I don't know," says Silverstein as Joseph moves out of sight. "He's out digging for worms and there's this diamond winking at him from the dirt? What do you think the chances are for something like that happening?"

Sophie is silent, mourning the loss of her diamond wedding ring, the one meaningful souvenir from her marriage, lost six months now, glittering no doubt in a garbage heap off of the Belt Parkway, gleaming among the milk cartons and vegetable peelings and chicken bones, a feast for the seagulls. She can still see it perfectly: the narrowest band of white gold decorated all around with diamonds the size of pinpoints. She had wrapped it in a tissue one night just before kneading ice-cold ground beef into a meatloaf for her dinner. Somehow the tissue had been thrown out, tossed down the compactor along with the rest of that night's trash, picked up the next morning by a truck and carried off to the garbage mountain near the parkway. Pleading over the telephone to someone at the Department of Sanitation, begging for a stranger's help as she never had before, she'd listened to an anonymous voice, nasal with contempt, saying, "Madam, what do you think this is, the lost and found? Just do us all a favor and tell your husband to buy you another ring." Rarely does she think of her husband, of anything even distantly connected to him, but the loss of this wedding band stings so sharply, a wound that she believes will never heal. Now for the first time, she finds herself imagining the ring's rescue: a seagull swoops down beautifully from the sky, seizes the diamond band in its mouth, then flies, guided as if by some mysterious sympathetic radar, to Sophie's windowsill. And there is Sophie, waiting with palm outstretched, to close her fingers tightly over the perfect circle of her wedding band.

On the table, between two water glasses, lies Sophie's fist, nails pressed painfully into the soft pad of flesh of her palm.

"You going to give someone a punch?" teases Mac. "Thinking about the time the old man got fresh with you?"

"I'd like to give *you* a punch," says Silverstein. He unwraps Sophie's fist, traces the crescent-shaped marks left behind by her nails.

"Me?" says Mac. "What for?"

"Just on general principles," says Silverstein. "For general, all-purpose obnoxiousness." To Sophie he says, "My son, God bless him, comes on strong. Either you love him or you hate him, don't you think?"

"I want to thank you, Mac," says Sophie, "for bringing us here for your father's birthday. A nice meal in a restaurant, with linen napkins on the table and five different forks. . . . It's a beautiful thing."

Mac smiles. "Seems like a good time for a toast," he says, and raises an empty wineglass, nodding at Sophie and Silverstein to do the same. "To my father, on his eighty-fifth birthday. Much happi—"

"That was last year," says Silverstein. "This is number eighty-six."

"Impossible," Mac says as they all put their glasses down. "Last year you were eighty-four and this year you're—"

"Last year," says Silverstein, "you and Audrey gave me the sterling silver tray with that peculiar message on it: 'To my father: eighty-five years young. With all the love we can muster—your devoted children.' "

"Run that by me again," says Mac. "I seem to remember Audrey buying someone a very expensive tray, but that's about all I remember."

"A very practical gift," says Silverstein. "Sometimes, when I'm entertaining Sophie, I fill the tray with crackers and cheese and before you know it, the inscription's all covered up and it's just a plain ordinary innocent-looking sterling silver platter, which no one would be embarrassed to have in their home. Of course, once the cheese and crackers are eaten up . . ."

Mac rubs his temples, then his eyes. "I'm sorry," he says. "If you don't like the tray, maybe you could have it melted down and made into candlesticks or something."

"I'd like to hear a few words from Mr. Silverstein on the occasion of his eighty-sixth birthday, please," says Sophie. "Something honest and very wise."

Silverstein picks up a fork and stabs it into the tablecloth. "We come into this world, each and every one of us, knowing we're going to die one day," he says calmly. "And let me tell you, at the age of eighty-six, the idea still doesn't appeal to me, no way, José."

There's a tingling in Sophie's hands and feet, turbulence somewhere in her middle; her breathing quickens to a pant. She does not want to be alone, does not want ever again to face the solitude she has lived with so comfortably all these years. The pacemaker is supposed to regulate her heartbeat perfectly, but laying her hand over her heart, she can feel a commotion in there. "Monroe," she says softly, then a bit louder. Raising her head to see what has caught his attention, she gazes up at the sight of Ann Landers and the man in the painting coming toward them, directly to their table. "Monroe," she says again. "I'm going to marry you after all."

Ann Landers (not Ann Landers at all, but the owner of the restaurant, it turns out) and her husband arrive at just the right moment to hear the news. "Congratulations," they say, offering handshakes to everyone at the table, and also a complimentary bottle of their house wine. Sophie understands that this could not possibly be Ann Landers she is looking at, but still she would like to pull the woman to her side and ask for a little advice. "Go get 'em, Toots," she can hear the real Ann Landers saying, "and for God's sake, hurry!"

16

"Don't kiss me," Laura warns as David shuts the door to his apartment behind her. "I've got a cold."

"No big deal," David says. "With or without your cold, I'll still be dead in a couple of months." But he does not kiss her, only holds her against him, breathing in the perfume she'd streaked through her hair with her fingertips a few minutes earlier. When she pulls back from him, reluctantly, but knowing he is better off sitting down in a chair than standing there with her, she notices that he is in jeans and a sweatshirt and running shoes and socks. This is a surprise: lately, since his release from the hospital six weeks ago, he has been in a bathrobe and slippers, with pajamas underneath, whenever she comes to visit.

"You must be feeling okay today," she says. "Tell me I'm right." They settle next to each other on the couch, knees and thighs touching.

"What?"

"You're dressed in street clothes. I haven't seen you like that since before you went into the hospital."

"These fancy clothes," he says, "are for the benefit of my son, who, even as we speak, lies prostrate in bed with the flu. I don't like him to see me walking around in my bathrobe when the rest of the world is dressed and looking presentable."

"He's home?" says Laura, instantly feeling panicky. "From school?"

"Home from the moon. Of course he's home from school. He has the flu. Or thinks he has the flu. Maybe it's just a trigonometry test. But what has that got to do with us? With you?"

Laura gets to her feet. "You're crazy," she announces.

"Probably," David says, yanking her back down, down into his lap, only for a moment, but long enough for her to feel all his bones, sharpened to extraordinary, heartbreaking points.

Laura shifts to an armchair next to the couch. She is afraid of a sixteen-year-old boy, a stranger, a stranger's eyes narrowing at the sight of her in his parents' living room. *His* living room.

Kicking off one shoe, David stretches his leg out until it rests on her thigh. Automatically, her hand goes out to him, slips underneath his fuzzy sock and massages his ankle. "Don't you care?" she whispers, and then the whisper turns to a hiss. "It's wrong of you not to care." Gently she lowers his leg to the floor.

"Just in time," David sings, "I found you just in time . . ."

In walks Ethan, bare-legged and barefoot, a red T-shirt reaching to his knees. Across the front is the word "Marijuana," the "M" exactly like the one in the McDonald's logo; below that, it says, "Over 69 Billion Stoned."

"I came out for some juice to take with my aspirin," Ethan says.

"Come over here so I can feel your head," David says. "But don't breathe on me, please." Ethan approaches slowly, guardedly, as if detecting the possibility of danger. He puts a hand on David's shoulder to steady himself. He turns in Laura's direction, not saying anything, then looks at his father.

"Are you going to introduce me or are you going to pretend I'm not even here?" he says, shaking David's hand from his face.

"I'd say about a hundred and one. Not too bad."

"I'm not invisible," Ethan says. "And neither is she."

"Forgive my rudeness," says David. "I was just concentrating on your not feeling well. These days, I can only concentrate on one thing at a time, it seems. Anyway, this is my friend Laura."

"And you're Ethan?" says Laura, sounding only partly convinced, as if she needed proof that he truly belonged here in the house of a dying man.

"How come you know all about me and I don't know a thing about you?" Ethan says. He is off to the kitchen, where, still visible to Laura and his father, he props the refrigerator door open with one shoulder and drinks straight from a large carton of Tropicana, wiping the juice from his chin with the back of his hand.

"Very considerate," says David. "You're sick and you drink from the carton like that?"

"I don't know anything about you, really," says Laura. "Only your name." But of course this is not true. *Your father is going to leave you,* she silently tells him. *Get that through your head and then move beyond it, to a place where you can be comfortable together. Your father has been waiting there for you; don't you see him waiting with his arms outstretched, eager for anything you can give him?*

Ethan shrugs, moves to the dining room table, where he picks up a magazine and begins to flip through it, his back toward

Laura and David. A broad straight back under a wrinkled T-shirt, shoulders stiff with anger, pride, disdain. *I know who you are*, his shoulders tell Laura.

She is angry at David for his selfishness, for allowing her to come here when all that was needed was a phone call to keep her safely, wisely, at home. Where she belongs. "I've got to pick my daughter up at school," she says, checking her wrist for the watch she'd forgotten to put on this morning. (Too busy running perfume-scented fingertips through her hair.) *My daughter. My husband. My son. My wife. No names, please.* David never refers to Ethan and Barbara by name, as if referring to them by title only, they are somehow less than real; only shadowy figures, incapable of feeling pain. In David's company, Laura almost always does the same thing, though it sounds false to her, cold and formal. Unloving. When she was first married, she got such a kick out of using the words "my husband," would feel a flicker of pleasure every time she pronounced the words, telegraphing the message, *I'm married. Can you believe it?* After a time, when the first year or two of her marriage had passed, she was back to calling him Zachary again, knowing for sure, believing finally, that she was a woman with a husband.

A husband she has betrayed. Not cruelly, but unexpectedly. Almost unintentionally.

Sometimes she is able to convince herself that if what she is doing is wrong, at least it is venial. Living, as she has these past few months, with a little guilt and even more confusion, with a muddled sense of right and wrong, has been startlingly painful. She would not recommend adultery to her worst enemy. Or to the weak-kneed. For her it has been, oddly, a test of courage. She is someone who gets no thrill, large or small, from risk-taking. Only headaches, for which she's not even permitted to swallow a single aspirin. ("Headaches?" her obstetrician said on her last visit. "Have your husband rub your forehead for you. Just as effective as anything else. And a lot sweeter.")

She listens now to the sharp slapping sound of Ethan's disapproval as he turns the pages of *Esquire*, swiftly, one after the
other. He picks up the magazine in his hands, bends it back so
fiercely she is sure he is going to break its narrow spine. *Her*
spine, if he could. In a chair, at a distance of fifteen feet, he
sits, watchful, guarding his father. A self-appointed sentry. He
will keep watch for as long as she is there, Laura knows, and she
cannot blame him.

"Did I mention," she says, making a great effort to sound
casual, "that I'm going away for a couple of weeks? With my
husband, for his spring break?" She pauses, waiting for the slapping sound to begin again, but Ethan, too, is listening with
interest. "To Key West," she finishes.

"No," says David through his teeth. "You very definitely did
not mention you were going away with your husband for a couple
of weeks. How nice. Where did you say you were going?"

"Key West," Ethan says. "Neat town, neat bars." Lifting his
head, he smiles at Laura in a friendly, eager way. "You'll have
a terrific time."

"Well, the drive from the end of the Florida Turnpike down
to the Keys is supposed to be spectacular," Laura says. "According
to my husband."

"I wouldn't know," says David. "In fact, there are many things
I don't know."

Enough, Laura wants to say. She knows that if it were in his
power, he would not grant her permission to go away. Surely
not on a vacation with her husband. She stares at him, tries to
look severe, as if it were Mia she were hoping to intimidate. Who
does he think he is? Has he forgotten he is only her lover? David
does not know it, but she'd argued with Zachary about taking
this trip. A two-week vacation? she'd said. Why do you sound
so horrified? Zachary asked, puzzled. What could be wrong with
taking a vacation? She argued that it would be too expensive,
and that traveling with Mia would hardly be a vacation at all.

But here were Zachary's plans: they would fly to Miami and stay with his parents for a week, then leave Mia there with them, and drive down to Key West alone. His parents? She pointed out that they were elderly and temperamental and growing more unpredictable by the day. Where would they find the energy to cope with a willful and perverse four-and-a-half-year-old? They'll manage, Zachary told her. No one ever died at the hands of a four-and-a-half-year-old.

She could not argue with him after that, could not risk sounding as if she were holding something back from him. *Where have you been*, she heard Zachary saying so softly, so bewilderedly. He had not meant to frighten her, only to let her know that he had missed her, that after ten years of marriage he had not been listening as carefully as he'd meant to. It was an apology, really, and also a gentle accusation. *Where have you been? Within walking distance*, she wanted to say. *But farther than anyone ever could have imagined.*

With or without David's permission, she was going away with her husband. She went to a store called Great Expectations and bought a maternity bathing suit that looked, on her, twenty years out of fashion. After she brought it home and studied herself in it too long and too closely, she began to weep. She cried for David, for the two impossible weeks of their separation. She lay at the foot of her bed and fell asleep, dangerously near to the time she had to collect Mia from school. She dreamed strange middle-of-the-afternoon dreams. In one of them, she was swimming leisurely laps in her in-laws' pool when her mother-in-law appeared in the water balancing a portable phone on her shoulder. It was David, saying he had crossed over into another world and would not be back again. Would not be calling again. Her mother-in-law treaded water beside her, nodding her head approvingly. In another dream, it was David's wife who called. "How did you get my number?" Laura kept saying, but Barbara would only say, "What do you think, I'm an idiot?" When she awoke, it was to the sound of a ringing telephone. But of course it was only Mia's teacher, calling to say that her daughter had been waiting for her for over half an hour.

David walks her to the door now, saying not a word.

"There's always the telephone," she whispers; then, over her shoulder, she calls out "goodbye" to Ethan.

"Goodbye yourself," he answers, pleasantly enough.

17

"This marriage," says Adam, "is never going to come down off the rocks. It's going to stay there forever."

David has heard this before from Adam; their session has just begun and already he feels as if he cannot listen another minute. Laura has been gone two days. Thrusting his hand into his pants pocket, he fingers the tiny piece of paper where her in-laws' phone number is written. He has promised not to call her, and will stick to his promise. Between his fingers, the paper feels soft as cotton, in danger of disintegrating entirely. He cannot keep his hands off it. She will be back in twelve days and after that there will be no more vacations, at least not in his lifetime. He will not allow it. A while ago, Laura had asked him what he was like before he fell ill, and he told her that the loss of control over his own life had shaken his confidence so that he hardly recognized himself anymore. "I was more obnoxious than I am now," he told her, "quicker to bully people when I wasn't getting what I wanted from them." Perhaps not a person she would have liked at all.

He has noticed, recently, with curiosity and pride, his old self surfacing again. Arriving exactly on time at the oncologist's office yesterday, he was informed by the receptionist that according to her records, he had no appointment and would have to return to the office sometime later in the week. "Listen, you smug little incompetent," he whispered ferociously to the woman, "you better check your records again, because when I say I have an appointment, you damn well better believe I have an appointment." A blind man sitting close to the receptionist's window swiveled his head in the direction of David's whisper, his face alarmed, clearly wondering who this maniac was. David wanted to reassure him that he was not a maniac, but simply a dying man flexing his atrophied muscles. The receptionist's apology, when it came, was less than he had hoped for but gratifying nevertheless. "You're right," she said, stunned. "You were right and I was wrong."

"Reid complains we're like an old married couple," Adam is saying. "At the breakfast table, we grab sections of the newspaper and then barely say a word to each other. Then we're off to work, without much of a kiss goodbye. At night we watch television, or, more accurately, I watch him watching television. He sits there with the remote control in his hand, flipping through thirty-five channels an hour. Who can watch television like that?" Adam is out of his seat, pretending to study David's diplomas on the wall. "It was what I always thought I wanted, to live with someone so closely they'd become a kind of second self. That kind of intimacy seemed so exciting. It was only Reid's little betrayals that made me so miserable; everything else was minor. But he's been on his best behavior for months now, and you know what? I don't care so much about pleasing him anymore. I wanted to be like an old married couple—I thought it was something to aspire to. But now it seems like we hardly have anything to offer each other anymore. I'm just so surprised, I guess."

David remembers a book, from the early seventies, that proposed a woman greet her husband naked at the front door with a pitcher full of martinis when he came home from work. And that she cover her body with whipped cream and suggest to her husband that he lick it off. The best way to counteract boredom was to act like an idiot. He smiles, considers telling Adam this.

"What do you think you should do?" he asks instead.

"You tell me." Poised glumly at the corner of David's white Formica desk, legs crossed, Adam lights a cigarette and blows smoke over David's head.

"I think you should be asking yourself whether or not you still love him."

Adam mentions a fight they'd had a few days earlier. "In fact, he wouldn't talk to me for the entire weekend," he says. "On Monday morning I hand-delivered a dozen roses to his office."

"That's very romantic," David says, "but I don't know that it's love."

Smoke slips noisily from Adam's mouth like a sigh. "You want to know if I could survive comfortably without him. I guess I'm just too afraid to find out."

It's your life, David is tempted to say. His impatience is curdling into contempt. Where is his sympathy, the one thing he'd never expected to lose? It is possible that he is no longer fit to counsel anyone, that people should not be entrusting their lives to him.

Adam can take his fucking life and shove it, for all he cares right now.

Denial
Anger
Bargaining
Depression
Acceptance

What does Kübler-Ross know? *She's* not dying. *She* has a future. How dare she presume to know what he is feeling.

He looks at Adam, who is nibbling away at his thumbnail, unmindful of the scattering of ash that has fallen silently upon the desk. Sweeping it to the floor with his cupped hand, David says, "Forgive me."

18

Zachary is behind the wheel of a rented silver Rabbit, one pale sharp elbow poking out from the window. Beside him, Laura twirls a pair of wraparound sunglasses, arranges them on her nose, then pulls them off. To the east is the Atlantic Ocean, to the west, the Gulf of Mexico. There is nothing to see but water, patches of muddy brown surrounded by luminous turquoise. Above, in contrast, a perfect blue sky seems unremarkable.

Laura slips off her shoes and props her feet up against the dashboard. "Do you think she'll be all right without us?" she says.

"Mia? I guarantee you she doesn't mention our names twice while we're gone. With all those new toys they dumped into her greedy little hands, she'll probably forget we even exist." Zachary touches her thigh. "It's a wise parent who knows enough to take a vacation from his child."

On the radio, John Lennon is singing about the joys of fatherhood. Listening to him, Laura thinks of her daughter's farewell to her this morning: first Mia looped her arms around her and pressed her head against Laura's belly, then she opened her mouth wide and grabbed Laura's shirt between her teeth. "What the hell do you think you're doing?" Laura said as she retrieved her shirt, studying the tiny damp teethmarks. "Biting the baby," said Mia cheerfully, "what did you think?" And then there was Zachary's mother taking Laura aside and asking earnestly, "Do you want me to keep a record of her eliminations while you're away?" "Excuse me?" said Laura, having no idea what was meant by the question. Her mother-in-law frowned at her, suggesting Laura was seriously out of touch with matters of real importance. "Her bowel movements," her mother-in-law explained. "Aren't you going to want to know if she keeps to her regular schedule or not?"

"Sometimes," says Zachary, "it's nice knowing that home is far away." A pelican flies over the roof of their car, heading swiftly for the Gulf. Soon they are off the causeway and onto a two-lane road, and a sign appears, announcing that they are entering Islamorada. Trailer parks, each like a small-scale inner city, are crowded together, half hidden by clumps of palm trees. At the side of the road, in front of a ramshackle appliance store with an open-air porch, Laura sees a mannequin standing in a wedding gown and veil, looking forsaken.

Home. Where David sits nearly motionless, watching precious time pass. Two weeks is nothing, she'd told him, meaning to comfort him. A cruel thing to say to a man who may not have even two months to his name. The ultimate impoverishment.

Whittle away a man's future and he's left suspended between life and death, with nothing to hold on to. For David, there is only love, and it's coming from the wrong place, the wrongest place in the world. She should know better. She does know better. But still he is what she thinks of first when she awakens every morning. She has not been sleeping well since they met. In the middle of the night she slides her pillow up against the bedroom wall, leans back and stares at ordinary objects, trying, in the dark, to make sense of them, to make sense of something. The harder she stares—at Lucite-framed photographs of her daughter, at a silk-screen lampshade, at the gray-green face of a portable TV—the more ill defined everything looks. One night, before they'd left for Florida, Zachary suddenly rose from a sound sleep, letting out a soft cry and sitting up beside her in a hurry. "What do you see?" he said. "What could you possibly want to see?" A way out, she might have said. She was desperate to tell him all the things he would not want to hear. Instead, she shut her eyes and reached for his face, hands studying the beloved arrangement of hard bones and soft flesh. The pointed chin, much like her own. The slightly crooked mouth. The high, sharp cheekbones. The small smooth forehead. All memorized long ago. The face of a man she could not possibly, under any circumstance, live happily without.

"Hungry?" Zachary says in a while. Fast food beckons everywhere; a familiar nontoxic ugliness that is in its own way comforting.

"Mia would be in seventh heaven," Laura says. "Chicken McNuggets, Whoppers, Roy Rogers Double R-Bar Burgers—"

"Stop," says Zachary. "You know how I get when I'm tempted like that."

It is Burger King they settle on, but a Burger King like no other. The interior of the restaurant is a replica of a cabin cruiser, with a fake wooden dock and a dropped plastic ceiling, blue as the sky it is meant to represent. The walls are decorated with life preservers and driftwood.

"I'm seasick," Zachary announces as they get on line to order their food. Carrying their meal in tall white paper bags to a booth, he walks on unsteady legs, threatening to collapse at any moment.

"How about some Dramamine?" Laura says. She thrusts a pair of limp, pale French fries halfway into his mouth. They dangle from his lips like broken cigarettes. "Chew," says Laura. Obediently, with a little whoosh, Zachary sucks them in.

"Eat fast," he says. "I'm thrilled at the prospect of getting out of here in thirteen minutes or less."

In vinyl swivel chairs across the aisle, two teenagers in Burger King uniforms watch attentively while a third, older woman shows them royal blue velveteen trays full of jewelry: plain gold chains, children's rings set with tiny chips of garnet or turquoise or jade, crucifixes, Saint Christopher medals, silver charms shaped like telephones, ballerinas, and poodles. The woman showing the trays sees Laura looking in her direction, and smiles. "You interested?" she says. "Come over and take a peek." Laura smiles back, shaking her head. "Oh, come on," says the woman. "I'm not going to bite you." She hoists a large plastic bag up from the floor and sets it in her lap. "I've got some truly special stuff in here," she says. "Stuff you've got to be real sophisticated to appreciate."

"She's got you now," Zachary whispers. "Just be careful she doesn't get your life story out of you." This is a joke: Laura is usually so uncomfortable in the presence of strangers that even the briefest encounter sets her on edge. Unlike her mother, who, with no prompting at all, will pull out a wallet plump with snapshots and provide detailed histories of every one of her children and the heartache each has caused her. Supermarket clerks and salesgirls are her favorite audience; in a restaurant she will lean across the table to comment on a stranger's clothing or hairstyle, then immediately turn the conversation around so that *she* becomes the focus of attention. Laura has seen it happen over and over again, the impassive expressions of strangers hardening into boredom as her mother launches energetically, and without self-consciousness, into the secrets of her life. What, Laura wonders, would Ruth Elaine feel compelled to reveal about her? She can see her mother signaling to a waitress in a coffee shop, urging her to take a close look at a photograph of her younger daughter. Sweet, says the waitress. Her mother sighs dramatically. *Pregnant and insane*, she says. *A lunatic. Who does she pick for a lover? A man who can give her nothing. Worse than nothing; heartache.* That's too bad, says the waitress. Is that iced tea with or without lemon? *Cancer*, says Ruth Elaine. *Tumors. A young man, too. Not old.* The waitress glances up at Ruth Elaine, then back down to her order pad. That's a shame, she says. One bran muffin, lightly toasted? *This is a man you risk a marriage for?* Ruth Elaine says. If it's love, says the waitress, what are you going to do?

"Take it," says the woman with the bag full of jewelry. "Try it on." She hands Laura a necklace strung with miniature plastic globes; eight perfectly formed worlds two inches in diameter. Laura covers up all of Russia with her fingertip, travels the length of South America in an instant. "Isn't that the cutest little United States you've ever seen?" the woman says. She is about Laura's age, and is wearing a lot of makeup, most of it white, but her hair is in curlers, tightly covered by a green chiffon scarf. Where could she be going tonight? A church supper? Out to the movies with her husband? Possibly nowhere at all, a depressing thought.

"How much?" says Laura, passing the necklace back and forth from one hand to the other. She is hoping the woman will say ten dollars, a perfectly good reason not to buy it.

The woman pats a curler at the back of her head, then moves her hand forward, counting out a row of seven. "I'm Lou Ann Deegan," she says. "Is five bucks okay? That's only a dollar profit I'm clearing." She lowers her voice, and the two Burger King employees bend their heads toward her. "My husband's been out of work for thirteen weeks now. Having him home all day, it's like having another kid around the house. He trails after me while I'm vacuuming, yapping away about how we shouldn't waste the time from nine to eleven-fifteen every morning while the kids are in preschool, how we should, you know, take advantage of a nice empty house. Once he actually pulled the plug on the vacuum and tried to wrestle me down to the carpet. I told him, 'Eugene, if you want a clean house, and you always say you do, then you just better plug that Eureka back in where it belongs.' "

The girls from Burger King giggle. "And did he?" one of them says.

"I'll take it," Laura says, and reaches across the aisle for her pocketbook.

"Eugene hates for me to be selling this stuff," says Lou Ann. "He thinks it's humiliating for me to be out here every afternoon pushing this stuff on people. As it is, we're eating corn flakes for dinner, or eggs and toast. He doesn't know it, but starting next month, I'll be selling toys, expensive ones, imported from Italy and Switzerland, places like that. I'm going to have a toy party right in my living room and do a real nice presentation in front of my friends. Thinking about it makes me a little nervous, to tell you the truth, but mostly I've got a lot of confidence in myself. You've got to, these days. Otherwise, before you know it, you're slipping way down under and you can barely make it out of bed in the morning. Like Eugene. He mopes around, wanting sex in broad daylight, which he's absolutely positively not going to get from me. At least not on a steady basis. I've got more important things to do, like keeping a house clean and making a little money wherever I can. 'The problem with you, Eugene,' I tell him, 'is that you're still thinking high school was the high point of your life, that hanging around in your baseball jacket with the guys, checking out the cheerleaders practicing in the auxiliary gym after school every day, looking up those real short skirts, was the one true time of happiness in your life. Wake up, Eugene,' I tell him. 'It'll be seven years you're out of school, this June, and then eight years and then nine and you're not ever going to be back there where you were, no matter how hard you wish for it.' "

"Seven years," says Laura, who last saw the inside of a high school gym fifteen years ago. She cannot believe how young Lou Ann is. Certainly too young to be walking around in public with a headful of curlers. She hands her a five-dollar bill, which Lou Ann folds meticulously into a fan, then smooths out flat against the table.

"Time enough for Eugene to wake up, wouldn't you say?"

Returning to her own table, Laura slides in opposite Zachary. "What am I going to do with this thing?" she whispers. "Do you think Mia will wear it?"

"Not if she's got any taste."

Lou Ann appears, and grips the edge of their table with both palms. "I forgot to mention that I was one of the cheerleaders Eugene was always so interested in. JV and varsity. I even had a little silver megaphone I used to wear around my neck on a chain. One day last year it dropped off while I was washing the dishes. The whole thing, chain and all, slipped right out through my skirt and down to the floor, and then just disappeared. I carried on so, that Eugene actually had to move the refrigerator away from the wall, because I was sure that was where it had gone to. He was a real sweetheart that day, even though we never found what we were looking for. I have to say that most of the time he's the best thing in the world for me; it would be wrong to say anything else."

Laura nods, but does not speak. Lou Ann is up at the counter, paying for lunch with her five-dollar bill. From the back, dressed in tight black jeans and shoes with high heels, she looks unfamiliar, someone Laura has never met. She imagines her seven years earlier, dressed in her cheerleading costume, a vivid smile at her lips, confident, like Eugene, that this is the life she was meant for, and that it is unalterable.

"Eugene who?" says Zachary.

Ernest Hemingway's house in Key West has not a single air conditioner, though it does, as the tour guide points out, have a sixteenth-century birthing chair brought back by Hemingway from somewhere in Europe. The guide, an overweight man in high-waisted Bermuda shorts, tall black socks, and a white see-through shirt, refers to Hemingway as "Ernest."

"Ernest," he says, "was thought by many to be the greatest American writer ever."

"Oh yeah?" a tourist standing in front of Laura and Zachary calls out. "If he was such a genius, how come he wasn't smart enough to get a little air conditioning in here?" There is laughter from the group, but Sid, the guide, does not acknowledge it. He wipes perspiration from his face with a pink tissue and begins to discuss the architecture of the house, which is Spanish Colonial, he says, set on an acre full of exotic plants and trees from all over the world. He leads the group of twenty tourists down a narrow staircase and out of the house, where it seems, at least momentarily, to be somewhat cooler.

"Here," he announces, "you see the first swimming pool built in Key West, fed by saltwater wells almost two hundred feet deep. Ernest's wife had it built for him in the late 1930s while he was off on a trip, and it cost twenty thousand dollars, far more than what they'd paid for the house itself."

"Is it open to the public?" asks the man who'd complained about the heat. His shoulder-length hair is gathered in a thin red rubber band at the back of his neck. Circling his waist are the pale arms of a woman wearing a parachute suit and Dr. Scholl's sandals.

"A swim is absolutely out of the question," says Sid. "Now, do you want to hear the rest of the story or not?"

"I could care less," the man mumbles. Now, Laura sees, there is an unlit, homemade cigarette between his fingers. "Compared to Faulkner," he says loudly to his companion, "the man's work really appears quite simpleminded." As if this were her cue, the woman takes out a book of matches and lights the cigarette for him. Immediately, the air is scented with burning pot.

"No smoking," says Sid. "And if you're so hot for Faulkner, why don't you do us all a favor and take yourself on a little trip up to Mississippi." The man moves away from the group with his companion, but does not put the joint out. "This is a wonderful story," Sid continues, "so listen carefully. After Ernest got a look at this twenty-thousand-dollar swimming pool, he turned to his wife and said, 'Well, you might as well take the last penny I've got.' He reached into his pocket for a penny and stuck it into the wet cement of the patio we're standing on right now." Sid gestures to a spot just beyond Laura's feet. "Take a look for yourselves."

"The man certainly did have a way with words," a woman's voice says. No one laughs except Laura and Zachary. A thin gray cat with orange eyes weaves itself through Laura's bare ankles, startling her. Everywhere on the grounds there are sleeping cats—under trees, on rattan chaises longues, on puddles of shade in the grass. "A living memorial to Ernest," Sid says. Imbedded into the cement of the patio are tiny sets of paw prints. For Laura, the sight of all those cats—there must be more than fifty of them—is too much. An extravagance beyond reason. Goose bumps flower in an instant along her arms and legs.

"We've got to go," she says, grabbing Zachary by the back of his belt. "Now."

"Too hot?" Zachary says. There's a rustling in the shrubs behind them and then the man with the ponytail streaks past, followed loyally by his friend. Into the water they dive, letting out whoops of pleasure. Soon the man's arm shoots out above the water, revealing a clenched fist. "Screw Ernest!" he yells. "This is great!"

Sid runs to the side of the pool. "Get out of there, you ignorant asshole!" he orders. The people in the pool are doing the backstroke now. They yell for the rest of the group to join them. A handful of tourists, mostly men, kick off their shoes and jump into the water. Sid has disappeared into the house, but soon returns with a pair of gray-haired ladies in navy blue skirts and plastic-coated name tags pinned to their chests. One of the ladies claps her hands together. "Please," she says. "Please don't make me call the police." A tour guide in charge of another group emerges from the house and waits for his tourists to arrange themselves on the patio. ". . . fed by salt-water wells almost two hundred feet deep," he is saying. He ignores the splashing and shrieks behind him. ". . . Twenty thousand dollars," he continues, "far more than what they'd paid for the house itself."

Without a word, Zachary takes Laura's hand and leads her to the pool. They slip into the water, where Zachary does two laps and Laura stays put in a corner, squinting against the sun. "Ernest would be flipflopping in his grave," she hears Sid moan. She sees herself dripping water on the dirty tile floor of the local police station, holding tight to Zachary's hand. The police chief is trying to decide on a charge. Aggravated silliness, Laura suggests. In New York, a smile comes to David's lips as she tells him the story. *He wishes he could have been there, he says. He has forgiven her for leaving him. In her absence, something miraculous has happened: the tumors have shrunk to nothing. Nothing! he says triumphantly. His wife is able to look him in the eye again. She spends all her free time looking him straight in the eye. What she sees there is hope. And, unmistakably, love. David's voice is very quiet, nearly a whisper. You, he tells Laura. It was you who brought me back when I crossed over into that other world. Not me, she says modestly, but she knows he has told the truth. He no longer has any need for her, which pleases them both. Well, he says. She digs her hands deep into her pockets. Well, she repeats. An awkward moment that will soon be gone. See you, she says finally. Heading down the street toward home, she does not turn back for another look. Something like happiness seizes hold of her, and she begins to run, past her apartment house, past buses and taxis and dozens of people raising their heads at the sight of a pregnant woman flying so gracefully over concrete. Out of breath at last, she slows to a stop in front of a little neighborhood park without trees. She sits down on a swing, a thin narrow crescent of rust-colored rubber. Everything hurts—eyes, chest, knees. Everything aches. Happiness? No, that was self-deception. She has saved David's life. Healthy, an ordinary man once more, he is not for her. Surely she has known this all along. And it is true that the love she has felt for him was more like pain, really. Soon the pain will lift, leaving her lightheaded. Exhilarated. Out of love, out of pain. The swing she is seated on begins to move; there is the lightest touch of someone's hand at her back. Swiveling around, she is stunned to see David. He has come all this way to tell her something. What? she says. In slow motion he opens his mouth to speak. You tell me, he says. You tell me exactly what it is you want. This is easy: I want everything, she says. The best of all possible worlds. He comes around to the other side of the swing. He sweeps her up and against his chest as if she were nothing, weightless. You have got to be kidding, he sighs. Saying this, he looks unspeakably sad. He lowers her delicately to her feet. You have got to be out of your mind, he says.*

Water splashes in her face now. "Did I get you?" says Zachary. "Sorry." They hoist themselves out of the pool, gather up their shoes from a disorderly pile of Top-Siders and sandals and sneakers. Tourists in dry clothes are staring at them, some with curiosity, others with disapproval. Laura is embarrassed. Her pink-and-blue-striped maternity shirt clings to her middle, emphasizing her pregnancy. There are dry clothes and towels for them back at the motel, a fifteen-minute drive away. In the meantime, there is nothing to do but make their escape as quickly as they can.

"I think," says Laura as they run through the gates of Hemingway's house and out onto the street, "that Sid may be contemplating a change of careers."

Zachary laughs. "Why are we running?" he asks. "Who says we have to feel like fugitives?" They have reached the car now, parked in front of a battered-looking bungalow planted on an unkempt lawn. A brand-new, very expensive Audi rests in the driveway. Two roosters parade awkwardly near the car, hooting their contempt.

The neighborhood they are driving through now is full of tiny houses, each on a sadly overgrown lawn; in the side yards of several, goats are tied to fences and chickens can be seen wandering. There isn't a person in sight, except for an old black woman seated at the curb in a metal chair, dozing in the heat. Soon they are on a main road that takes them through a commercial area, past the St. Mary Star of the Sea School and the Margaret-Truman Drop-Off Launderette, which looks, Laura is disappointed to see, like any other Laundromat.

At the motel, a stripped-down version of the dozens of clean, cheap motels they have stayed at through the years of their marriage, they flop down naked on the cool sheets of a double bed. Fifty dollars a night and there's not even a black velvet painting above their heads, just blank yellowish-white walls, marked here and there by hairline cracks.

" '. . . and a crack on the ceiling had the habit/of sometimes looking like a rabbit,' " Laura recites, staring up at the ceiling with her arms folded behind her head.

"You're not supposed to be thinking about Mia," Zachary says. "Remember that."

"What am I supposed to be thinking about?"

Zachary puts a thumb at the center of each of her breasts. "Sex, of course." His mouth is on the freckled gap between her breasts, breathing humid air against her. "Cheap thrills in a cheap motel." It is late afternoon. On the catwalk outside their room, footsteps, heavy and light, can be heard. Strangers casting shadows on the tan shades over their windows. The rise and fall of strangers' voices. "No you may not have a Nestlé's One-Hundred-Thousand-Dollar Bar," a woman's voice says. "The subject is closed."

Laura thinks of Eugene wanting sex in broad daylight, of Lou Ann turning him down, perhaps once too often. The last time *she* had sex in the afternoon was on the floor of David's office. Lovers will take it anywhere they can get it, on hard floors, on prickly rugs, in underheated or blazing hot rooms. Married people look for comfort first: soft pillows, dim lighting, Stevie Wonder on the tape deck. After ten years of marriage, you know precisely what it is you need to get things right.

"Put the bedspread up over the windows," says Laura.

"What?"

"There's too much traffic out there, too many people going by. Their shadows are making me nervous."

"Close your eyes," says Zachary.

"I keep thinking they can see us. I know they can't," she says apologetically, "but what if they can?"

Zachary leaps from the bed and drapes a sand-colored wool blanket over the shades. Naked, his thinness fully revealed, he looks like a young, unfinished boy, someone who has hardly lived at all. Her own body, at this moment, is womanly in a way it never is except in pregnancy—sharp edges rounded off everywhere. Together, their bodies are a ludicrous match.

"What's so funny?" Zachary says as he scuttles back into bed.

"Bodies," she says. "Yours and mine."

"Go ahead and laugh," he says, pretending to be insulted. "I'll have you know there are at least a hundred women who would love to get their hands on this particularly perfect body."

"How about this one?" she says, making a grab for him just below the end of his spine.

Getting up for a shower several hours later while Zachary sleeps on, she pauses at the rear window for a look at the speedboats docked in the water outside. It is dusk. The lights of a Ferris wheel, part of an amusement park a few lots down, have just turned on, and she listens to the shrieks of its passengers, watches the bright wheel turning fast in the distance. Inexplicably, she is homesick, like a child in summer camp who longs to be back in his own room, where even the darkness is familiar. She misses David, misses the urgency of his love. If she could, she would send him a postcard announcing these things. It's far too dangerous, of course, to send even a blank postcard. Even so, she rummages in her bag for a card she'd picked up at the Hemingway house. There is a color photograph of the home, and in the corner, set in an oval, a pen-and-ink drawing of Hemingway himself in a fisherman-knit turtleneck sweater. You are loved 159,000,000 miles an hour, she writes with her fingertip. She imagines Rodney, the doorman in David's building, sorting through the morning mail before it is sent up to the tenants. He rests the postcard in his palm and puzzles over it a moment. A smile crosses his face. Of course! How lucky for the sick man on the fifth floor to have found himself a woman who would not be afraid to write such a thing.

Rodney is beaming. He must see for himself the look of pleasure on Mr. Graham's face. He rushes into the elevator, the postcard pressed against his heart.

19

Waiting at the bus stop at ten in the morning, Sophie eyes a teenage girl eating Rice Krispies and sliced banana floating in milk in a plastic container. "A smart breakfast," she says approvingly. The girl gives Sophie an unfriendly look and moves away from her, out of the Plexiglas bus shelter. Just as the bus pulls up to the curb, a blond woman with a baby in a stroller appears. She unstraps the baby, tucks him under her arm, and struggles to fold up the stroller.

"Would you like me to hold the baby for you?" Sophie asks.

The woman smiles and shakes her head. "English, no," she says.

"Hurry up with the tea party down there," the bus driver yells.

Sophie edges into the bus, taking each steep step with a sigh. Her legs, which have always been heavy, seem to her to have swollen to twice their normal size lately, though her doctor has assured her this isn't so. Her knees hurt, and her toes—just a little arthritis, according to the doctor.

She drops a token into the glass box, nodding at the bus driver, who is thickset and broad-faced, and who stares beyond her to the woman with the stroller.

"You fucking nitwit," he says. "Get the fucking stroller in here so we can get a move on."

"Sir?" says Sophie as the woman enters the bus. "What kind of a way is that to talk to a perfectly decent young woman? If you were a gentleman, which clearly you are not, you would have—"

"Put a lid on it," says the bus driver. "Either that or get off my bus."

Sophie slides into a blue plastic seat up front that says "Won't you please give this seat to the elderly or the handicapped." She hates to have to sit there, hates knowing this seat is for her, set aside for her in writing by some thoughtful person from the New York City Transit Authority. She stares at the back of the bus driver's gray head. Filthy human garbage, she thinks. It is not until she has left the bus that it occurs to her she might have taken down his badge number and the number of the bus, and placed a phone call to his superiors. And then what would have happened?

"Nothing," she says out loud. She has gotten off the bus after only seven blocks and is standing in front of a U-shaped red-brick building on an ivy-covered lawn. Magnolia trees are in bloom on either side of the building's striped awning, and there are circles of red and yellow tulips planted near the entrance.

She is here, as she usually is, once a month or so, to visit her husband's sister, Kate. Kate is ten years younger than Sophie and senile. When Sophie's husband died, it was Kate who gave her $300 in cash and never asked for it back. Months later, when Sophie was able to repay it, Kate refused to take the money, saying reasonably enough that a widow needed all the help she could get. This was forty-six years ago, but Sophie still feels she owes her sister-in-law a debt of gratitude. One of these days she may even arrive with a $300 check in her hand and insist that Kate take it, settling things once and for all.

"Hello, Floretta," Sophie says when Kate's nurse opens the door to the apartment. Actually, despite the white uniform she wears, she is not really a nurse, but more like a combination housekeeper and babysitter. Sophie likes her, though not the way she talks to Kate, which is the way most people would talk to a baby or a pet poodle.

"Hello, you," says Floretta. "I got her up all pretty for your visit."

"My little petite doll!" says Sophie. Kate is nearly child-sized, dressed in something pink-and-white, a pink ribbon tied around her hair, which is braided and pinned up behind her head. Her shoes are black patent leather with a single strap across the front. She is sitting in a padded rocker in the middle of the room, hands folded in her lap.

"She go and wet herself twice today," Floretta reports. "Wet right through those big fat diapers, right through her slip and dress. The washing machine running twenty-four hours a day in this house, let me tell you."

"It's the OldTimer's Disease," says Sophie quietly. "You know it's not her fault."

"AllTimer's," says Floretta. "With an A."

"What difference," says Sophie. "My poor little petite doll." She kisses Kate's powdered cheek. "You don't know," she whispers to Floretta. "You don't know, but this is a college-educated woman right here in this chair. And it wasn't like today, when going to college doesn't mean a thing, when the biggest dope in the world thinks he has to go to college. What I'm—"

"What you whispering for?" says Floretta. "You think she paying any attention to you? She hardly ever talks, don't listen, don't remember. She not even here, not really. She way out in fruitcake city, that's where she is." Floretta gently opens Kate's hand, stretching out her fingers in her lap. "Look how nice those little nails look. I give her a manicure every week."

Sophie nods, glad to see that outwardly at least, Kate appears no worse than she did the last time she visited. "You've done well by her, Floretta," she says. "No one can say you haven't."

"She do try my patience some," Floretta says. "Yesterday, or maybe the day before, she flush some stockings down the toilet. A real mess. I had to get plumbers in here and they real happy at what they saw. I slap her wrist for that, but she don't say boo. Just looks at me with those round blue eyes of hers, like what she done was a surprise to her, too."

"You slapped her?" says Sophie. "What's the matter with you?"

"Just a little love tap, that's all I'm talking about."

"She was valedictorian of her high school class," Sophie says. "Just remember that the next time you go to give her a love tap."

"I don't care if she homecoming princess. Anyone who throw things down the toilet like that got to be told she been naughty."

She's not a child, Sophie starts to say, then decides that's the wrong approach. "She's a sick woman," she tells Floretta. "As sick as someone cancerous, but in a different way. You wouldn't slap someone cancerous, would you?"

"You want this job?" says Floretta. There are tears in her eyes, which she does not bother to brush away. She fingers the postage-stamp-sized plastic picture of Jesus at her neck, sliding it back and forth on its chain. "Because if you keep talking to me like that, you going to find this job listed in the want ads under I for 'Impossible.' " Floretta's face is wet now, but she ignores the tissue Sophie holds out to her.

"Gee whiskers," Sophie gasps, and then she is crying, too.

Shredding the tissue in half, she offers a piece to Floretta, who grabs it from her and stuffs it into her shirt sleeve.

Kate begins to rock slowly in her chair. "How many remain?" she says in a monotone.

"What?" says Sophie.

"Howard, Harry, John, Sophie," says Kate. "How many remain?"

"Just one," Sophie says. "Just me."

"The oldest," says Kate.

"The oldest of the four and the only one still here."

"Good," says Kate, a half-smile flickering at her mouth. "Good for you."

"I don't know how good it is," Sophie says, "but it's the way things worked out."

"What's this now?" says Floretta.

"She remembers my brothers. You say she remembers nothing, but that's wrong. She just named every one of my brothers."

Matching palms in front of her as if in prayer, Kate rests her chin on her thumbs. "How many remain?" she says. This time she sounds exasperated.

Floretta shoots Sophie a look. "Fifty-three," she says. "Plus the two in prison up in Ossining. That make fifty-five altogether."

"Good," says Kate. She smiles faintly again.

"It could tear your heart out," Sophie mumbles. She feels a little wobbly and looks around for a place to sit; Floretta, seeing what she wants, guides her into an armchair covered in an itchy blue material.

"It's life," says Floretta. "You want some tea?"

"Have you got any lemon?"

"There was a little mold on it the last time I checked."

"Forget it," says Sophie as Floretta wanders off. She pulls her dress down over her knees, places her feet together in their wedge-shaped shoes, custom-made at $160 a pair. "What do you think of these stockings?" she asks her sister-in-law. "Very special support hose. Made to order, just like the shoes. Seventy-nine dollars. For a pair of stockings! And do you think they make my legs feel any better?"

Kate, who sits facing her, slowly revolving one thumb around the other, seems unimpressed. She stares unblinking at Sophie.

"I'm going to tell you something now," says Sophie, "and it's big news. I imagine this will mean nothing to you, but it means something to me, so I'm going to pretend that you're your old sharp self and that you're going to give me the best advice I can get anywhere."

Sophie looks into the shining surface of Kate's black shoes, then into her hazy eyes, eyes that are as still and blank as the rest of her face. "I've decided to marry Silverstein," she says, "and I don't think it's a mistake. To live a few years in the close company of a decent human being couldn't be such a risk, could it? And it's good to spend time listening to a man saying he loves you. It feels good. It used to make me so mad, I had no patience to listen to that kind of thing from him. But it's different now. I feel very calm when we're together, as if things have been set right, finally."

"Money," says Kate. "Isn't that what he has? I remember that's what they always said about him."

"To me that's nothing," Sophie says, waving her hand in front of her. "Tell me something else you remember."

"We didn't have a telephone," Kate says. "My mother was having a baby, a baby that died when it was very young. Philip went out to a store on the corner to use their telephone, to call the doctor. I stayed behind with my mother. I was just a child and the way she screamed was terrible, something a child should never have to hear. I took the pillow from under her head and wrapped it over my ears, but it didn't do any good. By the time Philip got back, I was screaming too. We sat outside on the steps and waited for my mother to be quiet. Then the war came. All the men in the street were soldiers, waiting for their uniforms,

waiting to be moved out. All the women were crying. The streets
were full of people and none of them were happy. My mother
said to Philip, 'If you go with them and get yourself killed, I'll
never forgive you.' She was so angry, words came out of her
mouth like fire. Then he married you and it was the same. She
said to him, 'Remember: you can always get yourself another
wife but you've only got one mother.' You were there," Kate tells
Sophie. "You remember." She begins to laugh, not unkindly.
"Funny," she says. "A funny thing like that you don't forget."

"It's news to me," says Sophie. She tries to recall her mother-
in-law, a tiny woman like Kate, with the same blue eyes. Fragile-
looking, doll-like. Not a generous woman. When Philip died,
she invited Sophie and her sons to stay with her, then threw
them out after a couple of days, saying the boys ate too much of
her food, that she didn't like their table manners. Their shared
grief wasn't enough to keep them together in one household for
more than a few days.

*You can always get yourself another wife but you've only got
one mother.* Not hard to imagine her mother-in-law saying this.
Or at least wanting to say it. Sophie clenches her fist, lifts it
above her head, sees her mother-in-law swaying, raising a hand
to her cheek. The woman has been dead for years, long forgotten
by Sophie. And what does Kate, poor lost Kate, know about
anything?

"Didn't you hear me tell you I'm getting married?" Sophie
says. "Why don't you congratulate me?"

"Married?" says Kate, laughing harder now. "Who's going to
marry you?"

"Silverstein," says Sophie. "Monroe Silverstein."

"That's sweet," says Kate. "That's real nice. Do you think I'm
too tall to be a flower girl? You could fill a straw basket with
daisies and I could walk down the aisle throwing them like this"—
she flings her arms out over the sides of her chair and then over
her head—"and this. You could trust me," Kate says. "I'd start

out at one end of the aisle and finish up all the way at the other end, just like you'd want me to."

Sophie is out of her seat and at Kate's side now. "I miss you," she says. "And knowing you're never coming back makes me miss you even more."

Kate reaches up to untie the ribbon from her hair and hands it to Sophie. "This is for you. In case I don't come back." She regards Sophie apprehensively. "Where did you say I was going? Because to tell you the truth, I'd rather just stay here. Right here with my friend with the brown face."

"Floretta," says Sophie.

Shrugging her shoulders, Kate says, "If you say so." She grabs the ribbon back and winds it twice around her wrist. It is a narrow band of pink satin that gleams against her pale skin. "Tell me," says Kate, showing her wrist to Sophie, "are the Cossacks still persecuting the Jews?"

20

Dear Editor,

Question? Would you tell me if this is worth publishing? I wrote it for our monthly Hadassah luncheon. The Hadassah ladies cried, and I received a standing ovation.

Dear Sire,

I hope you will publish my short story for a lot of money because I want to get my mother a washer and dryer and a two-door refrigerator with a 2.45 cubic foot freezer with side by side doors that costs $589.99. And also I want to give her money to buy a new color TV set. The rest of the money will be for myself.

My father and two sisters are dead in a fire on account of the electric lights on our Christmas tree.

I have tried to write clear and bright to make sure that you understand my story.

Sir:

Briefly: I am an explorer in search of me. My story "Santa Claus Is Coming to Town" is about love, death, nature, and human relationships. I wrote it five years ago and then stashed it away as obsolete.

Please tell me it wasn't a mistake to send it to you.

Alone in her apartment with a shopping bag full of unpromising manuscripts, Laura swings one leg over the other, closes her eyes, and drinks deeply from a purple plastic mug filled with ice water. She sets it down on the coffee table in front of her, next to the three other mugs she has emptied over the past hour. Four eight-ounce mugs of ice water, every drop of which has gone straight to her bladder. This is in preparation for the amniocentesis she will undergo in a little more than an hour. She will go to the hospital alone, although Zachary has offered at least twice to cancel his classes and accompany her. She knows his presence would only make her nervous, for he is suspicious of hospitals and doctors, and always expects things to go wrong in their hands. Once, last summer, when she'd returned home from the dermatologist following the removal from her ankle of a small blue-black spot, entirely benign, Zachary had flung his arms around her, welcoming her as if she'd just come back unharmed from the war. "Of course I was convinced it was melanoma," he explained, "that the news was bad and would only get worse." When she asked him why, he could not answer her, could only say that this was the way his mind worked and always would.

She travels through life differently, generally assuming that things will go well. The night they'd returned from Florida, she switched on the answering machine and listened, enthralled, to the voice of her grandmother excitedly reporting her marriage to Silverstein. "Good luck to the old guy," Zachary said, rolling his eyes. "I give this marriage six months, tops." "Can I quote you on that?" Laura said, and went to call her grandmother, who joked that she'd nearly succeeded in carrying Silverstein over the threshold of her apartment. She was thrilled with everything, she said, except for the justice of the peace who'd married them. The man was barely alive, she complained—he had no spirit, no soul. He'd read the wedding vows woodenly, never even pausing to look up at her and Silverstein, to see who it was he was marrying. And afterward, when he noticed that Silverstein had removed a single tiger lily from a vase on the desk, and given it to Sophie to hold, the judge had made him put it back. "You should have waited for me." Laura sighed. "I would have made sure everything was perfect." "At my age," Sophie told her, "you just don't have the time to wait for anybody."

Laura slips on her raincoat now, unable to sit still anymore, and slow-steps her way to the elevator, thinking longingly of the bathroom she has left behind. Outside, a taxi pulls up in front of the building and a woman gets out in a hurry. She is wearing dangling earrings, one a miniature American Express card, the other a MasterCard. "The man's a maniac," she warns Laura, shaking her head so that the earrings tremble, and runs past her into the building.

"I am not," says the driver. "I'm not even half a maniac."

Laura gets into the taxi.

"She tried to sell me some coke," the driver says. "I had to listen to her sales pitch the whole trip uptown."

Crossing her legs tightly, Laura goes through her purse, looking for something distracting. She finds one of Mia's toys, a tiny camera that can be transformed into a robot. Maneuvering the metal-and-plastic parts, she turns it into a crude-looking robot, then back into a camera.

"I only do this job summers and holidays," says the driver. "The rest of the time I work in the public school system as a drug coordinator/rock teacher/guidance counselor. That's all I need, right—to get charged with possession. I explained everything to that chick who was in here before you, but she just keeps on pitching to me. So she lost a sale. Big deal."

"Do you like working with kids?" Laura asks. She raises the camera to eye level and looks through the viewfinder, where everything is blurred.

"The pay sucks," says the driver, "but yeah, I like it." He stares at Laura in the rearview mirror. "You're not going to take my picture with that, are you?"

"You don't want me to?"

"I'm superstitious, like those primitives in New Zealand or wherever, who think you've stolen their soul if you photograph them."

"It's a toy," says Laura. They are stopped at a red light. At the curb, two pigeons ankle deep in a puddle are fighting over a dusty slice of frankfurter. Laura shuts her eyes. Just a few more blocks and she will be at the hospital, where she will beg to be allowed to pee. She can already see the nurse shaking her head "no" sympathetically.

"Ever have an out-of-body experience?"

"What?"

"It's very important," says the driver, "to learn to leave your body while you're still alive, because when you're dead, you know, you leave your body forever and that's that. So why not get in a few trial runs?"

"Actually, I'd love to have an out-of-body experience right now," says Laura, laughing.

"What are you laughing about?" says the driver as he takes the cab around the hospital's circular drive. He stretches out his arm to open the door for Laura. "You think I'm an airhead, right?"

"I don't," says Laura, "really." She tucks some dollar bills into his shirt pocket. "If you could give me some tips on how to get me out of my body this very minute, I'd be eternally grateful."

"Forget it," the driver says. "I can sense that your mindset is all wrong. Get your shit together and maybe one day it'll happen for you, too. Just think of it: one day your body will be in the kitchen fixing dinner but the real you will be floating from room to room, high above everything, peaceful like you've never felt before."

"I'll look forward to it," Laura says. She enters the hospital and follows a winding corridor leading to an elevator that takes her down to the basement. She makes her way past abandoned mattresses and wheelchairs that are folded up and stacked against the wall. The first thing she notices in the doctor's office is a water fountain, where an Indian woman in Nikes and a turquoise sari is filling a paper cup. The sound of the water hitting the cup is too much for her to bear.

"Excuse me," she tells the elderly receptionist behind the desk, "someone's got to take care of me right away."

"Read a magazine," says the receptionist. "You'll be notified when the technician's ready for you."

"I don't want to read a magazine. I want to use the bathroom."

"See that unfortunate person over there?" says the receptionist, gesturing toward the Indian woman, who is poised over the fountain, filling a second cup with water. "She didn't listen, and insisted on going straight to the bathroom the moment she stepped in here. So now she's back to square one. Is that where you want to be, back at square one?"

Laura skims an article in a news magazine on China's war against adultery. She paces the perimeter of the office as she reads. A woman who claims to be pregnant with twins asks her to sit down.

"You're making me nervous," the woman says. "The thought

of twins makes me nervous. And it turns out there may even be
a third heartbeat." The woman looks close to tears. "I'm thirty-
nine years old," she says. "I have one child each from my first
and second marriages. If it weren't for that prenuptial agreement
about having a baby with my third husband, it would have been
smooth sailing for me all the way."

Laura sits down. She learns that in Shanghai, some adulterers
are sentenced to labor camps. According to Chinese officials, the
rise in adultery can be blamed on bourgeois notions from the
West. She smiles at the idea of love as bourgeois. She tears
the article from the magazine and slips it into her purse, hoping
it will make David laugh.

The receptionist frowns at this but says nothing. Soon she is
instructing Laura to go to the bathroom and get into a gown. A
technician in a green smock approaches her when she returns to
the waiting room.

"Won't you step into my la-bor-a-tory," she says, and shows
her teeth. "Please don't hesitate to compliment me on my Tran-
sylvanian accent."

"Consider yourself complimented." In the small room where
the procedure will be performed, Laura climbs onto a metal table
that is draped with sheets.

"Now let's find your baby," says the technician, and prepares
Laura for a sonogram, coating her stomach with warm jelly. The
technician begins to hum the theme song from *Hill Street Blues*
as the baby comes into view on the ultrasound screen. "That's
your child," she says, "lying there on its back like a lazy bum."
What Laura sees is something resembling a seahorse, a shadowy
figure floating in darkness. An arm travels upward; a thumb is
slipped into the baby's mouth. "Those bad habits start real early,"
comments the technician. She points to a small dark pulsing spot
on the screen. "That," she says, "is your baby's heart beating."

Laura watches, spellbound. It seems unlikely that this strange
underwater creature could be her child. Its heart beats on, stead-

ily, confidently. A suspension of disbelief is necessary; she feels herself letting go, moving toward acceptance and, finally, passion. Looking at the little fluttering heart, tears well in her eyes. "You see this every day, don't you?" she asks the technician, amazed.

"Sixteen times on Mondays, sixteen times on Wednesdays. After I measure the circumference of the baby's head and the length of its tibia, I'll take a picture for you." She manipulates a few buttons, notes a few things on paper, and hands Laura a snapshot. Floating on its back, one arm curved along the contours of its belly, the baby shows off its sharp-chinned profile.

"I feel as if we've been spying," says Laura, balancing the photograph on her stomach. "It does seem kind of invasive, doesn't it?"

The technician gives a little snort of impatience. "Pregnant women are so *weird*," she says, and looks around, as if there might be someone else in the room who would agree with her. "Why don't you go call your husband or something. And feel free to use the bathroom. We'll be ready to do the amnio in a couple of minutes."

Streaking into the bathroom and then out again, her discomfort instantly forgotten, Laura finds a pay phone down the hallway. She feeds the phone some change and is told that Zachary is still in class.

No message, she says.

She calls David, not the best audience for her excitement. Holding the Polaroid in her palm, she describes what she sees.

"I'm going in for radiation as an outpatient," says David. "Five days a week for two weeks, with weekends off for good behavior." He has never had radiation before and is fearful of its side effects. He sounds angry. She searches for the right thing to say but comes up short.

"I saw the baby's heart beating," she offers.

"What are you telling me?" says David. "I don't care about

your goddamn baby. It's just another baby, just another beating heart."

She flips the Polaroid over to its back, where there are questions to be answered, boxes to be checked off. Would she like to order regular-size copies, wallet-size, 5×7 enlargements? The wallet-size, one each for the grandparents, one for her own wallet and her husband's, one for her lover's. One night Barbara is going through his wallet and finds, jammed in among the credit cards, the oddest-looking black-and-white image on cardboard backing. *That?* says David. *That's just my lover's goddamn unborn child.*

"Laura?" David says.

"What?"

A man dressed in a clown outfit has a hand on his hip and is tapping a huge floppy shoe against the linoleum. "How much longer?" he says.

"A minute," says Laura. "Maybe two. How should I know?"

"I'm a self-absorbed sitting duck," says David. "You're familiar with the breed, I assume?"

"Not really," says Laura.

"Liar," he says, softly, gratefully.

"It's pregnant women who are self-absorbed. They think the whole world is interested in every little miraculous fetal heartbeat."

"Are you interested in this?" says the clown. He pulls a long thin balloon from his pocket, blows it up, and twists it effortlessly into a swan. "It's yours if you get off the phone," he says. His smile is enormous, extending almost to his earlobes, a flashy bright-red smile made of greasepaint.

"There's a clown waiting to use the phone," Laura says.

"What kind of clown?" David says. "You mean an idiot?"

"Let me find out." She takes the balloon from the clown's freckled hand. "What kind of clown are you?"

"A forty-five-dollar-an-hour clown. I'm great at kids' parties.

I'm a juggler, a puppeteer, a magician, a well-rounded guy, really. Let me give you my business card."

"His name is Henry Lee Umansky," says Laura, skimming the card. "Otherwise known as Ju-Jube."

"I love you," says David. "Don't think for a moment that I don't."

The clown moves toward the phone as Laura hangs up. He winks at her and rubs his hand over the thick strings of royal blue yarn covering his head. "Hey," he says. "Are you naked under that gown, or what?"

"Nice work, Ju-Jube," she says, walking off. In the waiting room, she deposits the swan on the receptionist's desk.

The receptionist smiles, strokes the swan's transparent orange neck. "You're next," she says. "Good luck."

Now would be the appropriate moment for hand holding, Laura thinks, for a quick squeeze from Zachary, a hurried kiss. Instead, she will have to be content with David's declaration of love.

The doctor, a bearded man in red Top-Siders, barely acknowledges her as she lifts herself up onto the metal table again. He is busy at the sink, scrubbing energetically before the procedure. He does not know her name or anything about her, she realizes, nor does he care to. Lying on the table, feeling soulless, without identity, she thinks of David, of all the hours and days and weeks he has spent stretched out on unfamiliar beds and tables, just another damaged body beyond repair. Soon there will be the radiation, one more source of fear and grief. She aches with sympathy, can feel herself swelling with it, but what good does it do either of them? Sometimes, when Mia has banged an elbow on a table corner or kicked one of her ankles with the other, she brushes aside Laura's words of comfort. "I wish it were *your* ankle that hurts right now," she says, exasperated. "I want you to hurt, not me." Is this what David finds himself thinking? She would not blame him for thoughts like these. His anger, when it surfaces, always frightens her a little. She is defenseless against it, without resources. Everything he feels seems legitimate to her. She is able to excuse every ungenerous thought, every moment of intolerance. Lately there have been more of these than usual. She does not know why, or even if he is aware of them. Perhaps he is testing her endurance, testing the limits of her love. Unlike Barbara, she will not fail him. She will meet his gaze without any trouble at all.

"Ready for a little action?" the doctor is saying. A second sonogram is done, confirming the baby's position and exactly where the best place is to steal some amniotic fluid. "I'm coming at you now," the doctor soon says, approaching with a needle that looks to be just about the right size for an elephant.

Hurt my baby and I'll tear you to pieces, Laura thinks as the needle descends, painlessly, into her belly.

The doctor finishes up, filling two syringes with fluid. He glares at the technician. "Who can turn the world on with her smile?" she is singing.

"I *hate* when you do that," the doctor says. Out goes the second needle. Laura looks for evidence that it was ever there and finds none.

"Me?" says the technician.

"Don't tell me, don't tell me. The theme from *The Odd Couple*, right?" The doctor moves away to label the syringes on a counter top, then turns back to Laura. "There may be a little cramping, and also a little leakage of fluid, but I doubt it."

"Wrong," says the technician. "It's the old *Mary Tyler Moore Show*."

The doctor groans. "I never get any of them right," he says.

"Excuse me," says Laura. She has slid down from the table and is at the door now.

"Did I mention you ought to take it easy for the rest of the day?" the doctor says. "No water-skiing and that kind of thing."

"I just wanted to tell you I'm fine," Laura says.

"Good good good," says the doctor. "Of course. Good to see

you." His smile vanishes when Laura steps on the toe of one red Top-Sider as she leaves.

Standing in front of the hospital a little while later, watching one taxi after another going past her, she is startled to see Ju-Jube the clown driving off behind the wheel of a shining late-model Lincoln Continental. Two German short-haired pointers on leashes trot by, proudly carrying Frisbees in their mouths. Overhead, the sky turns yellowish. A little girl who reminds her of Mia struggles to keep up with the tall man holding her hand. The girl is hanging on to a clear plastic pocketbook shaped like a flattened fish bowl and filled with blue-tinted water and plastic fish. Laura stops her to ask where she got the pocketbook.

"My Nanny gave it to me," the girl says. "Nanny who lives in Disneyland."

"*Near* Disneyland," the tall man corrects her. "And it's just another piece of useless plastic garbage, as far as I'm concerned. What does a five-year-old need a pocketbook for? You tell me."

A taxi stops in the middle of the street for her before Laura can answer. Rain falls lightly against the windows of the cab. Laura takes out the picture of the baby. She smiles, imagining the baby being shown the photograph a few years from now. Me? says the child, shaking its head. Frightened, the child begins to cry. Perhaps it is true that some minor miracles are best left unrevealed. No, this is a romantic notion Laura cannot possibly accept. The sight of the little unearthly creature thrills her. At home, she allows Mia to hold the photograph between her fingers, to turn it slowly in a circle, to bring it so near to her face that her breath almost clouds it. Finally, Mia tosses the picture to the floor.

"You call this a baby?" she says. "Give me a break."

21

The husband and wife in David's office are named Carlos and Heidi Rabbitt. Carlos is a pediatrician, a handsome, well-groomed man who is going to lose his wife if he's not careful. Heidi teaches in a nursery school. Her hair is always in a long dark braid down her back, and she is so tall that David has trouble picturing her crouched on the floor all day, listening intently to the high-pitched voices of her tiny students. The Rabbitts have been clients for almost three years and David can never predict what complaints they are going to bring to his office next.

"It's that line about the nursery school teacher in this Burt

Reynolds movie we saw on the VCR that made her stop speaking to me," Carlos is saying. "You know, Burt Reynolds and Jill Clayburgh have this blind date and she's introduced to him as an extraordinarily gifted nursery school teacher. I cracked up when I heard that, because let's face it, there are gifted artists and gifted surgeons and gifted athletes, but who ever heard of a gifted nursery school teacher? There just isn't any such animal."

"Do you believe he doesn't understand why I don't want to be married to anyone with an attitude like that?" says Heidi. Reaching down to the floor where her handbag sits, she removes a can of Coke and places it on her knees. She pops the top and squeezes the metal ring over her pinky. "Would anyone like a sip?"

"What attitude?" says Carlos. "All that's at issue here is one person's sense of humor versus another person's."

"The issue here," says David, "is respect." He waits for Heidi to agree with him, but she has swallowed too much Coke too quickly and is coughing so hard her eyes fill with tears.

"She doesn't respect *me*," Carlos says, "and my right to a good night's sleep. In the middle of the night, she wakes me up to tell me that one of the kids is coughing. I don't know what she expects me to do about it. Give the kid a glass of water, I tell her. You don't have to wake up a pediatrician at two-twelve A.M. for advice like that."

"You bet I'm talking about respect," says Heidi, nodding at David. "We had an agreement, not on paper, but a verbal one, about how many nights a week I would stay home and cook, and how many nights we would go out. We agreed on four and three, three nights out. This agreement was respected for exactly one week and then by the second week we've gone to five and two and who knows what after that. Why? Because when I say I've had it after eleven years of cooking, nobody takes me seriously."

"All over the world," Carlos says, sighing, "women cook dinner for their families. Night after night, week after week, year after year. Why me? Why should my house be any different?"

This "why me?," delivered with such anguish, makes David want to haul Carlos out of his seat and slam him around a while. If only he had the strength. Actually, much to his surprise, the radiation hasn't left him feeling noticeably weaker. Completed two weeks ago, the treatments did not nauseate him or cause his hair to fall out. His oncologist had no explanation, but gave him a look that said, Be grateful. *Of course* he is grateful, though not for that look from his doctor. He does not need to be told what his response to good fortune should be. Unexpected good fortune. *Laura.* He is relieved to have her back. While she was away, traveling with her lawfully wedded husband, he had fixed on the idea of having another child. Probably it was Laura's pregnancy that had given him the idea to start with. He enjoys the fullness of her belly, the hard strong feel of it against him when they embrace. Sometimes, though he feels guilty about this, he allows himself to fantasize that the baby is his, that he will be present at its birth, a comfort to Laura, urging her on past the roughest moments. (Of his son's birth, he remembers little. And why should he? After getting Barbara to the hospital and into a wheel-chair, he had filled out health insurance forms, and then kissed her goodbye, saying he was off to get some fish food for the tiger barbs and red swordtails in their tank. By the time he finished feeding the fish and returned to the hospital, Ethan had been born.)

Approaching the subject of a new baby with Barbara, he had tried hard to keep the emotion from his voice, to sound as self-possessed as a man who knew that he had logic and reason on his side. "What are you, crazy?" Barbara had said. "A child you may not even live to . . ." Her voice trailed off, and she left his side on the living room couch to turn up the stereo, to put an undeniable end to the conversation. He followed her across the room, sweeping the stereo needle with his cupped hand as far over the record as it would go. They both looked at the long white jagged scratch that had ruined Leonard Bernstein's own conducting of his overture to *Candide*. "I want to *give* you some-thing," David told her, taking her by the shoulders, moving his fingers up the warm delicate sides of her neck, up over her ears, until finally his hands rested at the top of her head. "Forget it," she whispered. But her arms wrapped around him and she nuz-zled her face against his, letting him feel her tears. When he reached for her hand to lead her into the bedroom, she did not object. It was somewhere around nine in the evening. Like lovers, they undressed each other and left their clothing scattered on the floor at the foot of the bed. On the other side of the wall a voice that sounded eerily like John Lennon's sang, "Ever since you've been leaving me . . ." David knew from Ethan that this was not John Lennon, but Lennon's son, Julian. Since his father's death, the son had really come into his own, Ethan had said. Here was a subject that might have led them somewhere important if only Ethan had allowed it to, but if there was any connection between a son who had lost his father and a son who was soon to lose his father, Ethan was unwilling to examine it. It *was* spooky how Julian Lennon's voice resembled his father's, David found himself thinking as he and Barbara quietly made love. He and Ethan had almost precisely the same hands and feet, the same-shaped fingers and toes and nails. Looking at Ethan the day he was born, he was astonished to see that this was so. Not something that was noteworthy or meaningful to anyone except David himself; not a talent or ability that had been passed down from father to son, but something that gave him comfort nevertheless. The song was over, the radio turned off, and there was silence on the other side of the wall. Perhaps Ethan was listening to the unfamiliar sound of his parents making love. David had no idea what Ethan thought of their marriage, or if he thought of it at all. Certainly his son hadn't seen much of anything resembling love pass be-tween them recently, not for months, even before David had met Laura. Thinking of Laura, even in the most general way, as he made love with his wife, reminded him that he was now betraying his lover, which in turn made him feel as if he were betraying Barbara. It was no good at all to be thinking of these things. He concentrated instead on the cancerous cells in his body. As he had been advised to do in a book he had read not long ago, he concentrated on zapping the cells with every bit of energy he had. Thrusting toward his wife, toward the very center of her, he visualized tens of thousands of cells getting zapped by the clean bright light of his will.

"You pig," Heidi Rabbitt is saying. "Don't you understand it's not so much the four and the three or the five and the two, but what they represent? They're symbols, not just numbers telling how many times a week I cook and how many times you give me a break."

"Symbols of what?" Carlos says. "What are you talking about?"

"Symbols of your incredible lack of sensitivity and so forth." A troubled look comes over her face for a moment as she struggles with a thought, and then David sees that she knows just what it is she wants to say. "Carlos isn't even his real name," she announces, beginning to laugh. "His name is actually—"

"Tell him," warns Carlos, "and this marriage doesn't have a leg to stand on."

"Sylvan," says Heidi without hesitation. "As in his late Uncle Sylvan and Aunt Cookie." She holds the empty Coke can in front of her husband's face and crumples it. "You can't imagine how terrific I feel," she says.

David watches as Carlos dips his head low and slumps his shoulders. "How do *you* feel?" he says.

"Like the deep black hole of my neuroses has just grown immeasurably deeper and blacker."

David sighs. "Not exactly the answer I was looking for," he says.

22

The house in the Berkshires is a large light-filled A-frame that smells pleasantly of sawdust. Barbara and Warren are here for the weekend—the first weekend in June—out in the woods now that surround the house, Warren picking wildflowers from the grass as Barbara looks on silently. She considers calling David to say that she has arrived safely after the three-hour drive from New York, then decides she will call later. Much later. When she feels up to it. She is disappointed that David refused to come up here with her, refused her offer to make a bed of pillows for him in the backseat so he could ride comfortably all the way.

"Three hours in the Datsun?" he said. "With my knees tucked under my ears? Who do you think you're talking to—some teenager desperate to hitch a ride to his girlfriend's?" She would not beg him to do anything he did not want to do, and said that she would go alone. "I'm sorry," he told her, not looking sorry at all, only relieved. The next day, she called Warren from work and was warmed by the edge of excitement in his voice. He and his girlfriend had decided to cool it for a while, he said, and a weekend in the country sounded perfect.

He presents her with an untidy bouquet of Queen Anne's lace and black-eyed Susans now, and also a kiss, delicately delivered just below one eye.

She has not been here in a long while, not since first learning that David was sick. In a panic, she had thrown a flannel nightgown and some sweaters into a shopping bag, taken the car at six in the morning and headed out of the city with the radio turned up high and the windows rolled down, her eyes hidden behind sunglasses, as if it were not fall but still summer. A summer long past, with David at the steering wheel, within her arms' reach, when they knew nothing but ordinary things—ordinary happiness occasionally giving way to ordinary disappointment. She'd stayed away for three days, waking each morning to the sight of silver birch and evergreens as far as she could see. Awakening in the middle of a silent forest—the loneliest place in the world, she thought. A half mile from the house was a cold green pond she walked to every day, and there was a supermarket she drove to in the afternoons along fifteen miles of winding roads that always made her feel just the slightest bit woozy. The things she brought back from the Price Chopper were chosen at random and purchased one trip at a time—a pound of prosciutto, a small wire contraption that could slice an egg into six parts, a plastic Donald Duck nightlight that kept her up all through the freezing night watching her breath cloud the air like smoke. The first morning she arrived, she'd walked aimlessly in the woods for hours, kicking hard at clumps of earth and moss-covered boulders and fallen tree trunks. After a while her toes felt bruised and beneath her sweater her arms prickled with insect bites. In the woods she crouched on a damp log and remembered the fierce painful grip of David's hand against her wrist in the hospital. You're hurting me, she'd whispered, and pulled her hand back, knowing in that moment of withdrawal that she would surely survive and that he would not, and that the distance between them would grow so vast that eventually neither of them would be able to recognize the other.

And yet even as the distance between them has widened, there are moments when she has never loved him more. When he said, last month, that he'd been thinking about the two of them having another child together, the pain she felt at simply watching his open, eager face had been too much and she'd had to walk away. A few minutes later they were making love effortlessly, passionately, as if it were the most natural thing in the world for them to turn to each other this way. His body had been pared down by the months of illness, his muscles gone slack, the hair on one arm grown back bristly after having been shaved for one test or another. Coming home to his body after staying away from it for so long was not like coming home at all. She pretended that what she was feeling under her fingers was the old David— she imagined the solid feel of him, the slight pouch of his belly, the hard weight of his thighs. Imagining so well what no longer existed was her secret; never would she tell David that she had replaced him with a sturdier model from another life.

"Hey," says Warren, taking the bouquet of wildflowers from her and bending to tickle the backs of her bare knees with it. "I'm really psyched for a swim. Let's get into our suits and go over to the pond."

"It's too early in the season," Barbara says. "We'll freeze, I guarantee it." But they go indoors to change, then descend the wooden steps that lead to the driveway lined with cedar chips at the front of the house.

"Forget the car," says Warren. "We can walk the half mile." Pressed to his chest is a tiny battery-powered television set he claims to have bought in a moment of weakness. Lifting his face to the sun overhead, he says, "It's a real trip, you know?"

"What?"

"Nature," says Warren. "Dirt, flowers, bugs. I can really get off on it, sometimes."

They walk through the woods along a dirt road for a quarter of a mile, then turn onto asphalt. In front of a log cabin at the side of the road is a sign that says:

FUDGE

WORMS

SANDWICH COUNTER

Warren smacks his lips together. "I prefer my worms on whole wheat."

"David likes his on toast," she says. "Or at least he did the last time we passed the sign."

"How's he doing?" Warren asks. He settles an arm at her waist. "Did he get through the radiation okay?"

"Do you care?"

Warren looks insulted. "Yeah I care. As much as it's possible to care about a person you've never met. And a person who just happens to be married to your lover."

"We're not lovers," Barbara says, removing his arm from her waist and flapping it down at his side. "Whatever gave you that idea?"

"Jesus," says Warren, "I just had this conversation with Annie last week."

"Did she throw another plate of linguini against the wall?"

"That was capellini," says Warren. "A very very thin spaghetti. One step away from angel hair."

"She told you she didn't love you?"

"Something to that effect."

"I'm sorry," says Barbara. "You don't deserve to have that conversation twice in one week. You're a nice person and I'm grateful to you for a lot of things."

"Maybe you and Annie would like to exchange phone numbers."

"I mean it," Barbara says. "Without you, I'd feel even more lost than I already do."

"You're not lost," Warren says, stopping in the middle of the road to kiss her. "You're just not ready to find your way back again."

They have reached the pond, where the water is warmer than Barbara expected, but still uncomfortably chilly. They swim to a wooden raft near the center and rest there for a while, then reverse direction and set out for shore, Barbara floating on her back, falling farther and farther behind Warren. When she approaches shallow water, waist deep, she stands up. The sand underfoot is velvety; slowly she curls her toes around it. She waves to Warren, who is perched on a rock just beyond the narrow bar of beach, the little TV set against his raised knees shining silver. She calls his name, once, twice, and then again, but her voice is lost in the space that spreads wide between them.

Warren has read through the menu in his hands at least four times and still cannot decide what to order. Perhaps the restaurant has nothing appealing to offer, or perhaps it is the joint he smoked a few hours ago that still clouds his mind. The restaurant, a converted barn, painted white, is named Lox, Stock & Baigel, and Barbara said she'd wanted to eat here because every time she'd driven past the building, the sign out front had made her smile. Not the worst reason for choosing a restaurant, or anything else, Warren supposes.

He looks over at Barbara seated so stiffly at the other side of the table and thinks about stroking the beautiful skin across her cheekbones. Cautiously his arm goes out, then freezes in mid-air; quietly he drops it back into his lap. He knew that things were bad when she'd refused to share the joint with him, dismissing him with a spiritless wave of one hand as she kept the phone up to her ear with the other. She'd held a whispered long-distance conversation with David for nearly an hour. Warren had given up eavesdropping after only a few minutes and retreated with the joint to a hammock slung between two maples just beyond the driveway. Smoking the reefer down to a tiny roach that stung his fingers, he watched the sun set high above the trees and thought of absolutely nothing at all. His arms drooped over the sides of the hammock and his fingertips touched grass. Something tickled the back of his hand, almost imperceptibly; lifting his hand onto his stomach, he stared at a silky-skinned salamander that stared right back at him. He thought the salamander resembled a midget dinosaur, and told him so, but the salamander showed not the least bit of interest in what was being said. It occurred to Warren that he might set the salamander on fire, to see for himself if the mythology were true—if, in fact, a salamander could actually endure fire without injury. But the matchbook was in his back pocket and he couldn't remember where his back pocket was. This struck him as hilarious, and when Barbara got off the phone and came out to find him, the screen door snapping loudly back in place behind her, his face was streaked with the tears of his laughter. The salamander had vanished; a loss which seemed, for only a moment, tragic. Then he remembered that there was something important he had to tell Barbara. "You know, of course," he announced, "that dinosaur means terrible lizard in Greek. *Deinos sauros.*" Barbara's face was impassive. "B.F.D.," she said lightly. "Big fucking deal in Latin."

"Morons," she is saying now, letting the menu drop facedown onto the table. "They can't even spell bagel right. And then they go and spell pastrami with an 'o' at the end."

"Pastramio?" Warren says, and laughs. Barbara's cheeks look as if they are painfully sunburned—if he puts his fingers to her skin, he thinks, he would feel the heat in an instant.

"I can't eat in a place like this," she says, and then is struggling from the table.

"You people ready?" A young waitress is standing over them, clicking a ballpoint pen with her thumb.

"My wife," says Warren, as Barbara rushes soundlessly along the varnished wood floor in her flat-heeled shoes. "I'm not sure that she's coming back." He smiles at the waitress's T-shirt, which is dark blue and says "I Survived Catholic School" across the front in white felt letters.

The waitress sighs. "Problems?" she says. "Irreconcilable differences? Well, you still have to eat, no matter what."

"Excuse me," says Warren, and pushes away from the table. Outside, crossing the dark parking lot, he thinks of how unfamiliar it feels to be hurrying after Barbara, uneasy and unnerved, his heart thumping. He is reminded of his parents' marriage: his father had been the explosive one, the one who lost his temper at inattentive waitresses and salespeople, at strangers who accidentally brushed up against him in a crowd somewhere. His mother usually ducked her head and said nothing, wise enough to stay clear of him those first few dangerous moments when he might have turned on her, too, and called her a jackass or worse in a voice loud enough for everyone to hear. His mother had known to approach his father just as his anger was evaporating, and then they simply picked up where they had left off, ignoring the obvious: that a grown man losing his temper that way was inexcusable.

But this is different. This is Barbara, who does not love him but who needs his comfort. He doesn't feel much like listening to all she has to tell him. Perhaps she wants nothing more than to rest all her weight against him in silence, eyes closed, while he lightly threads his fingers through her hair. Loving her, he should be able to do this with ease, but he cannot bear the thought of his hand falling so gently upon her. He hates it that he is less compassionate than he ought to be, less delicate in his under-standing. If he were a woman, he wonders, would his sympathy be more generous? Maybe it was true that women were instinc-tively given to a deeper kindness. He doesn't know. All he knows is that whatever it is he can give her, it will surely be a near miss, for he is like a dancer waiting with arms outstretched to receive his partner just an instant too late.

He finds Barbara leaning against the front door of the Datsun, shivering in her short-sleeved sweatshirt, the small swell of bone at the back of her neck a perfect white in the moonlight.

"I'm tired," she says. "It's such an effort sometimes." She raises her eyes to him. "It used to be easier."

"Easier," Warren repeats, "yes."

There is silence on the way back to the house, a silence he does not feel obligated to fill. The roads are dark and twisting and he worries that Barbara is taking them too fast. He imagines that they will crash and die and that David will be flown up to the Berkshires to identify the bodies. *Who the hell is this?* David will say, his grief doubled at the sight of this stranger who had shared his wife's last moments on earth.

Just some guy who happened to be in the car with her, the state trooper mumbles, embarrassed for David and for the two bodies arranged so carefully on stainless steel trays that pull out from the wall.

Her lover? says David.

The state trooper shrugs, offers David coffee in a white Styro-foam cup.

A voice from one of the steel trays says, Not lovers. Whatever gave you that idea?

"Will you please," says Warren. "Jesus Christ. Does the whole world have to know?" A small red fox with luminous eyes appears in front of the Datsun's headlights for a moment, then vanishes.

"Excuse me?" says Barbara.

"The fox," he says after a while. "I was just wondering if it was real."

Barbara laughs sweetly, surprising him. "You city boys," is all she says.

23

"You're telling me," says Aïda, "that big black boot over there is going to make those poor fat legs of yours nice and skinny like mine? That's a joke, right?"

"It's modern medicine," says Silverstein, patting the metal, hassock-shaped contraption through which a tube leads to the knee-high plastic boot covering Sophie's leg. "Sometimes you've got to respect it." In the living room, the three of them watch as the boot rhythmically inflates and deflates, presumably releasing the fluid from Sophie's leg.

"All I want is my ankles back," Sophie says. "Not that I ever had much of an ankle to begin with."

"It works by electricity," Silverstein explains to Aïda. "I don't understand it, but this electrical pulsing is supposed to reduce the swelling in her legs somehow."

"Sounds like black magic to me," says Aïda.

"Stop talking stupid," says Silverstein. "You're making Sophie nervous. Haven't you got anything better to do than hang around here talking dumb on a beautiful summer day?"

"Monroe," says Sophie.

"A *hot* summer day," Aïda says. "And you've got air conditioning." She walks backward to the little unit set into the window, lifts up her ponytail, and lets the flow of air cool the back of her neck. "I could stay here all day," she murmurs. She's in a black bikini bathing suit that shows how thin she is except for her ballooning stomach. With a deep groan she hoists herself onto the windowsill. "All this extra weight I'm carrying around is such a drag," she says. "And these varicose veins are disgusting. I cover them up with makeup whenever Jimmie's around because I know it makes him sick to see them."

"Is that what the doctor told you to do, cover them with something from Revlon?" Sophie asks. "Come over here and let me see what you're talking about."

"I'm going out," says Silverstein. "All this female talk is getting to me." Pulling his chair closer to Sophie's, he picks up her wrist and brings it to his mouth.

"There's a time and a place for everything, Monroe," Sophie says. "Didn't anyone ever teach you that?" But she likes the warm gentle feel of him along her skin, the sweet tentative way he always approaches her, as if he is still uncertain of just how much he has earned. "Go ahead and kiss me, Monroe," she says. "You've come this far, you might as well go all the way."

"Maybe I should leave," Aïda says, smiling, "and just take the air conditioner with me."

"Oh no you don't. That air conditioner's not going anywhere," says Silverstein. "You want an air conditioner, you go to an appliance store like everyone else." He drops Sophie's wrist without warning. "What do you think, you can come here and get everything for free?"

"This is my husband, talking so disgusting like that?" Sophie yells. "My husband, the one man in all the world who wants to make me happy?"

"Maybe Carmen's up from her nap," Aïda says quietly, easing away from the window.

"Talking like a pig, an ignorant animal, right here in my living room? I don't even know you, I don't even want to know you."

"I suppose if you want me to apologize, I could apologize," says Silverstein.

"Don't do me any favors, you."

"I could say I'm sorry right now."

"I'm leaving," Aïda says.

"You," says Sophie, "stay. He goes. Truthfully, I can't stand the sight of him."

"Where am I going to go, out into the hot street?"

"I wouldn't know," says Sophie. "That's entirely up to you." She is up out of her chair, detaching herself from the machine, slipping the boot from her leg. She follows a strip of linoleum into the bedroom, where she yanks open Silverstein's dresser drawers one by one, and begins tossing socks and underwear and a pair of his honeymoon pajamas onto the bed, along with some plaid shirts she knows Frances had chosen for him years ago. Leaning into the closet, she tears pants from hangers, and ties and belts. Gathering up an armful of his things, she sweeps past Silverstein and Aïda and out the door, down one flight of steps to the lobby and out the exit that leads to the courtyard. Metal trash cans are lined up against the wall; she lifts up the covers of two of them and stuffs Silverstein's belongings inside. A family she doesn't know well at all is having a picnic not far from the line of garbage cans. They are seated on folding chairs at an aluminum table, listening to music from a radio as big as a small suitcase, and drinking cans of Ballantine.

"Pardon me for disturbing your lunch," Sophie says, slipping her glasses above her eyebrows to brush away the tears. "I didn't mean to interrupt." She watches as a thin little girl of seven or eight lays a doll between two beer cans on top of the table, raises its floppy legs, and unfastens a disposable diaper from its bottom.

"Wet and stinky," says the little girl cheerfully.

A bare-chested man in mirrored sunglasses knocks the doll from the table. "Not here," he says. "Play on the floor."

"You killed my Cabbage Patch preemie," the girl says in a quivery voice. "You broke her neck and killed her." Picking up the doll off the ground, she nestles it against her. "My poor dead preemie," she croons.

"You want a sandwich, Nellie?" says the girl's mother. "You want a Yoo Hoo?"

"I want nothing," says Nellie. "I just want to sit here and be sad."

"Me too," says Sophie. "Oh, God, me too." A sleeve of brown-and-beige checks from one of Silverstein's shirts hangs limply over the side of a garbage can. Sophie approaches it, takes the cuff in her hand, where it sits for only a moment. She tucks the sleeve neatly into the garbage, setting the lid back on quietly.

"*You* want a sandwich?" Nellie's mother offers. "Ham or jelly?"

"Jelly would be all right," says Sophie. "And maybe some tea to go with it, though I don't imagine you've got any hot tea down here with you."

"Beer is nice, nice and cold on a hot day," says the woman. She helps Sophie into a chair and opens a can of Ballantine for her. Sophie looks into the can and shakes her head.

"Once," she says, "I became friendly with a man who liked to drink beer. A very good-looking young man this Morgan was. Tall and slim, with beautiful manners. Every night we were together he offered me a beer, and I always said no. I think that disappointed him, though he didn't say so." Sophie takes a small bite of her jelly sandwich. "If I could remember the rest of his name, that would be really something." Handing the sandwich back to Nellie's mother, she says, "You're a married woman?" Nellie's mother says something Sophie doesn't understand. "Well," says Sophie, "I was once, and now I am again. Just a few months it's been this time. Just a little bit of time, but it seems longer. Every day seems long; space that needs to be filled. In the morning there's breakfast, in the afternoon there's lunch, at night there's supper. In between, there's a lot of time to get into trouble, to disagree about the way things are done. I'm not a difficult person; I get along fine with myself. But to have another person on top of me all day, following me around, watching everything I do, asking questions—it's a difficult thing. When you're young, it's different. You go to work, there are children to take care of, so many things that need doing. A husband and wife have time together, but they're also apart. This man I'm married to, he's looking in my direction every minute. If I'm in the bathroom, he wants to know when I'm coming out. Sometimes I go in there and lock the door behind me. I read for a while or I stare out the window. If I'm in the living room and looking out the window, my husband says, 'What's so interesting?' 'Children,' I tell him, but that's not enough. What kind of children, he wants to know. Boys? Girls? How many of each? What are they doing out there? That's enough to put an end to my sightseeing, let me tell you."

"Bruno," Nellie's mother whispers, "don't talk to me at all, except to yell. 'Where's my shoes? Where's my keys? Where's my wallet?' " She shrugs her shoulders. "Maybe one day I'll say 'Find them yourself, dummy,' and won't he be surprised."

Sophie isn't listening. She is staring at the trash cans, watching the cats who are rubbing up against them, winding their long thin bodies around them over and over again, as if it were a sensual pleasure. "Osborne," she says. "Morgan Osborne." She remembers exactly what he'd said when she'd told him she was pregnant: "Is that so?" Raising his thick pale eyebrows, stretching out his hand to stroke her face. She was frightened then of what had to be done, and wanted to cry but did not. Instead, they made love one more time, both of them knowing she had already given him up. They had never had even a single argument and there she was walking away from him. It had all been impossible and unlikely from the start. They had chosen each other knowing that and it had not made them sad, only grateful. Nearly fifty years have passed and she is still grateful.

Upstairs, her apartment is cool and silent. There is a one-sentence note from Silverstein propped up against the radio on the kitchen table. The note says: "I did not mean to speak nasty to your friend, but you can't get angry like that, it's bad for the hypertension." She leaves the note where it is, then goes next door to Aïda's and lets herself in after two knocks. The kitchen is steamy and filled with empty soda bottles—on the floor near the window, under the table, and above the refrigerator. Sophie picks up a Coke bottle that is blocking her way to the table. There are two small roaches imprisoned inside, making their way to the opening; when she shakes the bottle, they fall to the bottom.

"Get rid of this," she says. "And let me see those veins."

Aïda is still in her bathing suit, and is eating fried banana chips out of a turquoise cellophane bag, pausing every few moments to suck her fingertips.

"Want to smell my scratch-and-sniff stuff?" Carmen says. She holds a little picture of a moose head under Sophie's nose. "Smell," she orders.

"What is it?" says Sophie, waving away Carmen's hand. "What are you doing to me?"

"Chocolate moose. Now try this one." She hands Sophie a picture of a cross-eyed watermelon wearing white gloves and sticking out a large red tongue. "Wacky watermelon," she says. "Do you smell it?"

"Delicious," says Sophie. "Thank you."

"You going to give the old guy his clothes back?" says Aïda, lifting her leg onto a chair so Sophie can study the lacing of swollen veins on the inside of her thigh. "I think he was worried you were going straight to the Salvation Army with them. He talked to me a little while you were gone, but I don't think he likes me very much anymore."

"He likes you fine," says Sophie. "He just forgets how to talk nicely sometimes."

"All I wanted was a little cool air on the back of my neck."

"You've got to wear special stockings on these legs," says Sophie. "That's what the doctor told you, didn't he?"

"Too hot for stockings, forget it."

"You want to get a blood clot and have to be operated on?"

"Are you my mother or something?"

"Your mother's in Puerto Rico, but this is serious, sweetie pie."

Aïda yawns, and puts her head down on the table, into the crook of her arm. "One time, when I found out Jimmie was screwing another lady behind my back, I took some of the shit he left in my apartment—a silver bracelet I gave him, some leather sneakers, a Sony Walkman—and sold it all in the park. I took the money and bought a whole lot of Chinese food. Carmen had an egg roll and I ate the rest, all in one night. I just kept eating and eating and then I threw up. I was sick like a dog, but I didn't mind so much. Even when I was so sick, it was better than picturing him with that other lady. The next day I went to her house. I grabbed her by the hair and pulled it real tight. She had a lot of earrings in each ear, maybe four or five. I ripped a little gold hoop right out of her ear and made her cry."

Sophie shivers in the sweltering kitchen. "Like an animal?" she says. "How could you do such a thing?"

"I told her, 'Let my Jimmie come near you again and I'll do a lot worse.' "

"There are ways and there are ways," says Sophie.

"Well, that was my way and it worked real good because I never had any trouble with that lady again."

"You're going to have trouble with those legs if you don't get yourself a pair of those support hose. A blood clot could travel straight to your heart and that would be the end of you."

"You set the old guy's clothes on fire, didn't you? You went down to the basement and torched them, right?"

"I'll go out to a surgical supply house and ask for a pair in the petite size. Then I'll come back here and stand over you while you wiggle yourself into them."

"You're not even mad at the guy anymore. You want to get those clothes back but you're too embarrassed."

"I'm mad at *you*," says Sophie. "To be so stupid is just plain dumb."

"Maybe he's out buying a new wardrobe right now."

"Monroe?" says Sophie. She has forgotten, until this moment, that he is gone, forgotten that she is the one who chased him away. She thinks of him wandering about the neighborhood, bareheaded in the fierce bright sun, plagued by the gritty uncomfortable feel of his wife's anger under his skin. His wife. That is what she is, though she can't, suddenly, imagine why. She is eighty-five years old, too old to share generously whatever she has left to offer. It is far too much trouble for her, these days, to keep her anger to herself, to pretend, in the presence of her husband, that everything he says and does will lead her straight to happiness. Surely that is what he wants to hear, deserves to hear—that he is the guardian of her happiness.

"It's a terrible thing I did," she says. "A foolish thing."

First she will get his clothes back, then, before it is too late, she will take care of the other.

Down in the deserted courtyard, she pokes about in the trash, hating what she must look like—a desperate old bag lady in search of her next meal, or, perhaps, salvation. After a while, after going through two pails' worth of garbage, she understands that Silverstein's shirts and pants are gone for good, though she suspects that if she keeps her eyes open, she will catch sight of her neighbors in their new clothes sometime soon.

His underwear and socks turn up stained with mustard and ketchup and speckled with bits of canned vegetables; corn and peas and carrots that stick unpleasantly to her fingers.

Empty-handed, she climbs the stairs on legs that do not want to go anywhere. "Get going," she says. "Move." Coming up behind her is the teenage boy from the third floor whom she sometimes pays a dollar to change the lightbulbs in her overhead fixtures or to unclog the drain in the tub.

"I have a business proposition for you, Marco," she says. "How about you giving me a lift up the stairs, and I'll give you a couple of dollars when we get to the top."

Marco is wearing a shirt of white netting; through it, the blue and green of the tattoo on his chest are visible. He flexes the muscles in one arm, releasing a strong scent of perspiration. "I'm strong," he says, "but not that strong."

"Not strong enough to give me a few big pushes?"

Marco takes her arm. "We'll go real slow," he says. "Tell me if you need to rest."

"My new boyfriend," Sophie says, leaning her weight into him without apology. "Isn't this nice."

Leaving Silverstein is actually a good deal easier than marrying him was, Sophie tells herself as she packs up a vinyl flight bag and a small suitcase. No special dress is required for the occasion, and there's no need to set aside time for a session at the beauty parlor. She simply gathers her things together, calls a taxi, and says goodbye.

"How many times do I have to explain this to you, Monroe?" she says. "Mistakes are made, but that doesn't mean you have to live with them." The taxi, when it arrives, will take her straight to Manhattan, where she plans to stay with her granddaughter until she feels like coming home again. This will be news to Laura, but Sophie isn't worried. What can Laura do to her—throw her out into the street? Knowing Laura, she will put out fresh towels and a new tube of toothpaste in the guest bathroom, and refrain from asking all the wrong questions.

"You can't leave today," says Silverstein. "Today is our three-and-a-half-month anniversary. One hundred and five days ago you promised to spend the rest of your life with me and I believed you."

"Get off the bed, please. You're wrinkling the bedspread."

"Frances stayed with me for fifty-five years," says Silverstein. He slides to the edge of the bed but does not get up.

"And that's why you miss her so much," Sophie says. "I understand that." She is going through her jewelry box, looking for something she can give to Laura, but all she finds are stray bobby pins and a couple of gold bangle bracelets that are badly dented.

"I don't," says Silverstein, "now that I have you. These three and a half months have been like a wonderful gift. Sometimes, when we're eating a meal at the table together, sitting so close our elbows bump, I look at you and think, Who am I to be so lucky? How is it possible that an old man can be so contented? My hands shake when I lift a teacup to my lips, I have to get up out of bed to go to the bathroom two and three times a night, my toes cramp up when I walk, but I have no complaints. I'm a contented man. And now you're going to go and make me miserable? Just when I've gotten accustomed to feeling good?"

"I'm just thinking," says Sophie, "about a friend of mine, Mrs. Weiss, a very presentable woman you might be interested in, excepting that she's a little on the religious side, always mumbling a little prayer before she sticks a piece of food in her mouth. But other than that, she's good company. Should I call her before I leave?"

"Call her for what? I'm not interested in this Mrs. Weiss or anyone else. I have a wife I love, what's the matter with you?"

"I don't know," says Sophie. Absently, she slips the bracelets over her wrist. "I don't think it's anything personal, though. Maybe it's just two people in this little apartment, elbows bumping into each other, no place to hide."

"We'll move," says Silverstein. "To a big apartment on Park Avenue, with a doorman to carry our packages to the elevator. With enough rooms so you can hide from me whenever you want."

"Is that what you want, a wife who needs to hide from you?"

"I'm not offended," says Silverstein. "Maybe I talk too much, ask too many questions. My whole life with Frances, I let her do all the talking. I hardly opened up my mouth at all. I could try to do that again, if that would make you happy."

"Maybe I ought to call for another taxi," says Sophie. "What if they forgot about me?"

Silverstein brushes past her to a large gold-framed photograph on the wall above the dresser. It is a picture of Sophie's grandfather, a severe-looking man with an extravagant beard that reaches to the middle of his chest. Silverstein straightens the frame, then steps back for a better look.

"Keep away from my grandfather," says Sophie. "You want to touch that picture, you ask permission first." She adjusts the frame so that it hangs exactly as it had before, slightly off-center on the wall. "He was a *shohet*," she says. "In Moscow. An educated man, people respected him. He killed chickens, broke their necks in just the right way so they would be kosher. One day, in this country, he got knocked over by a horse-drawn wagon, trampled under its wheels. He should never have died; he was one of the finest, educated, lovable men in the world."

"I don't care," says Silverstein. "What was that, seventy-five years ago? I don't care at all." His face hardens slightly and he moves away from her, swaggering toward the door. "I canceled it," he boasts. "I called as soon as you hung up the phone, and told them to cancel the cab. What do you think of that?"

"You have your nerve," says Sophie, and reaches for the phone on the night table. She will not admit to him that, in spite of herself, she is a little pleased, a little bit flattered.

"Don't you owe me *anything*?" Silverstein says.

Sophie dials the phone, orders another cab, and hangs up. "It's good to hear someone say he loves you," she tells Silverstein. "The words sound beautiful, they make you feel like a person, a human being. But I can live without them, I don't need them to know who I am."

"You're my wife, that's who you are," says Silverstein. "Am I right, or am I losing my mind?"

"You're only losing me, not your mind. And believe me, compared to losing your mind, losing me is nothing." She is thinking of her sister-in-law Kate, of the pink satin ribbon spiraled around her wrist, of the small manicured hands folded obediently in her lap. "It's a pathetic thing," she says. "A person has got to have his marbles until the very end."

"I'm worried about you, Sophie," says Silverstein.

"Why should you be, I'm not worried about you."

"You worried about me when Frances died."

"That was different, that was fifty-five years of your life come to an end. This is three months; this is nothing."

"Three and a half months, and why does everything have to be measured in time?"

"Fine, we'll measure it in inches." Sophie holds up her hand, spreads her thumb and index finger a half inch apart. "This is our marriage," she says, then thrusts her arms wide apart. "And this is you and Frances."

"Frances is dead," says Silverstein, walking forward toward Sophie and gently bringing her arms together. The next moment he is placing them on his shoulders. "I'm alive, and believe me, I'm someone for you to worry about."

Raising her head slightly, kissing him for as long as she needs to, Sophie pulls away at the sound of the intercom buzzing. "First I have to worry about myself," she says. "It's nothing to be proud of, but still, that's the way it is."

"Wait," says Silverstein. He follows Sophie to the door and watches her gather up her bags.

"What is it?"

"We haven't had lunch."

Sophie laughs. "Where is it written that you can't end a marriage on an empty stomach?"

"You could make me a little lunch before you go," says Silverstein hopefully. "Nothing fancy, just a few sardines out of a can, something like that."

The buzzer rings again. Sophie has to stand on her toes to speak through the intercom. "Two minutes, sir," she yells, "and I'll be right down." She gets a can of salmon from the glass-paned cabinet over the sink, and drains the oil from it before adding a tablespoon of mayonnaise.

"Watch out for bones," says Silverstein. "You wouldn't want me to choke."

"How do you know?" Sophie murmurs. "Do you know everything?"

Silverstein peeks over her shoulder and into the glass bowl of salmon, a bowl shaped like an apple sliced perfectly in half.

"Not enough mayonnaise," he says tearfully, and Sophie pretends, as she adds another tablespoon, that now she has done everything exactly right.

24

Dear Editor,

Enclosed is a rock opera I wrote for David Bowie. He didn't want it, so I thought maybe you would. It tells all about my philosophy on
1) women
2) life
3) love
4) triumph

P.S. I am not now nor have I ever been a David Bowie fan.

Dear Editor,

I thought you might be interested in my story, which is only three pages and therefore cannot possibly consume much of your time. I would in all modesty call myself prodigiously gifted. Think of it this way: if you publish my story and my potential is fully recognized and I attain notoriety, it will be your contribution to the art world.

Editor:

You may purchase the enclosed work of fiction for the bargain price of One Thousand Twenty-five Dollars. I have not written it for prestige purposes or to perform a public service. My only reason for writing it was so I could receive money for it.

P.S. Is heartache all the death of a pet brings? Read the enclosed story to find an answer.

At the tenth ring of the telephone, Laura throws down the manuscript she is reading, shoots Sophie a look of pure exasperation, and grabs at the receiver so wildly that the rest of the phone pitches to the floor. "Listen, Monroe," she says, before he can even speak a word, "it's clear that you're going about this the wrong way." Since Sophie's arrival yesterday, Silverstein has called incessantly, every hour on the hour until midnight, and beginning again at eight in the morning. He has spoken to Laura, to Zachary, and even to Mia, who'd said, "Hello there, Mr. Dummy, sir," and hung up on him. Sophie has been absolutely unyielding in her refusal to speak to him, insisting there is nothing she can say that will put an end to his calls.

"You can tell him," she instructs Laura now, "that the lease is in my name and that he better get busy and find himself a new apartment."

"He says he wants his clothes back," Laura reports. "Especially his honeymoon pajamas, the tattersall ones with the torn pocket."

"He knows they're in the trash, he knows he can't possibly get them back," Sophie says. "Hang up on him."

"Do it yourself," says Laura, laying the receiver down on the table and walking away from the phone. She cannot believe the ease with which Sophie has abandoned her marriage, abandoned her home, which she has always pointed to as the one place in the world where she could be happy. Whenever she came for visits, sleeping for a single night on the pull-out couch in Mia's room, she awakened impossibly early and waited with poorly concealed impatience for Zachary to finish his breakfast and drive her home. This morning, pushing aside Mia's clothing in the closet and making room for her own, she told Laura how wonderfully well she'd slept. Then she announced that the sink in the bathroom needed a quick going-over, and asked for a can of Ajax. And while she was at it, a little sudsy ammonia to take care of the greenish stuff growing on the wall above the bathtub wouldn't be a bad idea either, she said, smiling at Laura, admitting that, God knows, she had never gone in much for housekeeping, at least not in her own home. Feeling too leaden to put up much of a fight, Laura stood in the doorway and watched Sophie clean the bathroom. While she scrubbed, Sophie talked about her own grandmother, who became a widow after a marriage that lasted almost sixty years. Whisked off by one of her sons to his house in Fall River, Massachusetts, following her husband's death, she was imprisoned there somewhere on the top floor, coming down only for meals and never going outside at all. When she died and some women from the synagogue were called to wash and dress the body, they were astonished to learn that she had been living there for years. "And you know why that was?" said Sophie. "Because her son and his family were ashamed to have anyone know there was an old woman living in their house with them, that's why." Laura simply nodded, wondering how many years Sophie was planning to stay. Reading her mind, gesturing with a hand dressed in a pale green elbow-length rubber glove, Sophie said, smiling, "Now *this* is where I intend to die, right here with you." Laura hated it that Sophie was so cheerful in the wake of her collapsed marriage, hated the thought of Silverstein left behind without even the small comfort of a deeply felt apology.

She can hear his voice now, calling Sophie's name through the telephone receiver on the table, growing ragged with despair.

"Monroe," Laura says into the phone, "you've got to be patient."

"I'll be anything she wants me to be. The problem is, I don't think she wants me at all—not quiet or noisy or stubborn or sweet or whatever. I don't think there's any way I can be that would be the right way for her. She goes into the bathroom just to hide from me. I know what she's doing in there, reading, thinking, contemplating life's mysteries. Why can't she do those things out in the open? It's like she can't breathe just being in the same room with me. She needs air, she says. Open a window, take a walk with me, I tell her. Not *that* kind of air, she says. What other kind of air is there?" When Laura doesn't answer, Silverstein says, "See, you don't know what this *mishegos* is about, either. Maybe she has another fellow in mind, that's always possible, I suppose."

"What?" says Laura. She looks over at Sophie, who is sifting through a wooden bowl of nuts on the coffee table, picking out every walnut she can find. Taking one in each hand, folding her fingers into fists, she squeezes hard. Laura listens to the splintery sound of the nuts cracking, shakes her head as Sophie holds out her hands, offering her the fragments in their shells. Who knows what she's capable of, Laura thinks, admiring the hands that are stronger than her own; pressing down on the walnut in her own palm now, she waits for the hard shell to give way but it does not. What is her grandmother's secret? Adultery? She can just see Sophie sneaking out in the middle of the afternoon while Silverstein dozes, hurrying to meet some courtly old man who knows precisely how to hold her in his arms—not too tightly, but delicately enough so that she can slip out from under his embrace without a word.

"Anything is possible," Silverstein warns. "Like my friend Archie Resnick will tell you, you never know. Archie was at some wedding, never mind whose, and he's a wonderful dancer, so of course he's out there on the dance floor, twirling his partner round and round and to and fro, but one time he forgets to reel her back in again, and off the lady goes, boom, and crashes right into some ninety-year-old dame who falls to the floor, breaks her ankle and sues Archie and his dancing partner for $15,000 a piece. And he had to pay up, too, don't think he didn't. Fifteen thousand big ones."

Laura laughs out loud. She smiles at the impressive line of walnuts Sophie has opened for her and arranged on the table.

"No laughing matter," says Silverstein.

"No," says Laura. As she well knows, anything is possible, even those things that are surely not.

Sophie is worried about her health; it is all she talks of, or so it seems to Laura. After two weeks, the exhilaration at having left Silverstein has faded, and in its place is a hard, stubborn pessimism that Sophie lovingly nurtures, sitting in a chair all day with her feet up on a soft leather ottoman, wearing only a half-closed housecoat and a shiny flesh-colored slip underneath. She says that her legs weigh two hundred pounds each, that walking is out of the question and reading too, because she has suddenly, three years after successful cataract surgery, gone half blind.

Friends of hers are dying like flies, she says—last month, for instance, Rose Rosenblatt, a woman with a pacemaker like her own, just lay down in her bed one afternoon and never woke up again, leaving behind a failing husband and two divorced children. Sophie smacks her lips slightly in the telling, savoring the details, Laura thinks. Savoring the knowledge that it is she and not Rose Rosenblatt who is here to tell the tale.

But then, finishing the story, Sophie begins to cry. "I can't go on like this," she says. "I want to go down into the street, to see people, to shop for a new housedress, to get on a bus and look out the windows. But my legs won't move and I can't even see to read the street signs to figure out where I'm going."

"What about a new prescription for your glasses?" Laura says. "We'll find an ophthalmologist in the neighborhood and have you checked out."

"Don't bother," says Sophie. "Those doctors all say the same thing, that the glasses I already have are the best they can do for me, that my eyes, for an old person, are as good as they're ever going to be."

"Getting dressed might help," says Laura. "You might feel like going out if you put some clothes on."

"How do you think it feels to lie down in your bed and never get up again? Do you think maybe it feels good, to disappear so quietly? When you're my age, maybe that's what you should be hoping for."

Laura is down on the living room floor now, doing several minutes of scissor kicks followed by twenty modified situps. Her breathing is so loud she can scarcely hear Sophie's voice over the sound of it.

"One of the Charlie's Angels, the blond one, I think, did what you're doing through her whole pregnancy," Sophie says. "Her stomach was hard as stone and ooh was she proud. Funny what people are proud of today. Stomachs like stone, eating to win, well-organized closets. . . . What ever happened to just trying hard to be a mensch?"

Lying flat on the floor, exhausted, Laura rubs her hard belly as if it were a genie's lamp. What would she wish for if someone dressed like a belly dancer and smelling of incense suddenly appeared with a pad and pencil ready to take her order? To be restored to her former status as a mensch. One afternoon not long ago, after making love with David in a hurry, knowing Mia had to be collected at summer camp a quarter of an hour later, Laura felt so overwhelmed by guilt that for a terrifying instant she did not recognize her face in the mirror. As she stood in her underwear brushing her hair in David's bathroom, she could not remember who she was. She had lost herself for only a moment, but the goose bumps flared everywhere along her skin. She told David then what had frightened her and she saw in his face that he was frightened too, afraid that she had already decided to leave and never return. She comforted him, held his face in her hands and kissed the taut dry flesh of his cheeks, all the while feeling slightly sick to her stomach. "I'm really a coward who's been pretending fearlessness," she told him. She remembered something Mia had said just after being reprimanded more forcefully than usual. "It's so much easier to be good than it is to be bad," Laura had shrieked at her. "So why are you so bad?" "Are you kidding?" Mia said. "It's *much* easier to be bad." Amused, Laura had forgiven her immediately. But the truth was, it was ultimately less painful and less complicated to do the right thing. The virtuous slept better; they fell asleep effortlessly every night and slept through until morning. They did not suffer headaches and queasy stomachs and mouths that turned dry with panic. Laura knew this firsthand. She felt as if she had been David's lover forever, but she still remembered the sweet untroubled flow of her life before him. Maybe what she needed, she told David, was to organize a support group: Adulterers Anonymous.

My name is Laura and I am an adulterer. Adulteress? It has been three weeks since I last betrayed my husband.

Fellow adulterers seated in orderly rows of folding chairs applaud vigorously: Way to go Laura, keep up the good work!

"You've got to stop thinking of yourself like this," David said. "It's too dangerous." Dangerous for him, he'd meant. His luck had failed him; his body had failed him, his wife had failed him. Eventually, the chemotherapy and the radiation would fail him, too. There was only Laura, the keeper of promises. She showed up at his apartment Monday through Friday, as promised. She tended to him lovingly for an hour or so and then left, but always he knew she would be back. One day she would come and he would be gone, taken away by ambulance, and he would not return home again. He would disappear without warning and she would pretend that every bit of it had been imagined; the uncertain beginnings of their love, his death, whatever happiness illuminated the moments in between. This was the way she had envisioned it, over and over again. In its inevitability lay its comfort.

Of course she would never leave him, she told David. Running out the door of his apartment, already late to pick up her daughter, as usual. Somebody's mother. Somebody's wife. Somebody's lover. Running through the summer heat, hands held over her stomach. "Hope it's a boy," a shopkeeper yelled after her from his doorway as she ran past without a smile.

Her grandmother is standing over her worriedly. "Are you in pain?" she says. "You're not going to have the baby today, are you?"

"Of course not. I'm only resting on the floor."

"When I was in labor with your father," Sophie says, back in her seat again, "a neighbor, Fat Angie, an older woman with a big set of false teeth in her mouth, came by to borrow some applesauce. 'I'm in labor,' I tell her, but I gave her the applesauce anyway, a whole jar of it. 'Labor?' she says. 'I don't feel so well myself.' Then she proceeds to get sick all over my kitchen floor, half swallowing those big big teeth of hers while she's doing it. I had to reach way down into the back of her mouth to grab a hold of those false teeth so she wouldn't choke on them. Do you think she thanked me? No sir, all she does is call out her doctor's phone number to me. 'I'm dying,' she says. 'Call the doctor and tell him it's an emergency.' The doctor tells me over the phone that he's too busy to come and that I should take care of her myself. 'I'm in labor,' I say to him, and he says, 'In that case, leave your friend on the floor and get over to the hospital.' "

"Did you?" Laura says.

"First I mopped up the floor," Sophie says, "because naturally I didn't want anyone who came into that kitchen to think I was a slob. Then the two of us went to the hospital together, Fat Angie and myself, moaning and groaning all the way there in the taxi, neither one of us paying any attention to the other. Your father was born that night and by the end of the week Fat Angie had knit him mittens and a hat, and a beautiful sweater with little heart-shaped buttons. She was grateful, I suppose, for the way I yanked those teeth right out of her mouth and saved her from choking."

Laura thinks of her father, whom she hasn't spoken to in months. Perhaps she could drive Sophie up to Stamford for a visit, deposit her with her flight bag at her father and stepmother's door. Catch them off guard, without a word to either of them.

"Does he know you're married?" she asks Sophie, suspecting she already knows the answer.

"Who?"

"My father."

"Your father?" Sophie hoots. "I don't tell him anything and he does me the same courtesy, thank you. That way we have nothing to argue about. I wish we could like each other when we're together, but that's always been out of the question. Well, not always: in the summertime, when he was a little boy, on the very hottest days, he would climb up into the icebox and sit there, legs dangling, and we would talk about this and that, nicely, just the way a mother and a son should talk together. Then in a few summers he was too big to fit inside the icebox and all his sweetness was gone. When it comes to children there's no knowing what went wrong. You do for them and you do for them and that's as it should be. If you're lucky it all comes out right in the end. And if you're not so lucky and you lose them, for a few years or even for a lifetime, you don't go on mourning forever. You're attached to them just the same, no matter how many times they open up a fresh mouth to you and tell you that you don't know anything at all, that you know even less than the rest of the world."

"You haven't been to Stamford in so long," Laura says. "Things might go differently than you expect."

"Haven't you been listening to me? I'm too *sick* to go visiting all the way to Connecticut. Everything is wrong with me, nothing is right. I'm going to die soon," Sophie says furiously. "Don't you pay attention when people talk to you?"

"You're old, but you're not dying," Laura says, sliding herself up against the glass rectangle of the coffee table, ignoring the thick edge of glass that presses into her back. "You're near the end of your life, but you're not dying."

"Listen, you," Sophie says, "when you've come to the end of your life, you know it. You feel it; things don't look the same anymore. The whole world is going to be taken away from you and nothing feels worse than that. Even at eighty-five years of age you don't want to let go. 'Why can't I be different, why can't I be special,' you want to know. You want to be the exception to the rule, the one person who's not going to have to give it all up. Nothing works right anymore—heart, eyes, legs, feet—proof that it's time to shut down the works. But still you don't want to get into that bed and just disappear. I *know*, because I'm old and sick and I can't expect to get any better. So I don't want to hear you tell me I'm not dying when I know for certain that I am."

"It's not the same," Laura says. She wants Sophie to know about David, to understand that by his standards at least, she has led something like a charmed life. A life that seems to go on forever, taking its time, going nowhere special, but going on nevertheless. "There's someone I know," she begins, "not an old person, but someone still quite young."

Soon Sophie is nodding her head, admitting that this, too, is terrible, and worse, even tragic. "For a young person to be so sick, it can't be anything but tragic," she says. "But why am I hearing about this person I don't even know?"

Laura is silent, refusing to believe that Sophie doesn't understand.

"Don't you see?" Sophie cries out a moment later. "I don't care about him, some stranger. How do his problems make mine any better? They don't! And it's rotten of you to pretend that they do. If he died next week, next month, what does that mean to me? Only that someone else got cheated out of half a lifetime. So what? It doesn't make me any less afraid."

"He's my lover," Laura whispers. "This man who's going to die is my lover."

"Oh my," says Sophie in a voice that wobbles. She puts a hand up to her eyes, covering half her face. "*Mamele,*" she says. "My sweetie pie." In a trance Laura moves to her side, bends to lay her head in Sophie's lap. "A *zeisa neshumah* like you," Sophie says. A sweet soul.

"I'm not," says Laura. "I'm not." But still she likes to hear the words, repeated again now as Sophie's hand passes delicately along the top of her head and down the slope of her skull.

25

One night following dinner, just after Barbara has left to see a movie David has never heard of called *What Have I Done to Deserve This!*, George appears at the door dressed in a white jogging suit with a turquoise stripe up the side.

"No date tonight?" says David as he leads his father into the living room.

"It happens," says George, and winks. "Not often, but it happens. You wouldn't believe how many women there are out there in the street, especially now that it's summer. And most of them are in shorts and those aerobic shoes, even the ones that are my age. They dress the same as the twenty-year-olds, all those women hoping to pass for fifty-five or so. It's all vanity out there, but I'm not complaining." George smiles only briefly, then says, "I had a dream about you last night, cookie. The dream was that all of this was a dream. I never came to visit you here anymore; we kept meeting on the tennis court somewhere. We played doubles, triples, whatever, and we always won. We flew across the court without any effort, so strong and graceful people said we were beautiful to watch."

David glances at his father's balloon of a stomach. He thinks of himself walking the sixty yards to Laura's building and then back home again, breathless, his middle just a hollow space that quickly filled with pain. "I've never played tennis in my life," he says. "And neither have you."

"I'm not talking about life," his father says. "I'm talking to you about a dream. Don't you ever have dreams like that where you're strong and happy and there's no one to tell you otherwise?"

"Never," says David. In the beginning, when his illness had first been diagnosed, he had had those dreams often, dreams that awakened him while it was still dark and kept him up until light suffused the room again. Every dream was the same, uninspired and unoriginal but so intoxicating: at its center was a simple mistake, a misunderstanding between two doctors, the pathologist and the internist, both of whom delivered embarrassed apologies, eyes cast downward. You're a free man, one or the other of them said, giving David a push out into the street, into sunlight so startling his eyes instantly flooded with tears. He has not had these dreams in months. The exhilaration he felt in the midst of them was so real that he would awaken with a noisy, quickened heartbeat and pajamas dampened with sweat. He missed the dreams when they stopped coming, missed the happiness that was his for what was surely only a fragment of an instant but seemed substantial enough. Now all of his dreams have something to do with Laura; most recently, he and Laura having a child together, a solid long-limbed boy who grasped David's finger and would not let go. Even in his dreams, David knew he would not live to see the baby grow beyond infancy. It was terrible to ponder this; awakening in the darkness, he grieved for the dream baby who had seized hold of his finger and would not give it up.

"Well," says George, "I guess I bombed out with that one. I concentrate on saying all the right things to you, but sometimes it all comes out wrong and then I feel so useless, like some well-meaning casual acquaintance who doesn't know the first thing about what you're feeling."

"At least you talk to me," David says. "Try living in a house where the best anyone can manage is to leave notes for you in your shirt pockets."

"What kind of notes? 'Please take this to the cleaners for me'?"

David shakes his head. "I mean like, 'Dear Dad—I would appreciate it if you would stop trying so hard to get information out of me. I believe in a person's right to his privacy, which shouldn't be that tough for you to understand. Why is it so important for you to know what I'm thinking? It seems that whenever I'm here you're staring at me with the saddest face in the world, wanting to know things I just need to keep to myself.' "

"Wow," says George. "You memorized that?"

"I've looked at it five times today and it scares me more each time I read it."

"I'd tear it up," George says. "I'd force him to talk. A father has to know almost everything, especially the things his child is afraid of. What kind of father can you be if everything is a big secret? You can't go around guessing what he's feeling, it's not fair to either of you."

David remembers, as of course Ethan cannot, all those nights long ago when he lifted his sleeping son from the backseat of their car, from the floor in his room, from beds not his own, all those places he'd dropped off, unwillingly, to sleep, and from which only David could rescue him. The warm sweet leaden weight of his sleeping child against him, the limitless love that flowed miraculously from father to son, unasked for, but there for the taking. If only, David thinks, it were still possible to feel that weight against him. He wants a son he can carry in his arms, a child he can love effortlessly. Instead there is Ethan, inaccessible behind his bedroom door, where he sits large and silent as a boulder in a stream and just as responsive.

Leaving his father without a word, entering his son's room after a halfhearted knock, David comes upon Ethan on the rattan rug, headphones pinned to his ears, forehead dipped low, almost to the floor, then lifted up, then brought low again.

"Ba na na na na," Ethan sings. The pencils in his hands are drumsticks that strike the floor frantically.

David calls out his name. He claps his hands together twice. He puts his palms on Ethan's shoulder. At last Ethan turns to face him.

"I'm listening to the Boss," he says. "Want to try some?"

"Springsteen? Too loud for headphones." The drumsticks keep moving, but sluggishly now. "I got your note," David begins. Ethan slips the headphones down around his neck. "It wasn't what I wanted to see," says David. "Or hear, for that matter."

"I'm sorry, then."

"You don't sound it."

"God," says Ethan, "you're so intense. You listen so carefully to everything I say, it makes me nervous. What are you expecting to hear that's worth listening that carefully to? There's nothing I'm going to say that's so important to anyone."

"You're my child," says David. Then, seeing the look of irritation on Ethan's face, "My son." He stoops down, with difficulty, to lay a hand at the back of his son's neck. "We don't have forever," he says.

"How do you know that?"

"You know we don't."

"So why are you wasting your fucking precious time with that

Laura person?" The headphones are back over his ears now, the pencils tapping hard against the rug.

"You *listen* to me!" David yells. "And take those goddamn headphones off before I toss them right out the window."

The headphones remain on his ears. "You're so sick, right," Ethan says, "but you've still got enough energy to enjoy yourself. So I feel real sorry for you, right?" An unpleasant smile comes to his lips; a warning of what is to follow. "Hey, we're *talking*, man. It's what you wanted, isn't it, for the two of us to talk? Why don't we just keep on like this till we're all talked out?"

Even as David is yanking the headphones from his son, raising the window with such force that pain leaps to his side, he is thinking, I am the adult here, the father who loves you unfailingly, and this is what I have to let myself do, what I cannot stop myself from doing.

Charging out of the room in perfect imitation of a man in good health, he hears his son calling after him, brokenly, *prick bastard asshole*. Brushing past the confused, questioning face of his own father. Not even bothering to slam the door behind him. The elevator arrives, shoots him downward to the lobby, where a young doorman tips his hat vaguely, not knowing, David thinks, that this is a maniac who walks past him.

The city at dusk is no longer a place that is familiar to him; it has been months since he has been out at night. Sometimes, sitting out in the warm air just before dinnertime, gazing at the people returning home from work, everyone dressed neatly in suits, umbrellas and briefcases swaying, he felt a longing as keen and as pointed as unrequited love; an aching to be bound up again in ordinary life, in all its pettiness. *He saw himself on the steamy subway, his fingers wrapped around a metal pole, careful not to graze the hands positioned directly above and below his. The lights go out in the car and he sighs along with the rest of the passengers, all of them acknowledging that this is par for the course. And there he is in the supermarket, waiting for the cashier to figure out why the register drawer is jammed, the drawer with David's change locked up in it. He taps his foot against the wheels of his shopping cart, eyes the watch on his wrist, the clock on the wall. He is a busy man; finished at last with the day's work, off to hear the Philharmonic at Lincoln Center after he helps his wife prepare dinner. If he ever gets out of this absurd place. Eventually the manager arrives, carrying a knife which he will use to unstick the drawer. The manager, the cashier, and David exchange glances that say, What nonsense, what a foolish waste of time. Now we can get back to business.*

Standing in the subway, waiting on a supermarket line, hurrying home from work. He thought of these things dreamily, the way someone caught in a traffic jam would have imagined endless miles of perfectly desolate country roads.

Slow-moving as if he were trying in darkness to make his way safely down from a precarious height, he crosses the street now and walks south, down Columbus Avenue, stopping to look in the shop windows along the way. The window of a shoe store is taken up entirely by a six-foot-long sardine case, partially opened to reveal a dozen pair of floral-printed sneakers. He peers into a bakery whose walls are filled with bread sculpture—breads baked in the shape of palm trees, roosters, and turtles. In the display window of a women's clothing store he stares, astonished, at huge plastic flies, perhaps ten inches long, their shining green bodies and red eyes threatening under the fluorescent lights.

He passes a stationery store that has a plastic wading pool full of water in one of its windows; floating in the pool is a flashlight and the torso of an inflatable butler dressed in black and white, holding a tray with a martini glass balanced on it. At a telephone booth on the corner, a man with a baby on his shoulders is making a call; the baby grasps a handful of hair from the top of his father's head but the man seems not to notice. "They have great guacamole," the man says into the phone. "And a hundred and ten different kinds of wine on tap." David smiles at the baby, who smiles back, drooling into his father's hair. *Your fucking precious time*, he can hear his own son saying. He will not beg, or even ask for, Ethan's forgiveness. He had gone to his son propelled by love, seeking love, and had found only contempt and bewilderment. He imagines himself as death closes in on him, attended only by his stony-faced, unforgiving son, who hands him a note that is stapled shut. Too weak to open it, David watches the paper drift to the floor next to his bed. Ethan stares mutely but will not make a move to retrieve it. Then he looks up at David, hissing, *Get it yourself.* Where is Barbara? At the movies, seeing *What Have I Done to Deserve This!* one last time. And Laura? Nursing her baby in an overheated room, daydreaming of sleep, as her lover drifts toward death.

He has walked two blocks and is exhausted. He leans against a Honda Civic that has a parking ticket tucked under its windshield wiper. Propped up in the driver's seat is a stuffed animal he recognizes as the Pink Panther, a paw resting on each side of the steering wheel. "The least you could have done was talk your way out of the ticket," David says. Arms folded along his waist, legs crossed at the ankle, he gazes up at a second-story window into a tanning salon called Midnight Sun. It is nearly nine o'clock as he watches a couple of women, their backs facing the window, sitting in front of ultraviolet lights getting a tan. He laughs and laughs, is still laughing when, a few minutes later, the owner of the Civic comes back, a bearded man in baggy linen shorts and espadrilles and a Hawaiian print shirt that reaches to his knees. "Want to see something even funnier?" the man says, and rips up the parking ticket, scattering the pieces over his shoulder.

George is waiting for him when he returns home, too weary even to take his keys from his pocket and unlock the door. He sinks to the rubber welcome mat outside the apartment, colliding heavily with the door as he travels downward. Perhaps he will stay forever where it is safe, just beyond the threshold of his home. The door opens; George extends his arms and pulls David to his feet. "I hate the idea of you out there alone where nobody knows you're sick," he says. "What if you'd collapsed in the street and they'd mistaken you for a drunk?"

"Where's Ethan?"

"Out in search of his headphones." Helping him onto the couch, George props pillows behind David's head and under his feet. "Since when do you throw things out of the window like that? Someone might have been walking by at just the right moment and you'd have a nice lawsuit on your hands."

"The new me," David says. "Violent, unpredictable, and possibly dangerous."

George pats David's ankles, then hides his hands behind his back. "You want something to eat?" he says. "I could make you some Jell-O."

"Jell-O?"

"I was thinking something that goes down easy. Something you wouldn't choke on."

It is the thought of himself as a dangerous man that David may choke on. The kind of man who might come up behind anyone at all and give him a shove over the edge of a subway platform, into the path of an oncoming train. A man with nothing to lose because he's already lost it all.

"No thank you," David says, and pretends he is nearly asleep, a sick man's privilege. He feels his father's dry, prickly kiss on his forehead, hears his footsteps retreating into the kitchen. He listens to cabinet doors opening and then closing, to a spoon ringing metallically in its fall against the counter top; all the clatter of his father's love.

26

Laura recognizes the symptoms instantly: eyes streaked with red, a witless smile, an exuberance that cannot be restrained. "Will you look at my eyes?" David says the moment she enters his apartment. "Are they something to see, or what?" Seizing Laura by the elbows, he bumps noses with her and opens his eyes wide. "One black one and one blue one. After all these years, I just noticed I'm a freak of nature," he says proudly.

"Which is the blue one?" says Laura.

"Who cares? All I care about is getting to Bloomingdale's before it closes."

"It's ten-fifteen in the morning," Laura says.

"Then I guess we better hurry." David arranges the joint between his fingers like a cigarette, inhales, and holds his breath, eyes squeezed shut.

"Breathe," says Laura.

Exhaling, he begins to cough. "You know who gave this to me? A nurse in the hospital. A very very lovely person. A woman of infinite compassion. She told me it would make me feel better but I didn't believe it until a few minutes ago. Would you like a puff?"

"A drag," says Laura, laughing. "A hit."

"You're not laughing at me, are you?" David says as he raises the joint to Laura's lips. "Laughing at a dying man just isn't done, at least not in this part of the world. Maybe in other cultures, like Texas, it's permissible, but here it's looked at askance, like flossing your teeth in public. And speaking of Texas, did you know a pregnant woman was arrested in a department store there for shoplifting a basketball?"

"For her unborn child?"

"There *was* no basketball," says David. "There was only her basketball of a stomach, which the security guards mistook for stolen property. And now she's suing them for the pain and humiliation, which is, of course, the American way."

"Come on," says Laura.

"Come on and have another hit."

"What's my obstetrician going to say?"

"Does he speak English? If not, you won't be able to understand what he's saying anyway, so don't worry about it."

"What?" Laura smokes the joint in silence.

"I haven't been to Bloomingdale's in years," says David. "I'm tired of waiting."

"Why Bloomingdale's?"

"Because," says David, "it's like no other store in the world. At least that's what the woman on TV said."

"What woman?"

"I don't know, just some woman who gets paid to say things like that."

"I'm getting rid of this thing," Laura says, and goes into the kitchen, where she drops the joint down the drain, enjoying the sizzling sound it makes as it touches water. She opens the refrigerator door and takes out a head of iceberg lettuce and six different flavors of salad dressing. It occurs to her that she has never gone to this refrigerator before, never eaten even a mouthful of food in this apartment, or asked for more than a glass of water. She has never felt comfortable here, though she has walked naked through the rooms of the apartment, used its shower, the toothpaste lying in a shallow puddle on the bathroom counter, and once, a little bit of Barbara's sample-size Jean Naté After Bath Splash, which she found behind the sliding door of the medicine cabinet one morning while searching for some aspirin for David. What if Zachary has a lover whose fingerprints are everywhere in their apartment? A lover who has gone boldly from room to room, examining the thousand things that do not belong to her but to the life shared by Zachary and Laura. And Mia. Laura can see Zachary's lover naked, on her knees in Mia's room, going through Mia's Dr. Seuss collection, the bright boxes of cardboard puzzles, the small plastic suitcase filled with pieces of Lego. The woman's face is out of focus; it does not matter who she is or what she has done with Zachary, only that her hands have fallen eagerly on the bits and pieces of family life, a life from which she must always be excluded.

David is seated at the kitchen table with his hand in his shirt pocket, massaging his chest. "You never cook for me anymore," he says gloomily. "Not even a single salade Niçoise or a peanut-butter-and-Fluff sandwich on whole wheat."

"You must be confusing me with your wife," Laura says, and replaces the bottles of salad dressing in one of the shelves lining the refrigerator door. She tears off a sheet of paper toweling from the dispenser over the sink and returns to the refrigerator, where she wipes each bottle clean of fingerprints.

"What are you doing?"

"Getting rid of the evidence," she says. "Fingerprints."

"Fingerprints, of course," David says, bursting into laughter. He clutches at his side and she knows he is in pain. "I'm stoned," he says. "Are you?"

She studies the paper towel in her hand, decorated with gray-and-white drawings of cherries, apples, grapes, and pears. "Odd," she says. "No kiwi, and no clementines, either." She remembers a hand-lettered sign at the Korean grocer's last winter: "Cremen-tine, 5/$1.00." Now she is laughing too, standing at David's side with her face against the back of his head.

"You're not stoned," says David. "No way, buddy."

"I've got some new customers for you," Laura says. "How much do you charge, anyway?"

"Please. The word is clients—no customers." Laura's arms are dangling from his neck now, her hands at his heart. He kisses her fingers one by one. "Who's the happy couple?" he says.

"My grandmother and her new husband."

"I don't believe I know them. Are they Looney Tunes?"

"Sophie thinks she's going to die soon."

"There's a lot of that going around," says David evenly. "Es-pecially in the eighty-five and older set. Old-age depression, you could call it."

"She dumped her husband's perfectly good clothing into the trash, and then she dumped him."

"Send her over," David says. "And Señor Silverbean, too. If I can't help them, I promise I won't hurt them."

"If you can't help them, do they get their money back?"

"No exchanges, no returns. You put your life into my hands and hope for the best. Visa and MasterCard accepted, no personal checks. What about Bloomingdale's?"

"I'm sure they take checks," says Laura.

"I meant, are you ready to go?"

"Our first real date out in the world," says Laura, smiling.

"In that case, I'll have to dress for the occasion."

She follows him into the bedroom and sits watching while he gets into cuffed chinos, a blue-and-white pin-striped shirt, and a navy foulard tie. He has trouble getting the tie right; after three attempts, his face is shiny and stained slightly pink—several shades brighter than she has ever seen him.

She enjoys the sight of him leaning forward in the taxi to instruct the driver on which streets to avoid. The driver, whose I.D. against the dashboard suggests he is Arab, does not, at first, seem to comprehend much English. He ignores David's instructions as they are coming through the park and soon has them stuck behind an abandoned bus.

"Bloomiedale's," the driver says, throwing up his hands.

"Get out of the goddamn bus lane," David says.

Pulling the cab into the middle lane, the driver smiles at them in the rearview mirror. "Lady going to have her baby soon? Going to pop soon?"

"Not today," says Laura.

"Maybe today in Bloomiedale's," the driver says, and laughs. "My wife have one in the bathtub. The doctor says, 'Not today, go home and relax, take a bath.' In the bathtub she feels something happening so fast and pop, out comes my son. My other son always running with things in his mouth, sticks, pencils, toys. The day the baby is born, he runs, so happy, with a pen in his mouth, to answer the telephone. He falls and the pen makes a big hole in the top of his mouth, the roof. Sixteen stitches the doctor sews."

Laura puts her mouth to David's ear and kisses him; he smiles, but does not turn toward her.

"First baby?" the driver says.

Laura responds in an instant. "Yes," she says, and does not know why her answer gives her such pleasure. "We're going to name him Benjamin."

"We are not," says David. "Whatever gave you that idea?"

"Fine," says Laura. "Have it your way."

"I intend to."

With her wrists, Laura sweeps sudden tears from her eyes. "This is it," she says, "the one and only date we'll ever have."

"Actually, Benjamin is a very distinguished-sounding name. You can keep it if you want to."

"You're stoned and I'm not," Laura says. "It's a bad way to start off a marriage."

"The marriage is off," announces David as he pays the driver. "Too many complications." He nods at a pair of workmen on their break who are sitting on the sidewalk in front of Bloomingdale's. The men are eating packages of orange-colored Hostess cupcakes and drinking from little bottles of Perrier. "Enjoy!" David calls out, thrusting his arm into the air dramatically.

"What the hell is that supposed to mean?" says one of the men.

"I'm not telling," David says, and allows Laura to usher him into the store. He climbs a half flight of polished steps slowly, Laura's arm in his. "I need to rest a minute," he murmurs, and they stand at the front of the makeup department, gripping each other's hands. A girl about ten and her mother, both with tiny flowers made of glitter on their cheeks, walk by. Then the girl steps back, stopping beside a mirror on the counter, motioning to her mother to come and look. Silently, she smiles at her face in the mirror until her mother leads her away.

"Where would you like to go first?" Laura asks, staring at the sandaled feet of a tall black woman facing her from across the aisle. The nails of each of her big toes are covered with a thick layer of what looks like fourteen-carat gold. The woman is queenly, over six feet tall, her posture beautifully erect. Her golden toenails become her, Laura thinks—anything less extravagant would be inappropriate.

"Why can't we just wander aimlessly?" David says. "It's not my style, but in my old age it's what I feel like doing."

A crowd has gathered in the men's cologne department to watch a performer in tails and white-face impersonate a mannequin come to life. He moves his head to the left and to the right, eyes unblinking, and so mechanically that Laura can nearly hear the creaking of his gears, she thinks. Down comes an arm unhurriedly, then up; in his gloved hand is a sample-size bottle of cologne. He is giving them away free, and the crowd presses forward quietly.

"Take one," a woman urges her husband.

"I don't *wear* cologne," the man says irritably. "What are you bothering me for?"

"For free you can wear it," the woman says.

"For free *you* can wear it."

Laura collects a bottle and hands it to David. "Don't say I never gave you anything," she tells him. They take the escalator to the second floor. A harpist dressed in a pale pink sequined gown and silver flat-heeled slippers is setting up her sheet music on a metal stand in the middle of the handbag department. A few feet away, two college-age girls in floor-length flowered dresses are twirling matching parasols.

"Free umbrella with any purchase from our fragrance collection," one of them announces brightly. Turning to her companion she says, "I knew some people from California once and they made me sick. This one girl, this roommate of mine, she was a destructive psychopath and she like scared the shit out of me."

"Really," says the other girl. The harpist begins to play the theme from *Summer of '42*. "We were like *so* wasted last night," the girl says, stretching out the "so" to three syllables.

"Where were you guys?"

"What's the name of that place where they only have a men's bathroom and they have great munchies? Whatever that place is, that's where we were."

Her friend shrugs, and twirls her parasol listlessly. "Someplace in Soho, I think."

"Don't you girls know it's bad luck to open an umbrella indoors?" David says.

"This is a parasol, sweetie," says the girl whose roommate was a destructive psychopath. "They're trying to pass it off as an umbrella, but you wouldn't want to get caught with this baby out in a thunderstorm, believe me."

"I believe you." David steps closer to the girl. "Pretty costume." He touches her parasol, his hand lingering a moment too long for Laura, who grabs him by the wrist and hisses, "Let's go." The harpist is playing a song from *Annie* now, unmindful of the beading of perspiration along her powdered forehead.

"Bet your bottom dollar that tomorrow . . ." David sings.

The girls spin their parasols and wave goodbye.

"Those girls were very young," David says, sounding mournful. "Do you think they thought I was an old man?"

"How should I know?" Laura answers. They have arrived at another set of escalators, where a string trio in formal wear is playing "New York, New York." All three men are balding and are wearing black-framed eyeglasses; the expression on their faces is melancholy. Their music is impossibly cheerful but clearly the men are thinking of other things—unpaid bills, unfaithful wives, and worse.

"I'm as old as I'm ever going to get," David says. "Does it show in my face?" Staring into the nearest mirror for only a moment, he claps his hands over his eyes. "Don't look at me. Don't look at my face. Don't look at what's there."

"The light in here is terrible," offers the saleswoman behind the counter. "Very harsh, I'd say."

"You're panicking," Laura whispers. "You were high and now you're coming down." His panic unnerves her, deprives her of strength and courage. She is better off at home with Sophie, half listening to her fears of imminent death: what if the battery in her pacemaker dies, what if she falls and breaks her hip and languishes in a hospital where the nurses forget to turn her twice daily and she develops bedsores which become infected and ul-timately kill her? *You*, Sophie says, gesturing at Laura with her index finger. *How can you imagine what it's like to be so fright-ened?* And then there is Mia, who recently worried that the vacuum cleaner would suck her right up into its bag and turn her to dust, that the water flowing into the drain in the bathtub would carry her along with it down under the street to a place where no one would be able to find her, she insisted, not even the people who loved her most. "Would I let that happen to you?" Laura said, pressing her child to her so impassionedly that Mia began to cry. "I don't know," her daughter said, doubting the power of Laura's love to save her from the bathtub drain. "Would you?"

In a dream, David's head is in her lap and she is saying, with such certainty, as she strokes his cheekbones, *Would I let that happen to you? Would I?*

The certainty is that her daughter will be swallowed up by the vacuum cleaner before David will ever be rescued.

"You know you won't be at the funeral," he is saying to her now. "You'll be home with the baby asleep in your arms, watch-ing from the window as the hearse rides down the street, and you'll be saying goodbye in a whisper because what you'll want more than anything is for the baby to go on sleeping. You'll want that even more than you'll want to say goodbye, and so you'll barely raise your eyes to the window as the hearse takes off, because what good would it do anyway to imagine me like that, locked away under polished wood, wood so beautiful you'd want to run your hand along its surface over and over again."

Above their heads now a neon palm tree hangs suspended from invisible wire. Along one wall is a floor-to-ceiling painting of a cowgirl in a fringed halter top, a motorized cardboard gun in her hand, which she flicks up and down, endlessly. A guitar as large as she is is painted on the wall nearby.

"Why is everything so goddamn big?" David says loudly. "What kind of a place is this where everything is too frightening to look at? That woman with the gold toenails was nine feet tall, at least. Why do you take me to a place where nothing is like it's supposed to be? What am I supposed to do here?"

"You're tired," says Laura.

"I never leave my house anymore. I can't go out like everyone else, can't put one foot in front of the other and just go. I'm not that kind of person anymore. That's why my wife had to find a lover—a man who could put one foot in front of the other and escort her to the movie of her choice."

"Excuse me," a woman's voice says. "Where can I find Bloomie's underwear for like a three-year-old?"

"Do I work here?" David says. "Do I look like I work here?"

"You never know," answers the woman, whose hair is in shoulder-length pigtails. She is wearing a T-shirt that says, "Life is hard and then you die." She points at Laura's stomach. "And whatever your baby is, I hope it's a healthy one," she says.

"What's with the T-shirt?" David asks.

"A present from my ex-husband," says the woman. "He gave it to me the night we split up."

"You're well rid of him, I'm sure."

The woman sighs, and flips first one pigtail and then the other to the top of her head. "He said my relentless cheerfulness really turned him off."

"Was he in therapy?"

"Futilitarians don't go in for that kind of stuff. They just like to sit around and get stoned a lot."

David smiles. "I myself am really ripped, even as we speak."

The woman lets the fingers of one hand fall against Laura's stomach. "Don't forget to sober up before the baby's born," she says, and walks off.

"Didn't your mother ever tell you not to talk to strangers?" Laura says. "You can get yourself into trouble that way." She is one stair behind him on the escalator, riding down to the main floor. The outline of his shoulder blades is visible through his shirt, bones as sharp-edged as Zachary's; if she touches them, they will draw blood.

"I talked to *you*," David says. "You were a stranger."

Head over heels, the baby somersaults inside her. "Easy," Laura breathes, whispering one word only to this stranger she never talks to. She spends no time at all imagining this baby sheltered in her arms, greedily taking up all the time and space she has to offer. Time and space that are now David's, but will not be for much longer. Not without a struggle, anyway. She can see the sleeping baby, see herself hauling it in its wicker bassinet out the door and into David's building, into his apartment, where, together, they clear away a place for it in his bedroom, perhaps in the little dressing room behind it, near the bureau with Barbara's wedding picture arranged on top of it. Ignored, the baby sleeps on, while, close by, Laura and David make love guardedly, quietly, breathing without a sound.

A modern mother and her portable baby.

You took the baby out in that rain? Zachary says. In that snow? In that wind?

I had to go to the supermarket.

Are you out of your mind?

I don't know, she whispers. Possibly.

"I smoked a joint," she announces to David in the taxi homeward, and then again to her doctor a few days later.

The doctor, white-coated and red-faced, a drinker with six children, smiles at her with genuine sweetness. "Let's hope you enjoyed yourself, at least," he says.

27

Sophie slips on her reading glasses for a closer look at the papier-mâché figures seated on the bench in David's office. "And who are these people?" she says. "Friends of yours, I suppose." Silverstein laughs loudly at this, appreciatively, but Sophie ignores him. "Doctor," she says, "do you think you can do anything about these swollen legs of mine?"

"I'm not a doctor," David says. "You came here for help, but not that kind of help. Let's talk about exactly what it is you came here for."

"Well, first of all, I want you to know I'm heartsick when I think of you," says Sophie. She studies her granddaughter's lover, this dying man under whose spell Laura has so unwisely fallen. What Sophie sees is a pale young man with a delicate face; pale as eggshell and just as fragile, according to Laura. Maybe so, but who could tell just by looking at him—a sick and dying man who charges a dollar a minute to listen to the secret life of your marriage.

"You and I are two of a kind, sir," Sophie says. "Two sick people who aren't going to get any better."

"She's old," says Silverstein, "same as me. But it's not a sickness, doctor."

"There aren't any doctors here," says David. "Not a single one. Let's all try and remember that, please." Sitting behind his desk, he spins his wedding ring around his finger with his thumb; suddenly, the ring flies off, sails across the desk and comes to land on the tip of Sophie's broad black shoe.

"Excuse me," says Sophie, "but I can already see this isn't working out. I'm looking at my husband here and I don't feel any regrets about leaving him. I only feel uneasy being in the same room with him. I know he loves me, but it doesn't seem like a good thing, only like something dark and heavy, like a bad meal that sits way up near my heart, just sits and sits, refusing to go away." She crosses her ankles, and the wedding band slides, unnoticed by everyone but David, onto the carpet.

"I wasn't civil to a friend of hers, that's what this is all about," says Silverstein. "This little friend of hers, Aïda, wanted our air conditioner, and I wasn't very generous about it. She needs an air conditioner and a front tooth, and I promise you she'll get them."

"Dark and heavy, weighing down on me so hard I can't ever forget it's there. Does that sound like love to you?"

"Until a few weeks ago," says Silverstein, "I was a contented man. Then all of a sudden my wife decides love isn't what she wants after all. Not love, or marriage, either. What do you make of a person like that, doctor?"

David is crouched on the floor, scooping the ring up into his cupped palms as if he were bending over a stream to draw water. It shines there in his hands, reflecting light from his desk lamp, distracting him from Silverstein's voice. "Everyone's needs are different," he says finally, though it seems to him that the opposite is just as true. Rising unsteadily to his feet, the ring still in his hand, he grabs on to Sophie's shoulder for support. "I mean, everyone's needs are the same."

"Is this professional advice you're giving us?" Silverstein says. "I could get better advice from a drunk on a park bench."

"My advice," says Sophie, "is that you keep quiet and give the man time to think." She waits for David to take his hand away and then she says, "What do you know about varicose veins, doctor?"

"Not a thing."

"These professional people are good for nothing," says Silverstein. "Why won't you believe me?"

"He's an educated man, he must know plenty," Sophie says.

"About us? I doubt it. Why can't we just say goodbye to him and go home? We'll go to the Palace of Naples for dinner, just you and me." Silverstein smiles. "The Palace of Naples," he tells David, "is where Sophie and I officially became engaged. It was lovely—Ann Landers was there and we were given a free bottle of wine."

"Not the real Ann Landers," says Sophie, "just someone who could have been her twin sister."

"Dear Abby," says Silverstein. "Or whoever."

"I shouldn't have gone out that night," Sophie says. "I should have stayed home and cooked up some carrots and peas for myself and maybe a small piece of meat. But I wanted to get all dolled up and go to a restaurant, and that was my folly." She remembers the commotion in her heart, remembers thinking that she absolutely could not go on alone, that what she wanted was to awaken each morning beside Silverstein, a man who loved her and would tell her so, as easily and as openly as a child. For the moment, she longs to feel that way again—a little bit needy, someone who could turn to a man and feel entirely at home within the shelter of his arms.

She lifts herself out of her seat now and faces Silverstein. "Put your arms around me, Monroe," she says.

"Are you talking to me?"

"You're wasting time, Monroe."

He moves toward her in slow motion, throwing his arms up uncertainly, as if he is afraid Sophie will change her mind. "You shouldn't have left me," he says. "When you threw away my clothes, I thought, 'Maybe she doesn't like my wardrobe, maybe if I get a couple of new shirts she'll be happy with me again.' After you left, I washed and dried the dishes from lunch, and then I made myself another lunch because I forgot I'd already eaten. I wasn't hungry, but I kept on eating—a hard-boiled egg sliced in half and some horseradish—until I realized this was lunch number two. I asked myself, If Sophie were here, would she have let me go on eating or would she have cared enough to tell me I'd already had enough lunch for one day? I thought about it and thought about it all afternoon, but I couldn't be sure that you cared about me even that much." His arms stiffen around Sophie and then go slack. "Don't you even need me a little?" he says.

Sophie looks over at David. "I notice you're not saying much," she says. "How come?"

"Mostly I'm a listener, that's a lot of my job," David says, and fits the wedding band over his finger.

"So what have you been listening to?"

"A reasonable request for some answers."

"Reasonable?" says Sophie. "He's on top of me all day long. I'm washing out my underwear, girdles and stockings and so forth—ladies' things—and there he is poking his head over my shoulder, wanting to know what it's all about. Or I'm having a private conversation on the telephone, and he comes up to the kitchen table with his *Jerusalem Post*, sits himself down and tries to hear everything that's going on. What are we, Siamese twins? I think that's the way he'd like it, the two of us joined forever, maybe at the ear, seeing and hearing the same things at the very same moment. Isn't there such a thing as privacy in a marriage anymore?"

"Why should I have to be alone if I don't want to be?" Silverstein says.

"For three minutes a day you can't be alone?"

"There's nothing there for me when I'm alone; it's only time passing."

"Monroe," Sophie cries, wrapping her arms around him, "that is truly pathetic." She moves her hands along the stony ridges of his spine, enjoying the feel of a soft plaid shirt she's never seen before. "You bought a new blouse," she says. "Very handsome."

"Five of them," Silverstein says. "Chaps, by Ralph Lauren."

"I think," says David, "that we're making some headway here."

"Why?" says Sophie. "Because I complimented him on a new shirt?"

"The doctor thinks maybe there's a chance you'll come home with me, or at least have dinner at the Palace of Naples," says Silverstein. "He's optimistic—look at that little smile there."

David lets his smile broaden slightly. "I think that compromises can be made," he says.

Backing away from Silverstein, Sophie takes a seat on the bench next to the papier-mâché woman.

She envisions herself locked away in the bathroom at home, lying behind pink plastic curtains in the empty bathtub, reading a special large-print edition of the *Times*. Her back aches from the hard wall of the tub, but she is content there in her solitude. After a while, Silverstein's fist begins beating against the door, first one fist alone then both together, knocking so hard she worries the door will give way and come crashing down on top of her. *It's not right*, he yells, *it's not right what you're doing, leaving your husband alone out here, an old man who can't be alone for even three minutes.* She does not answer him, but goes back to her newspaper, whose print seems suddenly to have shrunk to its usual tiny size. Slamming the paper against the bottom of the tub, she climbs out and unlocks the door. Monroe, she says sharply and then she stops. He is seated there on the floor out in the hallway, chin sunk into his raised knees, seated so patiently, so expectantly, that her voice dims to a whisper and then cannot be heard at all.

"Don't you know me, Monroe?" she says out loud. "Don't you know I wouldn't have let you eat even a single bite of that lunch?"

They arrive at the Palace of Naples in time for the Early Bird Special—a full meal, including salad, coffee, and dessert, for $15.95.

"How's it going, you guys?" asks Joseph when he comes to take their order. He is, Sophie observes sadly, no longer wearing his diamond earring.

"Up and down, down and up," she says. "You know what it's like."

Silverstein takes a breadstick from a glass at the center of the table and jams it into the corner of his mouth like a cigar. "I'll have the fish," he says, "very plain, very—"

"What?" Joseph teases. "I can't understand you with that cigar in your mouth."

"The fish," hollers Silverstein, keeping the breadstick in place. "Very very plain," he yells, "as plain as they can make it."

28

"Of course I'm delighted that you called," Laura's mother is saying. "Though I have to admit I'm a little suspicious."

"Why?" Laura asks. She is sitting at the dining room table, which has not been cleared since dinner. Alphabet-shaped pasta swims in tomato sauce on Mia's plate; with her index finger, Laura arranges the letters to form her name. Her mother is someone to be endured, as patiently as possible. As a mother, she is a disappointment, but Laura has usually been able to forgive her without much effort. Recently, as the birth of her child approaches, she has been brooding over her mother's failings; her gloomy self-absorption, her inability after so many years to make peace with the end of her marriage, her refusal to travel forward toward happiness. Laura isn't quite sure why she has made this phone call, doesn't know what she hopes to gain from the sound of her mother's voice. A few minutes into the conversation, she realizes what should have been obvious to her all along—that she has called because she is soon to have a baby, and, like most daughters, is in need of a mother's compassion.

"Let's face it," Ruth Elaine says, "you never call me. If I didn't call you from time to time, we'd never be in touch at all."

"I called you tonight. Doesn't that prove something?"

"I suppose," says Ruth Elaine, clearly only half convinced. "So what do you hear from your father?" She keeps her voice mild, as if the answer to her question hardly mattered.

"Nothing," says Laura. The last time she spoke to her father, nearly six months ago, he'd called to tell her that her sister Wendy had written him a letter saying she was gay, that she had, in fact, always been gay, and that she was happily married to a window dresser for Lord & Taylor. Do you agree with me that this has to be your mother's fault somehow? he'd asked Laura. She understood then that this was the purpose of his call, to let her know that he was blaming her mother for one more thing gone wrong. Laura told him she had no idea whose fault it was, and that in any event, it was pointless to try to blame anyone. Disappointed, her father hung up on her.

"Absolutely nothing," Laura says.

"My social life's a big zero these days," Ruth Elaine says. "I go to work, come home, fix myself a little dinner, scrub out the bathroom sink, watch reruns of *Dynasty*, and that's it."

"Things will change," Laura promises. "They always do." She spells out David's name in pasta, then mashes the letters with a fork. "Grandma got married a few months ago," she says. "To Monroe Silverstein."

"No fooling!" says Ruth Elaine, sounding awed. The next

moment she is weeping. "Sophie?" she says. "She must be a hundred years old, at least."

"They split up for a while but they're back together again now." She is glad she cannot see her mother's face, grateful for the three thousand miles that separate them. In the background, on another telephone line, she can hear the faint voice of a woman saying, "So I washed the kid's mouth out with a little Ivory liquid. One squirt from the bottle, and I guarantee you he'll never say the 'F' word again."

"And that was the good news, right?" Ruth Elaine says. "What's the bad news?"

David's joke for Zachary: The bad news is your wife has a lover; the good news is he's dying of cancer. Hearing this, Laura's hand had struck David's cheek so hard that for half an hour afterward she waited, heartbroken, for the skin to turn black and blue. But the red soon faded to pink and then to his usual ashen color and then there was no evidence at all of her anger, no sign that for a moment she had hated him so much she could have killed him. He had only wanted to make her laugh, David said, and repeated the joke; this time, she laughed, seeing that it was, in its morbid way, funny, a private joke meant only for the two of them. She was ashamed of the way her hand had flown to his cheek, ashamed of the satisfaction she had felt at the sound of bone striking flesh. Only an instant later her chin was on his shoulder and she was dropping frantic kisses along his cheek until finally David said, Enough. Jesus, enough. He said it was mostly her fear at the thought of telling Zachary that had inspired the slap—an explanation that had not occurred to her. It is true that the thought of confessing to her husband chills her. She remembers his laughter, months ago, in their kitchen. Laughing, he'd said, What do you think, I'm going to be jealous of a dying man? This is what she will say to him, when the time is right: How can you be jealous of a man who was dying, of a man who is gone? You can't be.

She wants, so desperately, to be forgiven, to see Zachary nodding his head, to hear Zachary say, I understand perfectly; it's all right.

It is too much to ask of anyone, and she knows it.

"I want to come and stay with you when the baby's born," her mother says. "I want to be of some help."

Laura is silent for too long. "If we had a house," she says slowly, "it would be different. But it's only an apartment, just two bedrooms . . ."

"How can you be so selfish?" her mother cries. "I'm on cortisone again, my face is puffed up like you wouldn't believe. I'm a blimp and I'm all alone. Doesn't that mean anything to you?"

"I love you," Laura says.

"Like fun you do," says her mother, and hangs up.

29

Aïda is standing in the middle of Sophie's living room when her water breaks. "Shit," she says, watching as the carpet instantly darkens. "Do you think I ruined the rug?"

"Never mind about the carpet, it's garbage," says Sophie. "Where's Jimmie?"

"In school. Listen, I got to go shave my legs and under my arms, too. I don't want those nurses and doctors thinking I'm dirty."

"Can't we call him?" says Sophie.

"Who?"

"Your boyfriend, that's who. Don't you want him in the hospital with you?"

"What for? So he can hang around listening to me scream?"

Sophie slips an arm around Aïda and helps her into a chair. "There isn't going to be any screaming," she says. "Second babies generally just pop right out with no fuss at all." She doesn't tell her, of course, that there are always exceptions to the rule—that her younger son was born after a fifteen-hour labor that finally ended in a Caesarean.

"I'm a screamer," says Aïda. "When I was in labor with Carmen, the nurse told me I was disturbing the patient in the next room with all the noise I was making. 'What do you have to scream for?' she kept asking me. 'What good is it going to do you?' She was an ugly white lady, fat as a refrigerator. I asked her if she ever had any babies herself and she said no. 'Then you just shut your mouth about my screaming,' I told her. One minute later I see she's writing something down about me on her clipboard, something bad, I know, but I just keep right on yelling."

"You want me to go and get Carmen from her friend's house?" Sophie says. She pats Aïda's shaking knees, which are covered in thick, sand-colored stockings. "You may not listen to me about most things, but at least you've been a good girl about those support hose," she says.

"They are ug-ly," says Aïda. "They make me look like somebody's grandmother."

"Thank you very much for the nice compliment," says Sophie.

Aïda closes her eyes. "Let Carmen stay where she is," she says, and bursts into tears. "I wish I hadn't let Jimmie kiss me even once," she weeps.

"Sweetie pie," says Sophie. "Oh, sweetie pie."

"It hurts already," Aïda moans, starting to get up out of her chair. "I got to go home and fix myself up."

"Wait," Sophie orders. She leaves Silverstein a note saying she has gone with Aïda to the hospital. She attaches the note to the freezer door with a green-and-yellow plastic magnet shaped like a little pineapple. In Aïda's kitchen, Sophie prepares to shave her legs for her. First she smoothes coconut-scented shaving cream along her legs from knee to ankle. "Delicious, I bet," she murmurs, and puts on her reading glasses for a closer look.

"Hurry," says Aïda. "Please." She has changed into a clean pair of shorts and a shirt so tight Sophie can see the outline of her belly button. Her legs are stretched out on a wooden folding chair; Sophie is stooped over them, one hand grasping the side of the chair for balance. "You are the best in the whole world," Aïda says.

"The best what? The best lady-in-waiting?" Sophie smiles, and sets to work. When she finishes, she calls a taxi, then helps Aïda into the bedroom. "You tell me what to pack," she says. On the wall is a huge poster of Michael Jackson in a sleeveless vest and bow tie, and a Valentine's Day card decorated with Peanuts characters. "Hope Your Day Is Filled with Lots of Valentine Fun!" the card says, and is signed, "love, James." Aïda's bed is cluttered with soiled-looking stuffed animals, most of them bears with red plastic hearts for noses.

"Just don't forget Love-a-Lot Bear," says Aïda. "He's going to stay with me in the labor room."

"Which one is he?"

"The pink one, next to Tenderheart Bear. The yellow one is Funshine Bear, the green one's Good Luck Bear, the blue one is Wish Bear."

"What are these things?" says Sophie.

"Don't you know the Care Bears?"

"Are they from television?"

"They're from Jimmie," says Aïda. "He gets me one whenever we have a fight. I got Funshine Bear after he knocked out my tooth. The rest I can't remember."

"Very generous of him," Sophie says darkly.

"He *is* very generous."

Sophie dumps Love-a-Lot into an overnight bag. "Night-gowns?" she says. Aïda motions to a Formica dresser opposite the bed. There are stickers plastered along the front of one drawer—shiny pictures of a frog dressed in a diaper, a blond-haired pig with a baby bottle in its mouth, a ghost with a derby on its head. "Don't we have to call the doctor?" Sophie says.

"I'm a clinic patient. Whoever's around will take care of me."

"Are you sure?"

Aïda is rubbing her stomach with both hands. "Let's go," she whispers.

Outside, it is an unbearably humid summer day. The taxi that pulls up in front of the house has all four of its windows completely rolled down, Sophie notices. "Couldn't they have sent an air-conditioned car?" she says.

The driver is a young man in dreadlocks. He stares at Aïda, then at the overnight bag Sophie is carrying. "I'm a cab driver, not a doctor, you got the picture?" he says. "And this is a cab, not a hospital."

"Kindly keep your mouth closed, sir," says Sophie as she and Aïda get into the backseat. "It's only a ten-minute ride."

"You people make me real nervous," says the driver, and switches on the radio to a rock station. Sophie listens to a man's voice threatening to watch every move she makes, every step she takes. She looks down at the floor of the cab and discovers two greenish pennies, a chipped pretzel, a tiny pink mitten with a smiling face made of felt sewn onto the thumb. She squeezes her fingertip into the thumb and moves the smiling face around, trying to get Aïda to laugh. Aïda glances at her expressionlessly, then looks away.

At the hospital, in the gray-tiled waiting area, skinny children in shorts and stained T-shirts sit beside their silent parents in a horseshoe of plastic chairs. Sophie and Aïda take seats among them and stare along with everyone else at the tiny television set that is lowered from the ceiling. The local news is on, and all of it is bad: fires, corruption, a lovers' quarrel that ends in multiple stab wounds. The floor beneath their feet is littered with cigarette butts and ashes, though a sign next to the TV says "Smoking Absolutely Forbidden."

Aïda grabs Sophie's wrist. "The cramps are real bad," she says. "The worst."

"Contractions," says Sophie.

"What?"

"It's the uterus contracting," Sophie says.

"Just leave me alone," says Aïda, "will you."

When Aïda's name is called a few minutes later, Sophie feels a flash of terror. "Let me come with you," she says, and follows along as Aïda is brought upstairs in a wheelchair pushed by a man dressed all in green. He leaves them in a small ugly room, where a nurse hands Aïda a hospital gown and instructs her to undress. She pulls a curtain around the bed and Aïda disappears behind it.

"Are you her coach?" she asks Sophie.

"I'm her grandmother," says Sophie. "She lives with me."

The nurse nods. "There's no husband?"

"That's no concern of yours," says Sophie.

"She's so young," the nurse says evenly. "That's all I meant."

A resident has arrived to examine Aïda and check on her progress. When she is through, she parts the curtain and announces that things are moving along nicely. "Five centimeters down, five to go," she says. "We're halfway there—you'll have your baby in just a few hours, if we're lucky."

Aïda moans at the news. "I'll be dead by then," she says. "No way am I going to live that long."

Smiling, the resident rubs her eyes. "I've been on for almost thirty-six hours," she says. "I'm getting married this weekend and all I can think is that I'll be walking down the aisle with my eyes closed."

"Do you have a ring?" Aïda says.

The resident holds out her hand, revealing a diamond circled by sapphires. "I begged Jimmy not to go out and spend a fortune, but he wouldn't listen."

"Jimmie?" says Aïda.

The resident can't take her eyes off the ring. "In the right light sometimes, it glitters like anything."

"Is this a jewelry store or a hospital?" Sophie mumbles.

"Excuse me?" says the resident. She raises her hand toward the bright fluorescent lighting overhead and wiggles the ring from side to side on her finger. "We'll have you in that delivery room in no time," she promises.

It is nearly midnight. Sophie is at Aïda's side in the delivery room, dressed in a blue paper gown and mask. She has been with Aïda for almost eight hours; she is hungry and tired and has a headache that has moved into her eyebrows. Aïda has said some terrible things to her tonight, cursing in English and Spanish during contractions. Watching the course of the contractions on the monitor, Sophie felt like cursing herself. At ten o'clock, a doctor with a yarmulke fastened to his head with a plastic clothespin, put a needle in Aïda's spine. Sophie was sent out of the labor room during the procedure, and when she returned, Aïda was smiling. "I'm in heaven," she told Sophie. After an hour or so, the doctor came back and took the needle away and Aïda began to curse again.

Now a different doctor is in charge. He is a bearded gray-haired man and there are suede clogs on his feet. The heels of his socks are worn away so that his skin shows through, Sophie notices. Like Silverstein, the doctor is in need of a seamstress, and probably a maid and a cook, too. *Monroe*, she hears herself whisper. She wonders what he had for dinner tonight, worries that without her, he may simply have forgotten to eat. In her eyes, he is so thin that he cannot afford to miss even a single meal. When she spoke to him over the phone a few hours ago, all he could talk about was the air conditioner he'd been out buying for Aïda this afternoon. It was the top of the line, with all kinds of powersaver settings, he'd said excitedly. A wonderful baby gift for Aïda. Sophie did not have the heart to point out that the summer was nearly over, that the time when it really would have meant something to Aïda had already passed. But it was a generous impulse he'd had and she was proud of it, proud of him. In the weeks since her return home, she has not felt even the slightest need to escape from him. It is a mystery, but his presence has seemed a comfort. When she thinks of the things she said in front of Laura's lover, the marriage counselor, she is horrified. At the time, her words were true enough; in two months or two years they may be again. She cannot say exactly what it is she will want then. Perhaps she will want to hide herself away in the bathtub or perhaps she will want to hear, over and over again, just how much Monroe loves her. There are no guarantees—not for her or for Monroe or anyone else. For Monroe, that may be frightening, but for her it suddenly seems exhilarating.

"Push down," the doctor is urging Aïda. "You could have pushed this baby out an hour ago, if you'd wanted to. Now, push!"

"I can't," says Aïda.

"Come on and push that baby out!"

"I can't."

"You can," says Sophie. Lightly, she strokes Aïda's damp forehead. "You have to."

"Fuck you!" Aïda yells.

The doctor laughs. "You're wired for sound, you know. We're getting all this down on tape."

"Then fuck all of you!"

"Listen," says the doctor, "we're going to have to use forceps if you're not going to—"

"No forceps," says Sophie. "I was listening to Donahue the other day and a woman calls in—a very well-spoken woman, not some dummy—and says that her little girl is brain damaged because some doctor let a medical student use forceps on her baby. Brain damaged, what do you think of that?"

"Don't quote Phil Donahue at me, if you don't mind," says the doctor.

From deep in her throat, Aïda lets out a growl, and bears down hard.

"Way to go!" says the labor nurse. "Come on, baby!"

Sophie shuts her eyes, opens them a moment later to the sight of the baby emerging. *"Mazel tov,"* she says. *"Mazel tov,"* she says, smiling.

30

"Stretch it out, stretch it out," Jane Fonda orders gently. She is barefoot and is wearing leotards and leg warmers. A gold necklace glimmers near her collarbone. The woman is close to fifty, but David doesn't believe it. A human being that age couldn't possibly do a perfect split like that, he tells Barbara.

"Maybe it's all done with mirrors," he says.

"Double-time now," says Jane Fonda.

From her exercise mat in front of the VCR, Barbara moans and continues to reach for her ankles. "Double-time?" she says. "You have got to be insane, lady."

David clears his throat. He returns to his book, a paperback entitled *You CAN Get Well Again*. "Will you stop that?" he hears Barbara say. He assumes she is talking to Jane Fonda, and does not respond. Again he clears his throat.

"You're driving me crazy," Barbara says. "Is it absolutely necessary to clear your throat ten times a minute? What are you so nervous about?"

"Nothing much," says David. He checks his watch, and is surprised to find that less than an hour has passed since Laura's call. Sneaking away from her husband, she'd phoned to report that she was just about to leave for the hospital. "I'm already on my feet and pacing," David had whispered, making both of them laugh. Sitting in his living room now, watching his wife's bare leg swinging neatly through the air, he imagines Laura's pain, Laura sweaty and miserable and trying to breathe through the pain. He sees her husband's worried face, his shoulders hunched, fingers bent into tight fists.

He is sick with envy, so sick he is dying of it. The whites of his eyes have turned green, his arms and legs have taken on a greenish tint. If only he could feel warmly toward Laura's husband, feel warmed by the imagined sight of Laura and her husband together in the delivery room, he would be cured of his illness. They are killing him, those two, with their love for each other. He remembers something Laura had confessed to him months ago: as she fell further in love with *him*, she began to take more notice of Zachary's failings—his habit of leaving the kitchen with the refrigerator door wide open, of stuffing his laundry only halfway into the hamper, of dropping tangerine pits and peanut shells between the cushions of the couch—and began to feel enraged by them, as if she could no longer live with them, live with him. As if Zachary's sloppiness were reason enough to fall out of love with him and in love with someone else. But of course she was just fooling herself, she said—she loved Zachary no matter how often she found his tangerine pits between the cushions. David understood then that all along she had been searching for something that would explain why she had fallen in love with him, explain why a happily married woman would betray her husband not just once but day after day, week after week, month after month. What was wrong with her marriage? she wanted to know. What was wrong with her? All he could answer was that love didn't ever require an explanation. He knew it sounded romantic and fatuous, especially coming from a marriage counselor, but it was the one answer she could live with, and the one they'd both wanted to hear.

He stares at his wife, who is on the floor, heels over her head, head framed between her knees.

"Do you love me?" David says.

"Five-six-seven-energy," Jane Fonda counts.

Slowly Barbara unrolls herself, raising her legs into the air, then back down to the floor until she is flat on her back. "I've been having an affair," she says.

He nods his head. He feels a mixture of relief and sadness and curiosity, but no anger. "I figured."

"I don't see him anymore."

David nods his head again. "That's far enough," he says. "I don't want to know the rest."

"He was a tax lawyer, but a nice guy."

"Was? Is he dead?"

Ignoring him, Barbara gets up to turn off the tape. On her knees, she puts the machine on "rewind." With her back to him she says, "I'm sorry."

"It's all right."

"It's not all right," she says angrily, whirling around to face him. "How can you say it's all right? It's not as if we're talking about a book I lost, a dish I broke, shirts I forgot to pick up at the cleaners. I slept with a man I met in a movie theater. I went to his apartment dozens of times and let him undress me. I went with him into his bedroom and—"

"I know," David says. "But you said it was over and I believe you." The conversation is making him nervous; he wishes that, like Barbara's affair, it were over and done with. He knows he is supposed to show some sign of jealousy or resentment, a little bit of rage or passion. He imagines himself telling her the truth— that he is just as guilty, probably more so. *I've been having an affair* would not do it justice; to be entirely honest, he would have to say *I'm in love with someone.* He cannot hear himself uttering the words to her, multiplying the misery she has felt for so long now, the grief, the fear, the bitterness. Raising his head, he sees that she is staring at him, looking him straight in the eye.

"I hate you," she says. "You're sick and you're dying and nothing means anything to you."

"It's not true," he says.

She slips the cassette back into the VCR. "Are you ready to do the workout?" Jane Fonda says brightly. Barbara gets into position. "Stomach tight, buttocks pulled in," Jane Fonda commands, but sweetly. Following instructions, Barbara bends her head left, forward, right, back. There is a false smile on her lips, nowhere near as dazzling as Jane Fonda's. David approaches her; her smile fills him with pity.

"Don't you dare disturb me while I'm doing the workout," Barbara says.

"I need to apologize to you."

Barbara is jogging in place, clapping her hands together at every beat. "For what?" she says. "For getting sick and not getting any better? Forget it."

"For taking everything away from you."

By the time Barbara answers, she is nearly out of breath. "What?" she says.

"Happiness, love, sex . . . everything."

"Leave me alone," Barbara says. "Take a hike."

"What do you want from me?" David says. "What *is* it?"

Continuing to jog, but moving her arms as if she were climbing a ladder, Barbara says, "I just don't want you to die."

He has never, he realized, heard her say this; he needs, more than anything, to hear it again and again. "What?" he says. "Tell me."

She stands, motionless now, so close to him he can hear the breaking of her heart. "Don't you know I want to go with you?" she says.

31

Dozing in a hospital bed a day after the birth of her daughter Rosie, Laura dreams of David's death. She is at the funeral, her face unwashed, and her eyes ringed with gray-green circles of sorrow and exhaustion. Strapped to her chest in a denim sling is her newborn daughter. "How old?" says the stranger seated next to her in the chapel. "Three hours," says Laura. The stranger next to her smiles. "Babies are so portable nowadays," she says. "Pack a few diapers in a bag and away we go." The baby begins to knock her head against Laura's breastbone, whimpering softly at first, then wailing so loudly the man delivering the eulogy has to shout to be heard. "Young lady!" he yells. "You'll kindly escort your baby out of here this instant." Out of her seat, making her way to the back of the room, Laura covers the soft spot at the top of the baby's head with one hand. "Young lady," booms the man's voice. "I think you owe us all an apology." "I'm sorry," Laura mumbles, but the man isn't satisfied. "That's some apology," he says. "Now let's hear a bigger and better one, one that's loud and deeply felt." "I'm so sorry," Laura whispers, but it is a lie and there is no one in the room who does not know it.

A dark face is bending toward hers. "This will just take a half a second and then I'll leave you alone."

Awake, Laura blinks at the nurse. "What are you doing?"

"I'm here to check the fetal heartbeat," says the nurse.

Laura laughs. "Wrong," she says.

"Aren't you pregnant?" says the nurse. "What's that big stomach I'm looking at?"

"That's the twenty pounds I have to lose."

"You had the baby already?"

"Bingo."

"Congratulations," says the nurse doubtfully, and walks out the door just as the phone next to Laura's bed rings.

"Mommy?" says Mia. "Grandma told me not to call you."

"Sweet pea," says Laura. "I can't wait to see you."

"You come home *now*," Mia says. "Right *now*."

"How was camp today, sweetie? What did you have for lunch?"

"Buy me a toy and I'll tell you."

"Do you want to come and see the baby?" Laura says.

"Buy me two toys and I'll tell you what I had at snack time, too."

"Where's Daddy?"

"Sleeping. He's been sleeping for a hundred years."

"In that case, do me a favor and wake him up."

Mia is silent for a while and then she says, "There's someone I hate whose name begins with a *b*. You guess."

"I have no idea."

"You give up? Okay—b-a-b-y," says Mia. "She cries so loud she gives me a headache."

"How do you know? You haven't even seen her yet."

"B-a-b-y-s cry," says Mia. "I know *that*."

"Let me talk to Daddy, please," Laura says, and hears Mia throw down the receiver. Laura presses a button at her side and the head of her bed tilts upward noisily. Afternoon visiting hours have begun, and she watches the people coming through the door to see her roommate. A woman in a long-sleeved dress and a tan-colored wig walks past her, wheeling a tiny child in a stroller. The child is wearing wire-rimmed glasses whose lenses magnify her eyes, making her look bewildered. She too, is in a long-sleeved dress, and white tights. Behind her is a man with a blond beard and a yarmulke on his head. The little girl climbs out of the stroller and approaches her mother's bed, eyeing her uncertainly.

"Leah!" her mother says. "You look so big since yesterday."

The little girl smiles.

"Come and take a look at the new baby."

"I made him a present," says the little girl. "With sparkles and stars. But I had to leave it home."

The man in the beard kisses the top of his wife's head. He sits down at the edge of a chair and rocks his head and shoulders back and forth, looking as if he has instantly fallen into a trance, Laura thinks.

"I can't go through this again," his wife says. "They cut me open before the anesthesia started working and I went crazy right there on the table. I can't do it again—it's too many babies." She looks at her husband, who continues rocking in his seat. "I'm twenty-four years old," she says, "and I just can't."

"Sha," says the woman in the tan wig. She puts a finger to her lips. "Sha sha sha."

Laura turns back to the phone, but the line is dead. She tells herself it is just as well—she cannot think about Mia now, cannot think how to soothe her anger at all. Instead, closing her eyes, she savors the details of the birth—a fast, mean labor lasting only two hours, her whole body turning rock-hard with pain at each contraction. And then the surprise of the baby itself; for only an instant unrecognizable and unfamiliar, unloved. All three of them weeping together, she and David quietly, the baby furiously. Washed and dried and wrapped in a white blanket, she was an astonishing sight: clumps of silky black hair stood straight up from her head in alarm. Only David could say what he was really thinking. *She reminds me of Martin Sheen*, he said, laughing. *Our daughter looks like Martin Sheen.*

David? No, that was Zachary, glittering eyes showing above the paper mask he'd been wearing in the delivery room. She is sickened by her mistake, mortified at having robbed Zachary of his place beside her. Not an easy mistake to make. Or to forgive. She is tired, exhausted, really, and in pain. Her stitches hurt and her muscles are sore from the strain of giving birth. Even so. *Even so.*

She realizes David doesn't even know the baby has been born. She reaches for the telephone. It is mid-afternoon—if Ethan is home and happens to answer, she will simply hang up.

"It's me," she says into the receiver.

"Boy or girl?" David says. "Are you all right?"

"Girl, and I'm doing great."

"I've been thinking about you almost every minute."

"I'm fine," Laura says. She smiles at the little girl in wire-rims, who lowers her head in response.

"I'm coming to visit," David says. "Maybe tomorrow afternoon."

"Out of the question," says Laura.

"You came to visit *me*."

"That was different; you were sick and I had to see you."

"I have to see you."

"No you don't."

"Yes I do," David says, then laughs.

"What's so funny?"

"Our first fight," David says. "Isn't that romantic?" When Laura doesn't answer, he says, "I'll be going in for chemo at the end of the week. I'll call you when I'm feeling like a human being again."

"Better if I call you."

"As in: 'Don't call us, we'll call you'?"

"I had a baby yesterday!" Laura says with exasperation. "It's not like having your tonsils out. It's overwhelming, even the second time around."

"Something's happened," says David quietly. "Do me a favor and don't tell me what it is."

"It's just me, at this moment, in a strange place, that's all."

David sighs. "I'm going in for chemo at the end of the week," he says again.

"With hair like that," says Sophie, looking through the glass wall of the nursery, "what you ought to do is dye a little bit of it orange, a little bit of it purple, a little bit of it turquoise, just like those people you see sometimes on the television."

"I'd take it," says Silverstein. "It's a whole lot better than what I've got up there."

"What you've got, Monroe, is nothing."

"Mr. Yul Brynner had nothing, and look how far he went."

"He had talent," says Sophie. "He could do a beautiful polka. I saw him on the stage dancing barefoot with Gertrude Lawrence, and it was a spectacular thing."

"Ready to go back to the room?" Laura says.

Facing Laura, smoothing down the lapels of her bathrobe with both hands, Sophie says, "She's got beautiful coloring, your little daughter. Not too red, not too yellow. And very nice eyebrows, too."

"I didn't see any eyebrows," says Silverstein.

"Maybe you were looking at the wrong baby, Monroe."

"Let's go," says Laura, and turns away from the nursery. All along the hallway, women dressed in bathrobes, some still attached to their I.V. poles, walk hesitantly, one step at a time. At their side, keeping politely to the same slow pace, are fathers and grandparents, their voices hushed in the presence of so many sleeping babies behind glass.

Returning to her bed, Laura motions to her guests to sit down. The chairs she offers are covered with newspapers and books. Brown-edged petals from the roses Zachary brought are scattered on the floor, and also a stray wrapper from a straw and the metal pop-top from a soda can.

"Have you got a broom?" Sophie says, handing the books and papers to Silverstein, who immediately drops them to the floor. "You could do with a little housekeeping, I would say."

Laura shrugs. "Rumor has it that you were in the delivery room with—"

"Madame Butterfly?" says Silverstein.

"My little girlfriend Aïda," says Sophie. She frowns in Silverstein's direction. "And let me tell you something, it was a beautiful thing. Not all the mess and the blood and the screaming and hollering—that was ugly—what I'm talking about is that moment where they take the brand-new baby and put it right on the mother and you say to yourself, 'This is *it*—the most wonderful thing in all the world."

Laura nods, smiling. "Of course," she says.

"Sophie was Aïda's coach," says Silverstein proudly. "She was there for the whole show."

"Some coach," says Sophie. "Whatever I said or did, she cursed at me. Then when it was all over, she tells me how wonderful I am. But that's all right. The next morning, Monroe and I went out and bought some nice things for James, Jr.—crib sheets and little dressing gowns and the tiniest undershirts you've ever seen. And you should see what Jimmie picked out. After I looked at it, I had to go right out and get one for you, too." She hands Laura a small wrapped box, the paper patterned with ducks holding umbrellas over their heads. When Laura starts to tear the paper, Sophie grabs it back from her, saying, "If we open this right, you can use the paper over again."

"Depression mentality," Silverstein explains as Sophie returns the package to Laura. "Some of us who lived through the stock market crash of 1929 still haven't gotten over it yet."

Laura holds out a plastic heart in both hands and looks at Sophie. "Thank you," she says.

"This," says Sophie, "is a vibrating plastic heart. It makes a sound just like a heartbeat. You put it in the crib with the baby and it gets her right to sleep. Aïda just loves it."

"I can certainly see why," says Laura.

"Thirty-five dollars," Silverstein mumbles.

"Monroe," says Sophie.

"Maybe Jimmie has money to throw away on garbage, but I don't."

Sophie struggles to lift herself out of her seat. "I have a depression mentality?" she says. "I'm the one?"

"That's exactly right. I love you dearly, and that's what gives me the right to tell the truth." Silverstein turns to Laura. "Do you know," he says, "that she doesn't use soap when she washes the dishes?"

"I do sometimes," says Sophie, "in a big greasy pan, maybe. But most of the time plain water is just as good."

"Are you listening to this?" Silverstein says. "Do you hear this?"

Laura is looking at Silverstein's shirt, whose plaid reminds her of the curtains that were draped halfway around her bed in the labor room. She remembers Zachary's hand grasping the edge of the curtain as he watched her face during a contraction. Pulling at the curtain so hard that part of it slipped from the rod overhead, but still he did not let go. It was her hand he wanted to hold on to, but she would not let him touch her, could not stand even the thought of his touch. *Away from me*, she'd moaned. *Just keep away from me.* His face drooped for only an instant, long enough to let her see that she had hurt him. His pain meant nothing to her. *Tough luck*, she told him, and nearly laughed, because his pain was a joke, really, when compared to her own.

He forgave her everything, brushing it aside a few hours later when she tried to apologize. *Don't be an idiot*, he said pleasantly. *What kind of a guy do you think I am?*

"Rich men who live selfishly," says Sophie, "are, are—"

"Nice shirt," Laura says, gesturing to Silverstein. "Very pretty plaid."

"Mr. Calvin Klein," says Silverstein. "The softest cotton there is. Want to feel it?"

"—are a disgrace," says Sophie.

"I'm not," says Silverstein. "I just don't think a vibrating plastic heart is worth that kind of money."

Sophie considers this for a moment, then says, "The way I wash dishes is none of your concern, Monroe. Don't ever mention it again, if you know what's good for you."

"I only meant to say that a little Ivory liquid, a little Joy, a little Lemon Pledge now and then wouldn't be a bad idea at all."

"Lemon what?" hoots Sophie.

Laura smiles; Sophie laughs and laughs, tossing back her head to reveal a surprisingly smooth white throat. "You are something," she wheezes.

Silverstein looks on with pleasure. "I'm the happiest man in the world," he announces, "and don't you say I'm not."

Zachary arrives just before visiting hours are over, bringing more roses, a six-pack of Coke, and a small white envelope from Mia that is sealed with many layers of Scotch tape. There is a sharp metallic sound as he flings the envelope lightly into Laura's lap.

Holding the envelope up to her ear, Laura says, "What did you do—tell her she has to help out with the hospital bills?"

"Big mystery," says Zachary. "I have no idea what's in there." He leans back in his seat, arms folded under his head, legs extended so far that his feet are under Laura's bed. "Maybe when you check out of here, I could check in. It's my fondest dream to climb into a bed and stay there."

"Hasn't your mother been a help?"

Zachary sighs. "Try sharing your home with someone whose motto is 'Watch out for crumbs!' "

Smiling, Laura says, "You're taking her to the airport tomorrow night?"

"The night after, if I live that long."

"You know you couldn't have managed without her."

"She accidentally washed Mia's hair with half a bottle of cream rinse yesterday."

"But don't forget she had to fly more than a thousand miles to do it. Don't be so hard on her," Laura says. She tears open Mia's envelope and finds a gift of a dime and four pennies, and a homemade card ornamented with tiny rainbows. Inside, there is a message written in orange crayon:

I LOVE MOMMY AND
HATE MOMMY
FROM MIA

"Is honesty a virtue or one of the seven deadly sins?" Laura says. "I can never remember which."

Bringing his chair closer to Laura, Zachary leans his elbows on her bed as he pulls the sheets up over their heads. "*I* would never send you a card like that." Under the sheets, he leaves the lightest of kisses at her mouth.

"What will the neighbors think?" Laura murmurs.

Zachary gets up and draws the curtain around the bed. He slips off his shoes and swings his legs over the side of the mattress. "Kiss me, you fool," he says in a deep voice. He closes his eyes. "We could stay here forever," he says. "Just I and thou and thee and me and a six-pack of caffeine-free Coke."

"And the baby," Laura whispers, her mouth against his.

"What the hell," Zachary says. "We'll put them both up for adoption."

32

The baby is gazing up at Laura from inside her bassinet. One side of her mouth pulls upward into a goofy smile that charms Laura in an instant. "My beautiful girl," Laura says. "You don't look anything like Martin Sheen." Hearing this, Rosie crosses her eyes and begins to cry.

With an extravagant moan, Zachary rolls over to Laura's side of the bed. "It's not possible it's your turn to get up and feed the baby, is it?"

"You have the night off, you lucky duck."

"A thousand thank-yous, master," says Zachary. "And let me add that it couldn't have happened to a nicer guy."

Carrying Rosie into the living room, Laura switches on the TV set before settling down to feed her. The baby's lower lip curls as she cries, giving her a look of genuine sorrow. "You big phony," Laura says. "What could you possibly be thinking about except food?"

There is an elderly woman on the TV screen with a sea turtle cradled in her hands. According to the woman, the turtle, who is wearing a chartreuse polka-dotted dress and a fur hat, may very well live to be one hundred and thirty-six. The woman flips up the little dress to reveal a pair of ruffled pink bloomers, and the audience goes wild.

"Well I'll be," says the talk-show host. He wants to know whether a turtle is the kind of pet that inspires love in its owner. In response, the woman kisses the turtle's face. The audience groans; the woman lowers her face for another kiss.

When the phone rings a moment later, Laura answers it with her eyes still on the screen.

"Thank God I got you," her mother says. "Is the baby all right?"

"She's perfect," Laura says. "How are you?"

"I almost had a heart attack," says her mother. "I had a dream that the cat jumped into the bassinet and smothered the baby. I just had to call to make sure everything was all right."

"We don't have a cat," says Laura.

"Are you sure? The dream was so real to me. It was a purebred cat I saw, a scrawny Siamese with dark blue eyes."

"Let me check around the apartment," Laura says. "Maybe one slipped in through the window without my noticing."

"There's no need for sarcasm," says her mother. "Do you think it's easy for me, when my brand-new granddaughter and I are on opposite ends of the earth? How do you think I feel about that?"

· "Come for a visit, then. A short visit."

"Not me," says Ruth Elaine. "I'm staying right where I am, thank you. I have a wonderful doctor I'm seeing—a very lovely nutritionist. All he allows me to eat is cheese, and I have to say my health has never been better."

"Believe it or not, we have cheese in New York, too. There's some in my refrigerator at this very moment, in fact."

"You've missed my point entirely," says Ruth Elaine. "Without R.J., I'm a wreck. And he couldn't possibly come to New York. He's much too busy for a trip right now."

"R.J.?" The old woman on TV has brought out another turtle, this one dressed in a red poncho and a sombrero. His name is Juan Carlos, the woman says.

"R. J. Rosenfeld, M.D.," says Ruth Elaine. "A little overweight, but otherwise the man of my dreams."

"Great news," says Laura. "Was that hard cheese or soft?"

"Hard and also semi-soft. Do you know someone with asthma?"

"No one at all," says Laura. "But hold on while I burp the baby. I need three hands for that."

"I'll let you go, then," says her mother. "But I want you to know I'm still worried. Dreams can be prophetic, you know. If someone tries to give you a kitten tomorrow, don't take it."

"I won't," Laura promises, rolling her eyes as if she had an audience.

"And send pictures," says Ruth Elaine wistfully. "A whole walletful."

The turtle in the poncho and sombrero is naked now, swimming in a basin of water. He just loves to go skinny-dipping, the old woman says. One hundred and thirty-six years, Laura thinks. David's life will soon be over but the turtle will be skinny-dipping through the twenty-first century and beyond. She would like to take the goddamn mindless turtle and set it on its back, watch its flippers move helplessly through the water until finally, in silence, it gives up and dies.

Laura pitches the baby's empty bottle toward the old woman. It hits the TV screen and drops quietly onto the carpet.

In her sleep, Rosie lets out an extraordinary burp. She dozes against Laura's shoulder, unmindful of the warm tears that have dampened the hair blooming so wildly at the top of her head. Laura moves her cheek across the baby's. She puts her lips to the baby's ear. Delicately, she licks the beautiful soft curve of the outer rim. She will tell the baby everything. Or she will tell Zachary everything. *It doesn't mean anything to me,* she will say. *He doesn't mean anything to me.* But she longs to tell the truth, to hear Zachary say, *You?* He looks at her, stunned. *Why are you telling me this?* he says. *What do you expect me to say to you? You want me to comfort you because your lover is dying?*

She turns off the television set, ignoring the bottle at her feet. She walks back to the bedroom and lays the baby on her stomach in the bassinet. She covers her with one summer blanket and then another. She eases herself onto her own bed. In the hollow between Zachary's last rib and his hip, there is a resting place for her head. Uninvited, she spends the night there.

33

David has been waiting for two weeks to see the baby and now Laura has made him wait forty-five minutes longer. On her way to his apartment, she prepares one excuse after another but none seems right. It is a mild September morning, and Rosie is overdressed in a hooded pink bunting with a little white hat under the hood, and a thin satin-edged blanket draped around her middle. She has never gone visiting before: *in her baby book, below the heading "My First Visit," Laura will write, "To see my mother's lover."*

She puts the baby down on the floor of David's office before she begins her apology. "I meant to be on time," she says, "but . . ." Bending to unwrap the baby, she feels David's arms around her waist, and stiffens. "Your hands are so cold," she murmurs, though this is untrue. "Like ice."

David holds out his hands in front of him, palms up, then turns them over. "Nothing up my sleeve," he says. "Will you let me hold her?" He sits down on the bench next to the papier-mâché woman and smiles as Rosie is lowered into his arms. "How do you do, miss," he says. "Who's your hairdresser?"

"Her press agent says she's tired of answering that question."

"I'll bet," David says, running a finger along the arch of the baby's eyebrow. "As long as the punk look is in, she's all set."

Laura is beside him on the bench now. She smells his toothpaste, and, leaning her head along his shoulder, the pleasant scent of fabric softener in the V of pajama top peeking out from his bathrobe. He is wearing Weejuns without socks, and in each shoe is a shining subway token. His hair looks sparser than it did last month, she notices, his nose sharper, his eyes more deeply set. His face is dry and powdery-looking—she imagines that if she touches him, her fingers will come away coated with sweet-smelling dust.

"Have you been feeling okay?" she asks. The simplest of questions, whose answer she does not want to hear.

"I've been feeling lousy, ever since that last round of chemo. I haven't been out of my pajamas in days."

My health has never been better, she hears her mother telling her, and pretends the words are David's. She listens to him insisting that it is cheese that will keep him alive forever—valembert, fontina, cheddar, baby swiss, havarti with caraway, havarti with dill. He will eat nothing but cheese and live to be one hundred and thirty-six.

His photograph is on the front page of the *National Enquirer*, just below the picture of the human baby born with cloven hoofs and a rat's tail. *Cancer Patient Outlives His Great-Grandchildren*.

Customers on line at the supermarket in the twenty-first century shake their heads, thinking this is simply one more outrageous story in the *Enquirer*, but they are mistaken.

"I have a present for you," David is saying.

She looks up at him, startled. There has never been an exchanging of gifts between them, mostly because Laura considered it too dangerous, evidence that might someday be used against her. One time, months ago, David had tried to give her a necklace of gray-and-white porcelain beads that she had loved but had been too uneasy to accept. Unable to return it, he had given it instead to his wife, who, much to his relief, had shoved it to the back of her underwear drawer and never worn it.

"Don't even show it to me, whatever it is," Laura says. "It makes me so sad to have to turn it down."

"It's for the baby," he says. He returns her daughter to her, then opens a locked drawer at the bottom of his desk and takes out a small package wrapped in aqua-colored tissue paper, no box. Beneath the tissue, Laura discovers a tiny jumpsuit of lavender velvet with a white lace collar.

"It's lovely."

"My father has good taste, in baby clothes, anyway. I sent him out to the stores as soon as the baby was born." He touches Laura's arm. "You have to keep it."

Laura rubs the velvet sleeve against Rosie's cheek. She wants to go home and weep in private, but already there are tears welling up in her eyes. Silently, she settles the baby in David's arms. Blinking away the tears, she walks to the window and looks out across the street at Mia's school. She sees pots of geraniums lined up on a windowsill, and next to them, the slumped backs of a trio of rag dolls. Mia. For nearly a year she has turned her attention away from her, cheating her, and Zachary, too, day after day, letting them make do with whatever she had left over for them. It seems to her now that she had once stood shyly on the pavement in front of David's building, stood high on her toes and then spun herself around to face him, turning her back on the lives that meant everything to her.

"I'm not coming back," she says as she moves away from the window.

David is playing with the baby's hair, threading it through his fingers, murmuring something meant only for her.

"I just can't," Laura says, remembering her roommate in the hospital saying the words in the same voice as her own. And the woman in the wig saying *sha*, over and over again, as if it would do any good at all.

"Can't or won't?" says David. "You know goddamn well you can." Tears flare briefly in his eyes, then disappear. He blows softly on Rosie's hair, watches it stir under the delicate breeze of his breath. "It's the baby," he says. "It's giving birth, you and Zachary holding hands in the delivery room, all that Lamaze togetherness jazz, am I right?" When Laura doesn't answer, he says, "What can I say—'I'll kill myself'?" He waits for her half smile and then he says, "Clichés come to mind—you know, me putting my fist through the wall, me sitting around in my undershirt, unshaven, drinking whiskey straight from the bottle . . ."

"My God," Laura says, "it's been twenty years since I gave Timothy Fucarelli back his I.D. bracelet in front of the boys' bathroom."

"Timothy what?"

"There were two of them, Timothy and Artie, the Fucarelli twins. They both had bad skin, but they were on the junior high football team and that made them cool."

"You must have made a charming couple."

"When I gave him back his bracelet, he said, 'Start thinking of all the Saturday nights you'll be sitting around wishing you still had this I.D. on your wrist.' He swung the bracelet back and forth in front of my face and then he ran into the boys' bathroom with it and tried to flush it down the toilet."

"Shut up," David says. "You're talking too goddamn much."

Leaving the baby next to the papier-mâché woman, David rises from the bench. His elbow grazes Laura's breast, and she flinches. "What is it?" he says.

"My milk came in just a few days ago. It should have come and gone by now but it hasn't." David nods, and gently slides his hands under her sweatshirt. You're hurting me, she starts to say, but falls silent.

"No bra?" he says. Under his fingers her breasts are hot stone. "I want to put my fist through glass," he says, "don't you understand that?" His hands are traveling along her spine now. "You'll see me sitting out on the street, under the canopy," he whispers. "You'll see me there every morning and then one day you won't. Keep track of the days and weeks, and then you'll know. Or the doorman will know—doormen always know everything."

"No," she says. "It isn't going to happen."

The pain in her breasts is nearly unbearable as she embraces him. "Look at me," he says fiercely, but she looks beyond him to the street below where she is already walking past him, head lowered, chin reaching to her chest, eyes cast safely downward toward smooth pavement.

34

"Listen to this," the new doorman in David's building says. "This friend of mine, he's a customs agent at the airport, and last week he's going through a woman's suitcase and he finds a Diet Pepsi bottle hidden inside a velvet bag, the kind you get liquor in? The bottle is filled with dirt, maybe dirt from the Holy Land, because that's where the plane's just flown in from. 'What's this?' my friend asks the woman. 'Dirt from the Holy Land?' 'That's my boyfriend,' says the woman. 'What's he doing in a Diet Pepsi bottle?' my friend says, because of course he thinks it's a joke. The woman grabs the bottle out of his hand and bursts out crying. 'He got sick and died,' she says. 'I brought his ashes back with me, if that's all right with you.' "

Under the canopy in front of his building, David taps his foot. A girl in a boy's haircut whizzes by on a skateboard, holding a can of beer to her lips. The telephone in David's pocket rings, and he reaches for it eagerly.

"*I* thought it was a terrific story," the doorman says, and walks back inside the building.

The voice at the other end of the phone wants to reserve a table for two for seven-thirty tonight. "Something overlooking the water would be nice," the voice says. "Will that be a problem?"

"No problem," says David without hesitation. "Name, please."

"*M* as in macaroni, *A* as in alligator, *R* as in rhinoceros, *X* as in xylophone."

"Very good sir," says David, returning the phone to his pocket. He tries to laugh but cannot. He imagines himself in a Pepsi bottle, white chips of bone in soft dark ash. He believes he will die but not that he won't ever see Laura again. The phone is in his pocket: he can call her this very instant and beg for more time. He is a dying man but he is no beggar. After she left yesterday morning, he had gone straight to the kitchen and opened the door to the freezer, as if he knew just what he was doing there. Staring inside for a moment, he seized two cans of apple juice and hurled them to the floor. He reached deeper inside and flung a bag of baby shrimp over his shoulder, a half gallon of ice milk, four quarters of butter. The thought of himself as a demented housewife made him smile; one by one, every package in the freezer went skidding crazily across the floor. With ice-cold hands he cooled his forehead and the back of his neck. He felt slightly dizzy, and something was wrong with his eyes, as if he had been staring too long into bright light. He went to lie down on his bed and when he awakened it was early afternoon.

His son was in the kitchen, sweeping puddles together with a sponge mop.

"Defrosting the freezer?" Ethan said.

It seemed to David that this was the first time his son had smiled at him since the night his headphones had been tossed out the window. They had never spoken of Laura again, had barely spoken at all through the summer, each gliding by the other almost unnoticed.

"Aren't you home early?" said David.

"Teachers' Conference."

"Sounds familiar. I must have forgotten all about it."

"You look wiped out," Ethan said. "Maybe you should call the doctor or something."

"Maybe." David sat down at the Formica table and studied the ice milk that oozed from the collapsed carton under his seat.

Ethan continued sweeping puddles together. The soles of his sneakers left dirty prints against the wet tiles. "I've been thinking a lot about you and that chick Laura," he said.

"And?"

"You do what you have to do," he said. "It's no good if you don't."

David said nothing.

"Shrimp cocktail, anyone?" said Ethan, and threw the bag into the sink.

"When you were a baby," David began, "about two and a half, I think, I took you to the supermarket in your stroller one day. You were a real cute kid—very personable and friendly. We were walking by the fruit and vegetables and all of a sudden you yelled, 'I love you, lady!' to a woman standing next to us. I was embarrassed, but the woman said, 'I love you, too, honey,' and that was that, I thought. But you wouldn't keep quiet—you had to say 'I love you' to everybody we passed. Just about everyone smiled at you, patted you on the head, that kind of thing. Then an old man came and squatted down by your stroller. 'That's all very well and good,' he said, 'but it isn't necessary to love every-body you see. It's only necessary to love your father and your mother.' As he walked away, you yelled after him, 'I love you, too, honey!' "

Ethan let the sponge mop topple to the floor. Crossing the kitchen in two rapid strides, he was gone from the room.

A little boy holding hands with a silver-haired man walks past David now. "Me?" the boy says. "When I grow up, I want to be cool and wear a black leather jacket and watch X-rated movies on cable TV." David knows him—he lives in Laura's building with his mother, a short, chubby woman who always wears plaid pleated skirts, knee socks, and loafers, as if she were in parochial school. Enviously, he watches the little boy enter Laura's build-ing. *I just can't*, she had said. He and Timothy Fucarelli, prob-ably the only two she had ever dumped. *Laura.* He will miss the kisses she always dropped so gently along the path of his scar. Deprived of them, he will continue to wither and will die. De-prived of them or not, he will wither and die. At the oncologist's office several mornings ago, light-headed with pain, in frantic need of stronger medication, he found himself in tears before he'd even left the waiting room to see the doctor. A few minutes later, examining him with slow-moving hands, the doctor had sighed in a way that terrified him. "You've hung on so beauti-fully," the doctor said, his voice fading to a near whisper, "you almost had me convinced you were going to beat the odds."

He recalls a book he read years ago, where a man who knows he is going blind looks, for the last time, at beloved things—paintings, books, his own face in the mirror. Quietly taking leave of them all. There is comfort in such deliberateness, David sus-pects. And so he will move unhurriedly from one beloved face to the next, lingering as long as he likes. And then at last he will let go. Let go of Barbara and Ethan and his father. And Laura. Not Laura, who has cheated him of one last chance to linger in her arms. Hurrying out of his life with the baby clamped firmly against her shoulder and looking up at him amazed, she had forgotten to say goodbye.

The moment has come and gone too quietly, and he can only blame himself. *Stay right here*, he should have said. *Stay and watch me put my fist through glass.*

35

Laura is floating naked in darkness. She is in a tank of Epsom salt solution, listening to a tape cassette of celestial music entitled "You Are the Ocean." She hears two different kinds of flutes, a harp, and a cello, but is unable to pick out the sounds of the ocean. According to Alex, the aging hippie who runs the place, the music is perfect for relaxation and "the unfolding of joy." After collecting fifty dollars from her at his desk, he had led her into a steamy high-ceilinged room containing a wooden bench holding a stack of carefully folded towels. On the other side of a Plexiglas partition stood a shower, a very small hot tub, and the tank where she now floats drowsily. Tossing his sad gray ponytail behind him, Alex promised that the buoyancy from the salt solution would make her feel nearly as weightless as an astronaut in space. He pointed out, at the side of the tank, the soft plastic buttons controlling the music and lights, then disappeared.

She has never been so alone in her life. She waits for the joy to unfold but nothing happens. She hits a button with her palm and the music fades. In the deep soundless dark, she feels disembodied. Holding her hand up over her face, she struggles to see her fingers but cannot. This isn't what she came here for. She came seeking tranquillity, but what she is experiencing is a taste of death, a terrifying feeling that the world doesn't exist, her family doesn't exist. So this is what David is heading toward, a place so dark you cannot see the hand held up in front of your face. It has only been a day since she left him. She has brought pain to a dying man, the very worst thing in the world. He will never forgive her and that will be her pain. But perhaps, miraculously, she will be able to forgive herself. A *zeisa neshumah* like you, she hears Sophie saying. A sweet soul. Unlike Laura, a *zeisa neshumah* wouldn't dream of abandoning a dying man. This stranger Sophie has mistaken her for, this sweet soul, is someone who is willing to hang on forever, even after the dying man says *Go; it's over, there's no hope left at all*. Hearing this, a *zeisa neshumah* could not bear to let go, could not bear to turn away. Unlike Laura, who cannot get away fast enough. *Selfish cowardly bitch*, she whispers in the darkness. *You selfish cowardly bitch*. She could spend the rest of her life apologizing and it would not be enough. Not enough for Zachary, either, whom she has betrayed over and over again. It is too much to ask his forgiveness, madness to expect understanding. And so he will never know where she has been and she will love him all the more for it.

She draws her hand up out of the pool and feels the strangely silky water between her fingers. The only noise she hears is the rumbling of her stomach, a sound that unexpectedly makes her giggle. She is alive, floating bravely through space. Her eyes begin to close. Her mind is blank, a pristine and beautiful place untouched by thought. Time is passing with astonishing speed or astonishing sluggishness—it is impossible to tell which. *You will be at one with the universe*, she hears Alex promise. Hippie dippy silliness uttered so earnestly, it was hard not to laugh. She misses her baby, misses the feel of her cool silken ears, the sight of her sweet hands and feet. She yawns, and stretches her arms out behind her, disturbing the still water, sending drops of it into the darkness and across her face and into the corner of one eye, where it burns with surprising fierceness. She remembers that there is a squeeze bottle of fresh water sitting on the ledge of the tank and reaches for the button that will switch on the lights. Running her hand repeatedly along the wall of the tub, she hunts for the button but cannot find it. She is lost in a terrifying darkness. Her breathing quickens to a pant; in another moment or two she will have a heart attack and drown. No. In another moment she will find the button, because of course it is there, a circle of soft plastic waiting for her trembling fingers to seize hold of it. She has brought this on herself, endangered her life by traveling across town to a place called Serenity, Inc. For fifty dollars, she'd expected an hour free of all regret and longing. An hour to begin to forget everything that needs to be forgotten. But she will forget none of it and will never stop longing. The utterly impossible trick will be to remember without remorse.

Suddenly, she is hearing music again, a prearranged signal from Alex that her hour is up. And then his voice, coming, like the voice of God, from a hidden place high above her. "How you doing, huh?" he says through the intercom. "Was it like, euphoric?"

"I can't find the light switch," she cries.

"You don't have to yell. As long as the intercom is on, I can hear you just fine."

The room gradually fills with soft light and she sees that her hand, still groping at the side of the tank, had missed its mark by no more than a few inches. Emerging from the water, she leaves footprints along a walkway of towels that leads straight to the shower. There is a fine white powder of dried salt over her body. Licking her lips, she tastes the bitterness of Epsom salt. She feels as she does after making love, she realizes—exhausted, relaxed, amazed.

After a long shower, she dresses slowly and dries her hair with the blow dryer left out for her on a three-legged wooden stool. She unlocks the door and approaches the desk where Alex is seated eating from a box of dry cereal called G.I. Joe Action Stars. "I love this job," he says in a whispery voice. "It's a natural high for me, just seeing the smiles on all my floaters. I myself once floated overnight for nine hours. What a trip, let me tell you."

"I panicked," says Laura. "I couldn't find the light switch and I panicked."

Alex shakes his head. "You look wonderful," he says. "That's because your body's natural painkillers were stimulated while you were floating in there. I'm talking heavy flow of beta endorphins and a real decrease in ACTH levels."

"I thought so."

"Did you hear the sound of your blood traveling through your veins toward your heart?"

Laura studies the drawing of G.I. Joe on the cereal box. Blond hair in a severe crewcut, face set in a grimace, fists clenched, he is a sinister-looking figure. "So that's what that was," she says. "I thought it was the sound of my stomach rumbling."

Pushing the box of cereal toward her, Alex says, "Don't be afraid. They're fortified with eight essential vitamins and minerals. Really." His voice never rises much above a whisper, for which she is grateful.

"Thank you anyway," she says, and heads for the elevator beyond his desk.

He waves goodbye as she steps into the empty car. "All that sugar, but who cares," he calls after her.

Leaving the building, she is nearly run over by a man on a unicycle coming out of the coffee shop next door. "Watch it, you," he warns. She blinks in ordinary sunlight, which seems startlingly bright, as do the orange letters of a sign spelling out "Burger King," and the green sweater tied around the shoulders of a woman walking in front of her. At the next block a crowd has gathered around a street vendor who is hawking something Laura can't see. Stepping into the crowd, she stares, horrified, at two life-size, trembling rubber hands that are arranged on the pavement, one upright in a woolen cuff, the other peeking out of a paper bag, palm to the ground. "Repulse your friends and family!" the vendor urges. "Buy a bagful today! Batteries not included." He stoops to the ground, grinning at the sight of the rubber fingers twitching mysteriously at his feet.

Laura's eyes and ears are shut tight. She floats swiftly toward home, unnoticed and without any effort at all, weightless as an astronaut in the pitch-dark silence of space.

Dear Editor:

This story is a warning to all those women who are doomed to spend the rest of their lives alone with their hearts of stone.

Read it and weep.

Dear Editor,

Although I am at present working in the luggage business, my writing is me. I have recently turned to nutrition, yoga, and meditation. I am studying at the School of Actualism and LOVING LIFE!!!!!

Sir:

Enclosed is an editorial type reflection of Death Row, where I have been for the past 6 years. They say I killed my wife but this is untrue. I loved my wife even though she was a nympho and slept with many of my friends and strangers too. Some people may think that is a good reason to kill their wife but not me. I say live and let live.

Thank you.

"Put those manuscripts away and help me get this kid to bed!" Zachary yells from Mia's room. "No more fooling around and I mean it!"

"N-o w-a-y, José," Mia says cheerfully, and jumps from the couch to her bed and then back again as Laura approaches. "And anyway, you didn't even brush my teeth."

"You hold on to the infanta and I'll catch the jumping bean," says Laura. She darts across the room to Mia, who instantly leaps back to her bed, saying, "Get away from me, you mutant."

Zachary's face is in the baby's hair. He draws back, then bends to touch his forehead to hers. "I'm so in love with this baby." He sighs. He carries her out of the room; a moment later, he reappears with Rosie still in his arms. "Don't call Mommy a mutant, please," he says.

Mia jumps up and down on her mattress halfheartedly. "All right," she says as she collapses on her stomach. "But I'm not letting any mutants brush my teeth tonight. I'm too tired. I'm just going right to bed."

Alone in the room with Mia now, Laura lies soundlessly beside her. She gazes up at the ceiling, her hands behind her head. "I want to turn off all the lights," she hears Mia say, but does not answer her. She is flat on her back on her daughter's narrow bed, watching David from the slightest distance. She sees him in his chair outside under the canopy, dressed in pajamas and a bathrobe, subway tokens glittering in his shoes, looking as if they might, at any moment, carry him anywhere at all.

"I want to turn off all the lights in the universe," Mia says.

ABOUT THE AUTHOR

MARIAN THURM has published fiction in *The New Yorker, The Atlantic, Mademoiselle, Ms.*, and many other magazines. Her work has also been chosen for several anthologies, including *Best American Short Stories* and *Editors' Choice. Floating*, a collection of her short fiction, was published in 1984. This is her first novel.